HALF THE TRUTH

Also by David J. Walker

Fixed in His Folly

HALF THE TRUTH

DAVID J. WALKER

ST. MARTIN'S PRESS
NEW YORK

PUBLISHED BY THOMAS DUNNE BOOKS
An imprint of St. Martin's Press

Library of Congress Cataloging-in-Publication Data

Walker, David J., date
Half the truth / David J. Walker.
p. cm.
"A Thomas Dunne book."
ISBN 0-312-14611-6
1. Private investigators—Illinois—Chicago—Fiction. 2. Chicago (Ill.)—Fiction. I. Title.
PS3573.A4253313H35 1996
813'.54—dc20 96-21728

First edition: November 1996

10 9 8 7 6 5 4 3 2 1

To Ellen, again

Any fool can tell the truth, but it requires a man of some sense to know how to lie well.

—SAMUEL BUTLER, *NOTEBOOKS*

Half the truth is often a great lie.

—BENJAMIN FRANKLIN, *POOR RICHARD'S ALMANAC*

Speaking of truth, while Sir Thomas Overbury actually shows up in the history of literature, the Chicago restaurant that carries his name, as well as Cragman College and a number of other institutions, show up nowhere else but in this book. That's true of the characters who people these pages, too.

And while we're on the subject, the truth is that I owe special thanks—for various kinds of help in getting this fiction told—to my editor, Elisabeth Story, with whom I've had the good fortune to work; to Jenny Notz, for her part in creating that good fortune; to my agent, Jane Jordan Browne, who has wisdom and energy enough for two; to my erstwhile coach, Marsha Haake, who'll see right through to your heart if you don't watch out; and to my friend, Harry Bonin, who is larger than most of us, in so many ways.

HALF THE TRUTH

CHAPTER

1

It was just past midnight, the threshold of an October Friday, with cold, blue moonlight splashing through oak leaves still too stubborn to drop off their branches. Not far away, birch logs were burning in somebody's fireplace, scenting the thin, crisp air with the promise of warm peace and the comfort of home.

As always, the Lady had left that Thursday's supermarket coupons for me, bound carefully into a tight roll with a red rubber band. This time, though, there was something different. The roll lay half-buried in the crabgrass, just off the left edge of the cement slab by the coach house door.

And that's what sent me back for the gun in the toolbox.

I'd just ridden home from Miz Becky's Tap, still too crazy about my new used motorcycle to mind the sudden early freeze, and humming "Shine On Harvest Moon." So what gets harvested in October, anyway?

Thinking corn for sure, and maybe pumpkins, I leaned the BMW into the crushed-stone drive at the Lady's Evanston mansion, then cut the ignition and let the big bike roll silently along to shelter under the wide eaves of the coach house.

It was only after I'd rocked the bike up on its center stand and started toward the door that I noticed the coupons lying in the weeds. They should have been up on the slab, snug against the bottom of the door. Maybe it meant the Lady hadn't been as careful as she always was. And maybe it meant someone had gone through the locked door ahead of me.

So I turned back to the BMW, unlocked the hinged seat, and swung it up and open to get at the toolbox. The gun, wrapped in soft cloth, was a Beretta, a compact semiautomatic with .22 LR cartridges in a seven-round magazine. I hadn't thought much about it since Happy Mallory, despite her husband's dismay at her hiring "a cheap fucking private dick," hired me to look for her long-lost son. Before that one was over, we'd all come to question her choice, for various reasons.

But that was the past, and now, with the Beretta under my belt and the coupons wedged into my jacket pocket, I unlocked and pulled open the heavy oak and beveled-glass door.

What we all called the "coach house" was basically an attic apartment over a garage that had bays for six cars and a workshop area no one used anymore. At one end there was a separate entrance and an enclosed stairway that led to a small landing with one door. I had signed a lifetime lease with the Lady—her lifetime, not mine—and later I had the landing and the doorway rebuilt. I'd paid plenty to be able to unlock the door quickly and quietly, swing it open with my foot, and have a clear view of the interior from an unexposed vantage point. After that, I could turn and run like hell down the stairs and out the door if I had to.

I'd even practiced that routine, maybe a hundred times. I'd been very nervous then, all the time. And not without reason. I'd lost my law license and gained some resourceful enemies. But time went by, and the client who'd started that particular trouble had his throat slit in Joliet Penitentiary. I'd hoped those bad days were over.

But you never know. So, feeling slightly foolish, I went through the routine. The door flew open and slammed against the wall.

No need to turn and run.

A small fire lay dying in the fireplace, and within its flickering light there were two women. The one on the couch was a stranger. The other, standing by the window overlooking the driveway, was my wife. Her name's Cass. We'd been living together off and on—mostly off—ever since the wedding. I insisted she keep a key, since this was "our" place. But she hadn't used it for longer than I wanted to calculate.

Cass turned to the woman on the couch. "See?" she said. "Didn't I tell you if we left a clue he might come through the door that way?"

My most recent excuse for our inability to mesh lifestyles was that Cass was too normal. A puzzle, really, given her set of rather eccentric parents. Her father was once a world-class chess player of some renown, and her mother a sort of scatterbrained chess groupie. They'd named her Castle.

Cass nodded toward the window. "A motorcycle, Mal? Whatever possessed you? What did the Lady say about that?"

"A BMW," I answered. "A gift—or a fee, actually—from a client. The Lady hasn't said anything about it at all. But she's certainly got nothing against fun."

Pushing the door closed behind me with my heel, I put the Beretta and the coupons on the shelf of the ancient wooden hall tree to my right. My windbreaker went on one of the tarnished brass hooks. Crossing the room, I feigned nonchalance, but was as bewildered as ever by how Cass, even in zippered sweatshirt, jeans, and inexpensive running shoes, dominated the space around her. My pleasure in her simply being there was all too familiar.

"You've been playing, too," I said, as she pushed away from a too-brief embrace. I took a tennis ball from her sweatshirt pocket and bounced it off the oak floor.

"How clever of you, Sherlock," Cass said. She smiled, then frowned. "I've brought you a client."

Why the hell she'd bring me a client, when she kept claiming what I needed was a real job, was a mystery. Maybe I wasn't the only one in this twosome that didn't always make sense.

"I don't want a client. I don't need a client." Actually, though, the money I'd gotten from Happy Mallory was about gone, and you can't pay bills with a used BMW. This potential client did look very promising from a financial angle—not to mention every other angle. Still, I wasn't anxious for work. "I don't have time for a client," I added.

Cass was undeterred. "Sharon Cooper, meet Malachy P. Foley. And Mal, don't *say* things like that. Sharon might think you're serious."

"I *am* serious," I said, turning toward the woman on the couch.

The dying fire glowed softly in the globe of the brandy glass cradled in her hand. Her skin was the smooth, rich brown of strong coffee with barely a hint of cream. With a grace that seemed utterly unconscious, she swung free the long legs that had been tucked under her on the couch, set her glass on the low table in front of the fire, smoothed some invisible wrinkles from her wool plaid skirt, and rose to greet me.

"But," I said, "maybe I could make an exception."

With the plaid skirt she wore a plain white blouse and a tailored jacket that even my innocent eye could tell came with a price tag that would have paid my rent beyond the foreseeable future. She had the long neck, high cheekbones, and all-around classic features of a *Vogue* cover girl. Her jet black hair was pulled back tightly from her face and fastened into a chignon.

"Maybe you can help me, Mr. Foley," she said. The sparkle

in her eyes came from new tears, just ready to overflow. "I'm afraid, you see, they might actually kill me."

After that, as though we were all just a scene in an old-time movie, she sighed and collapsed gently backward onto the couch, unconscious.

CHAPTER

2

"NOT SO UNUSUAL," I said. "A strong masculine presence will do that sometimes."

"I've never noticed that, myself," Cass said. "But maybe it helps if your victim hasn't slept for two days. Not to mention the B and B I gave her to settle her nerves."

I didn't offer to help as Cass arranged Sharon's limbs into a more decorous and comfortable position on the couch and tucked a blanket snugly around her. Self-restraint.

I distracted myself by pouring two glasses of wine from a bottle labeled "Cabernet Sauvignon." The bottle and the label came from California, the wine from some high Andean foothills. Technically, I guess, it wasn't a Cabernet. But it was fairly smooth, with no more than a trace of chemical flavor. And it had another quality I had learned to appreciate in a wine—it was cheap. I'd bought as many bottles as the Lady's discount coupons allowed. Handing Cass her wine, I nodded toward the couch. "Are you sure she's okay?"

"Oh yes. Just asleep." Cass sipped her wine. "She's very attractive, isn't she? Did you know she's also quite wealthy? Do you think you can help her?"

She spoke in a series of questions, as she did so often. She usually expected an answer to only the last in the series, but I always tried to answer all the questions, and in the right order. It's a game I played, to prove to myself I had billions of still-operative brain cells the cheap wine hadn't gotten to yet.

"Yes, she is," I said. "I thought she might be. And . . ." I had to concentrate. "And I have no idea." I rewarded all those hardworking little cells with a gulp of Andean red.

Cass hooked her arm through mine and walked me to the wall of windows. The fire had subsided into a hissing glow. From the darkening room on the high second floor of the coach house, through the mostly bare branches of the trees, we could see Lake Michigan, the breeze scattering chips of moonlight over the surface of the water.

" 'Like shining from shook foil,' " Cass said.

"Wordsworth?" I tried, but without much hope.

"Uh-uh," she said. "Hopkins." She teaches English literature. "Now, about Sharon. She was one of those child prodigies—a violinist. Now she's a member of a string quartet, the Leopold Ensemble. Ever hear of it?"

"No, I can't—"

"They play mostly chamber music, I think. But anyway, that's got nothing to do with the problem. The thing is, she's in an absolutely impossible situation and . . . well . . . I told her you'd help her. You will, won't you? She has no one else to turn to."

I freed my arm and brushed aside the hair that had fallen over her forehead, then leaned down and touched my lips briefly to the skin just in front of her ear. "Isn't it 'no one else to whom to turn'?"

She twisted her head away and drank some wine. "Haven't you heard of how grammar evolves? But really, do you want to hear about Sharon, or not?"

The breeze was bending the tops of the trees and rattling the ancient windowpanes. I could feel the curves of Cass's body against my side.

"Yes, I have. And yes, I'll listen, even though I'll probably regret it." I threw down another swallow of wine. Only two questions, and getting harder to remember them in order already. "But let's talk about Sharon later," I said.

She started to melt into my side. Then suddenly, as though remembering something, she stiffened and moved away. "Really, Mal, it's . . . well, it's getting late and I have an early class tomorrow. I've got to get home."

She *was* home, damn it. But we'd been through that too many times to mention it again. Instead, I followed her into the kitchen, where she rinsed her glass and set it in the sink.

"Sharon can tell you herself much better than I. It all has to do with Jason. That's her brother. He's gone, or disappeared or something. And some people are after him. And now they're going to kill her if she won't tell them where he is, and she doesn't even know if she knows where he is. And, anyway, I've got to run."

She put her hand in her sweatshirt pocket and frowned. I followed her out of the kitchen.

"Ah," she said, retrieving the tennis ball from the floor and stuffing it into her pocket. "Bye, Sherlock," she whispered, and was gone.

I missed her immediately.

Outside the windows, the breeze had grown into a wind. The strong, tall trees were bending and straining and thrashing their limbs. The ripples on the lake were probably whitecaps by now.

I set the timer on the coffeemaker and went to bed.

SOME SIX HOURS LATER I stepped into a pair of jeans, and followed the scent of fresh coffee to the kitchen. I took a package of English muffins out of a mostly empty refrigerator, split one, and dropped the two halves into the toaster. I added milk to a steaming mug of coffee and went to check on Sharon. Despite a chill in the room, she looked comfortable enough, with the blanket wrapped tightly around her.

Staring at the woman on the couch, I thought about Cass. Each time she left, it got a little worse. Each time it felt closer to the final time.

Back in the kitchen, I buttered the toasted English muffin and scooped on some of the Lady's homemade strawberry jam. You could say the Lady's my friend, but she's far more than a friend, actually. Almost a mother, or at least that nearly perfect aunt nobody ever really has. And she makes great strawberry jam. It'll never replace Cass, but the jam was a comfort nonetheless.

Saving the last two muffins for Sharon, I refilled my mug. In the space beyond the kitchen that I call the music room, I dug out my headphones and plugged them into the electronic piano that sat at right angles to a scarred old Steinway upright. With the stereo phones hugging my ears, I could hack away and not disturb the sleeping Sharon. It lacks the sound and touch of the acoustic piano, but the electric keyboard did let me look out through the windows.

The view reminded me of the previous night. Same trees, same lake, but daylight. And no Cass.

I tried a sip of the too-hot coffee, and set the mug on the floor beside me. I imagined I was back at Miz Becky's, a bar with no charm at all to anyone but the locals who hung out there, which suited Becky just fine. What suited me was Becky feeding me free pretzels and beer—up to a point—to sit at the beat-up piano in the corner two or three nights a week and practice in front of her customers.

I slid my fingers across the keys and started through my repertoire, knowing the coffee would be cold before I thought of it again.

It was nearly noon when Sharon came into the kitchen. I'd had time for a run along the lakefront and a shower. I'd even taken the Lady's coupons and restocked my meager pantry.

"I'm very sorry about last night, Mr. Foley," Sharon said. "I guess I just sort of faded away."

"No problem," I said, handing her a mug of freshly brewed coffee. "Sugar and cream are on the counter—milk actually."

"No thanks," she said. "Black is fine."

I held my tongue and tried not to gawk. Even the way she sipped coffee was something to behold. She had an innate grace that made each move flow into the next, like a ballet dancer.

"You were saying, just before you faded away, that you hoped I could help you."

"Oh, I guess it seemed possible last night. Cass was so sure you could do something. I . . . I even had her take me to get some money. But it's a very long story and . . ." She turned and walked to the window, her back to me. I wasn't sure if I could actually see her trembling, or if it was just some sort of subliminal vibration in the space between us. She was scared as hell.

She turned and held the mug cupped in both palms, as though warming her hands would ward off the chill of her fear.

"Maybe we can talk about it some other time," she said, as though that made some sense. "I'm sorry to have bothered you. You must want to get to your office."

"I don't have an office. Or, if I do, this is it."

"But Cass said you were a lawyer."

"I don't practice law anymore. My law license is suspended."

"Suspended?"

"I had a client. A pretty bad guy, actually—a rapist for sure, maybe a cop killer. The supreme court decided the attorney-client privilege didn't apply to one of our conversations and ordered me to reveal what he said. My opinion was different. That was a few years ago and neither the court nor I have changed our mind so far." I sat down. "Anyway, Cass didn't bring you here because she thought you needed a lawyer."

"Maybe I wasn't listening to her very carefully. I'm not sure why she brought me, or why I agreed to come. But it was a mistake. I should be going."

She stayed right where she was.

Maybe I'd had too much coffee, I don't know. But the woman was getting on my nerves. I stood up and started pacing around the kitchen.

"Look," I said, "I don't know what's bothering you. And awake or asleep, you certainly add to my decor. But make up your mind. If you want to go, fine. Don't look to me to stop you."

She stood up slowly and placed the coffee on the table. By then, I was really hoping she'd leave. I had a feeling her missing brother was an invitation to trouble that nobody in his right mind would want to get mixed up in. My problem is I have a hard time turning down invitations like that, once they're extended—even when there are lots of other things I'd rather do.

She stood silently for a moment, then sat back down. I'd been afraid of that.

The problem was, and we both knew it, she had nowhere else to go. If she had, Cass wouldn't have left her on my doorstep. She picked up the mug again, then set it down without drinking. She poked at the spoon lying in front of her, lining it up parallel to the edge of the table.

If she'd kept it up much longer, I might have said, "Spit it out, kid. You can trust me." Fortunately, though, I outlasted her. She took a deep breath and then the words tumbled out, as though she had to say everything before she changed her mind again.

"There's nowhere I can go. I have no family nearby. I'm afraid to involve my friends. I don't have any clothes except what I've got on, and I can't go back to my apartment. I'm scared, I'm hungry, and I don't know what to do." She ran out of breath.

"Well," I said, pressing down the lever on the toaster, "how about an English muffin?"

A spark of indignation flashed through her eyes. "Look, Mr. Foley, I'm not kidding. These people will kill me."

"It's Mal," I said, "and I'm not kidding, either. I happen to *believe* in English muffins, especially with the Lady's homemade strawberry jam, and maybe a glass of milk. You don't need any more coffee. It's whole milk, though. I may be the only one left in the world who drinks whole milk."

"You're serious, aren't you?"

"Very. You need some food, and you need to relax a little, settle down, and tell me what the hell you're talking about."

I piled jam on the toasted muffin and pushed it across the kitchen table. Sharon took it and ate it. With a glass of milk. Then a second muffin. More milk. Credit the Lady's jam again.

Neither of us said a word while she ate. When she was finished, she sat staring at her plate, her hands in her lap. She looked like a schoolgirl getting ready to ask to be excused from the room.

She looked up at me. "Who's the Lady?" she asked.

"A friend," I said.

Finally, she stood up. "I play the violin," she said. "Have you ever heard of the Leopold Ensemble?"

"Of course," I said, "a string quartet, chamber music." She

looked surprised, and flattered, too, so why not pour it on a little? "You mean . . . you play with *them?*"

"Yes. Some friends and I began the group. But . . ." She turned, and I followed her into the living room. "I want to show you something."

Near the end of the couch where she'd spent the night she stooped to the floor. When she stood and turned to me, she had a black leather violin case in her hands. There were tears in her eyes and she was trembling again, quite visibly now. She held the case out with two hands, as though handing me a baby.

"Open it," she said. "I can't."

I took the case. She sat down on the couch and I sat next to her. I laid the case on the coffee table and the two of us stared at it for a moment. There were three catches that held it tightly closed. Leaning forward, I loosened one, then another. At that point, there was a hint in the air of why Sharon was afraid. I released the third catch, and opened the case.

The violin was beautiful, its wood gleaming with a light that seemed to come from within. It lay, delicate and fragile, in a lush, velvet-cushioned bed. But it wasn't alone in bed. Stretched along beside the elegant neck of the instrument, squeezed almost flat into the cobalt blue velvet, was a rather small, but otherwise ordinary, gray rat. Its head lay at a grotesque angle to the rest of its body, wrenched nearly off its neck. The rat's red-veined eyes bulged wide in fear and death, and the blood and other fluids coagulated near its body's orifices made it clear the creature hadn't been quite dead before it was crushed into its coffin.

I lowered the top of the case gently. Sharon was staring into the fireplace.

I went into the kitchen, opened the door to an unheated

back stairway, and put the violin case on the floor. With the help of scissors, gloves, and lots of paper towels, I separated the rat, the violin, and the case. The violin and the open case I left, apart from each other, on a shelf at the top of the stairs, with the window wide open. The rat, inside multiple layers of plastic bags, I left on the floor, to go out with the garbage later.

Back in the living room, Sharon hadn't moved from the couch. I pulled a chair around to face her.

We talked for a long time, and when we finished she gave me some money—a very large sum of money, in fact. It was nearly enough to convince me that money was the reason I agreed to help her—and not some immature compulsion to prove I wasn't afraid.

Out in the hall by the kitchen I picked up the little package from the floor and held it to my nose. Through all that plastic, the smell was faint, but unmistakable. Back in the kitchen, I opened the freezer compartment above the refrigerator. As usual, there was plenty of available space. I laid the plastic-wrapped rat in the freezer.

Because, as Fats Waller used to say, "One never knows, do one?"

CHAPTER 3

Leaving Sharon in the coach house, I spent some time at the library at Northwestern University, in the newspaper archives. After that I headed out to seek an appointment with Breaker Hanafan.

Breaker knows more than most people about what's really going on in Chicago, a lot of things you don't read in the papers—until after they've happened, maybe. He's what the press used to call "an underworld figure." That gives him a unique vantage point. He's like a man who lives in a sewer and learns what's happening above by studying the feces dropping down around him.

Although I'd once had something of an understanding with Breaker, we'd been out of touch for a while and I'd heard getting in to see him was more difficult than ever. He'd attained some success and, with it, a lot of worry. Even for someone whose job description included making enemies, he'd gotten a bit paranoid. I'd need someone to pass on the word that I wanted to talk to him.

Within a few hours, I'd found someone. Two of Breaker's lieutenants, in fact. But things weren't going well at all.

One of the two was, to put it bluntly, fat and ugly. He kept blinking his eyes in a sort of squinting way that used his whole face. It looked like he had a migraine headache. Not long into our conversation, I was hoping he did.

The fat man kept his heavy hands busy. At about ten-second intervals, his left palm would sweep back the thick black hair that kept falling in oily clumps over his bulging forehead. His right fist was wrapped around a piece of plumber's pipe—and not that plastic stuff that's outlawed by the city's building code. He gestured and poked with the pipe, unconsciously punctuating his conversation. It wasn't funny, but it reminded me of that comic punctuation routine of Victor Borge's. For the fat man, commas were a wave of the pipe to his right; periods were a downstroke. My big problem, though, was his exclamation points. Those were forward thrusts with the pipe, about chest high. Since my back was shoved up against the car and we were less than an arm's length apart, I was wishing he'd take it easy on the exclamation points. They were making dents in my rib cage.

The fat man was enraged. "You know [wave], that was a real stupid thing to do [downstroke]. You're a real dumb fuckhead [thrust]! You must not know shit about nothin' [thrust]! You're fuckin' crazy [thrust]!"

Each exclamation point put the pipe into my chest like a punch press. I didn't hear anything crack, but you can't always believe your ears. With my eyes watering and my breath coming in short gasps, I forced my hands to stay at my sides below my waist and said nothing.

"Do you unnerstand me?" the fat man raged. The question mark was a new move, a quick lift under the chin, with the round end of the pipe boring a hole into the soft skin just in front of my windpipe. He held the pipe perpendicular to the ground, forcing my chin up. "Do you *unnerstand* me, you dumb fuckhead?"

I couldn't have answered, even if I could have thought of something to say. He was lifting me up on my toes with the pipe, forcing my jaws together.

Finally, he gave up looking for an answer and shook his head disgustedly. "Jesus Christ, Mick, what a dumb fuckhead this guy is." Repetitive, but at least the downstroke let me lower my head.

Mick seemed barely more than a teenager. His features were gathered together in the middle of a wide face that was too large for the scrawny neck that held it up. His hair, thin and blond, was combed straight down over his forehead and would have reached his eyebrows, if he'd had any eyebrows. His thin lips curled down on both ends. His eyes were pale gray, sad, and streetwise beyond his years. "Let's go," he said. "We got no time for this shit. We gotta get Breaker his car back."

"Whaddaya mean? This fuckhead tore up my ticket. He must be crazy."

"I know, I know. I seen him too, didn't I? He don't look crazy, but maybe he is. Anyway, you don't need that ticket. No cop around here gonna mess with this car."

"I know, but that ain't—"

"Will you come on? Breaker's already pissed you messed up the fuckin' Ford. We gotta finish the rounds and get his car back to him like he said."

They talked to each other as if I weren't there anymore, giving me a chance to catch my breath. Thinking maybe I *was* crazy, after all.

I'd been waiting for Breaker's collection agents for over an hour, peering out through the murky window of a bar across the street from the Monumental Theatre, a northside porno movie house. I'd worked my way through too many Old-Styles when a late-model Jaguar sedan pulled up to the No Parking sign in front of the theater. The fat man had heaved himself out of the driver's seat and taken a parking ticket from the pocket of his rumpled suit coat. As he was fixing it to the windshield of the Jaguar, I hurried across the street.

"Excuse me," I called, my voice loud enough to attract

furtive glances from the pair of sheepish conventioneers at the ticket booth.

But the two goons had ignored me and headed toward the theater entrance. That's when I did what any crazy person in my place would have done. I took the ticket from the windshield and tore it in half.

"Hey," I called, trotting around the front of the car and waving my arms, "you forgot your parking ticket."

Both men turned then, just as they reached the theater doors. I held one half of the torn ticket between the thumb and forefinger of each hand and, as they stared at me, I let the halves flutter to the sidewalk.

I had gotten their attention, all right, together with a set of bruised upper ribs and a raw hole under my chin.

But now, only moments later, they were talking to each other as if I weren't standing there on the sidewalk with my back pressed against the side of the Jaguar. Short attention spans.

". . . so forget it," Mick was saying.

"Aw, Christ," the fat man said. "I guess you're right." He looked at me again and shook his head. "But he shouldn'a tore up my ticket. It was my last one."

The two of them turned away. I relaxed and took a deep breath. Just as I did, the fat man whirled back around and drove the end of the pipe hard and deep into my belly. I crumpled to my knees. Any possibility of making a sound rushed out of me with my breath. I couldn't keep my crossed wrists from instinctively pressing against my abdomen. But I forced my head upward and refused my body's demand that I roll up into a ball. I kept my eyes on Breaker Hanafan's two goons.

They didn't seem impressed.

The fat man laughed and tossed the pipe through the open passenger window into the front seat. "You shouldn'a tore up my ticket, fuckhead," he said, and the two of them disappeared into the Monumental before I'd gotten a chance to tell them I wanted to see Breaker Hanafan. Didn't even bother to lock the car. Like Mick said, no one was likely to mess with it.

I figured they'd be inside long enough to count the day's take—assuming they could count—and extract Breaker's percentage. I took some time to catch my breath, first crouching on the sidewalk, then gradually straightening and twisting from side to side, testing my chest and stomach muscles. The people walking by didn't seem to think twice about a man kneeling on the sidewalk clutching his gut, or struggling to his feet, holding on to a car. On that dingy block, I fit right into the scene.

Once I was able to breathe freely, I reached through the Jaguar's open window and took out the fat man's pipe. I walked to the front of the car and carefully smashed each and every light, working methodically—headlights, parking lights, turn signals. It was satisfying, somehow. So satisfying that I went to the back of the car and smashed the rear lights also.

It was Breaker's car and I wanted Breaker's attention. But I admit I lost control a little. Inside the rear window was the eye-level brake light. Thinking I should do a thorough job, I took the pipe in two hands and went to work on the rear window. It exploded into thousands of tiny safety-glass particles, and I smashed the interior brake light. If anyone on the street thought I was acting strange, they kept it to themselves.

My time was running out, but I wasn't thinking clearly. I circled the Jaguar and removed every window, one by one, then the mirrors. The only remaining glass was the passenger-side front window. It was down, and I would have needed the ignition key to operate the electric window. Nothing in life is perfect.

I placed the pipe back on the front seat, together with one of my business cards.

By the time I stumbled across the street to the BMW, my stomach was heaving and I felt light-headed. I knelt on one knee then, and vomited—mostly beer, maybe some remnants of strawberry jam—into the gutter. Raising my head, I stared back at the Jaguar. With no windows, no lights, the car had a forlorn, demoralized look. But it was only a car. It didn't feel anything.

Later on I would wonder about my behavior—wonder a lot. But just then, after I'd finished throwing up in the gutter, I was already beginning to feel much better. I hadn't invited Sharon Cooper and her missing brother into my life. I had lots of other things to do, things I enjoyed. But she'd showed up—with a big stack of money, and just the sort of problem I don't seem able to walk away from. So, when you can't do the things you enjoy, you ought to try to enjoy the things you do.

I rode off on the BMW, going through the gears smoothly, leaving the Monumental Theatre, the sad-looking car, and the vomit behind. The quiet throbbing power of the bike was soothing. Breaker Hanafan wouldn't be happy, but I'd get the face-to-face meeting I was looking for.

The ball had started to roll, and there'd be no stopping it now.

CHAPTER 4

I WAS PEERING into my bathroom mirror at the circle under my chin, when the phone beeped at me. Walter Barkley, a friend who's always been into gadgetry, had convinced me to let him set up a phone-mail system. I didn't much need it. But Walter had a great time.

If it beeped for a while and I didn't pick up or punch any buttons, Cass's recorded voice would answer. "Thank you for calling Foley Enterprises. If you wish to speak to someone in our Investigations Division," making the words sound capitalized, "please press two now. For our Entertainment Division, press three. For legal representation, although our Legal Division is not presently accepting clients, you may press four and someone will assist you. If you need to hear this message again, you haven't been paying attention."

That last part was my contribution.

I got about a dozen calls in a heavy week. Callers who pressed two or three got a different voice, Walter's girlfriend, inviting them to leave a message. Callers who pressed four—very rare these days—had their calls transferred to the office of Barney Green, a lawyer in Chicago's Loop. We'd been partners once and I wouldn't say I got anything out of those cases, since the rules prohibit Barney from sharing a legal fee with a suspended lawyer. But I never got hurt by sending him a case, either.

Anyway, the phone beeped. I didn't answer it and when the message began, the caller must have pressed seven, which wasn't on the list of choices. Cass on tape was interrupted by Cass live. "Mal? Are you there? Can you hear me?"

I picked up the phone. "Hi."

"It's me," Cass said. She paused. Finally she asked, "Well?"

"Well?" I asked back at her.

"Come *on,* Mal. Are you going to help her? Can you find Jason?"

"I'm going to try," I said, covering two questions with one answer. "In fact, I've already . . . reached out to a possible source of information. Meanwhile, Sharon has to stay out of sight for a while and needs to buy some clothes. Want to help with that?"

"Are you kidding? I'll be there in half an hour, with my shopping shoes on. We can stay at my folks' place for the weekend." She hung up.

"I love you, too," I said into the dead phone. "Why don't you come back home?"

BY FIVE-THIRTY, Sharon and Cass had driven off to ransack the malls. Sharon didn't look well. Maybe shopping would be therapeutic. We decided to meet for a late Mexican supper at Juanito's, about halfway between Evanston and the Wisconsin border, not far from Cass's parents' home.

That gave me several hours. It made no sense to sit around waiting to hear from Breaker Hanafan. Although he couldn't ignore my message, he wasn't the type to call and make an appointment. Meanwhile, there were things I could do. So, Friday night or not, Miz Becky's would have to get along without its piano player.

It was another crisp, clear fall evening, with a growing chill in the air that made me wonder whether I should take the car and leave the BMW behind. However, never one to make the wise decision, I pulled wool trousers over a pair of long johns, and dug out my wool-lined leather jacket and a pair of warm gloves. As I fired up the bike and headed down the driveway, I went over in my mind what Sharon had told me.

She came from one of that handful of truly wealthy black families in Chicago. Her father, Alexander Cooper, had started as a dentist. But he had an inquisitive and inventive mind, and before long he had a patent on a root-canal gadget the world's endodontists found they couldn't do without. The royalties rolled in, and Dr. Cooper sold his practice to concentrate on his inventing.

At the age of forty, he met Melissa Gatreaux Futrell, fifteen years his junior. She'd come to Chicago from New Orleans to attend the Goodman School of Drama, grew into a local star, and was about to move on to New York or L.A. when, instead, she married the dashing inventor. Sharon came along. Then Jason.

The two kids had it all—plenty of money, good looks, intelligence, and devoted, if somewhat preoccupied, parents. But the very advantages that helped Sharon discover her gift and glide easily into adulthood proved stumbling blocks to Jason. He was determined to show he was no better than anyone else. When good grades came despite his not trying, he had to prove he didn't care by "acting the clown," boisterous and uncooperative. In short, Jason sounded like a pain in the ass—on his better days.

By high school, Jason was beyond the control of his parents, who were caught up in a whirlwind of social and civic activities. Basketball was the only thing he let himself excel at. He was a natural athlete, whom every new school was delighted to have—but none for very long. His bewildered parents cleaned up one mess after another, trotting him from school to school.

Jason finally ended up at a place called Pepperton Military

Academy, a boarding school in rural Wisconsin, with a high percentage of social misfits among its student body. He spent two years at "Pepper Mill" and, much to Sharon's surprise, he thrived, despite his initial fierce struggle against "a bunch of bullshit rules, weird white dudes, and Mickey Mouse uniforms."

Sharon believed Jason's success at Pepper Mill was due to his basketball coach, Frank Parkins, the only black on the faculty.

I remembered Parkins from his basketball playing days, but most of what I knew came from a profile of him in the *Chicago Tribune* I found on microfiche in the archives at Northwestern. Parkins himself had attended Pepper Mill on a grant established by a born-again Christian who owned a chain of liquor stores in Milwaukee's black ghetto and felt driven by the Lord to "give something back." Parkins went on to the University of Wisconsin, where everyone said he'd have eaten the Big Ten alive if he'd had any support. Signed by an NBA expansion team, he soon dropped out of sight, bouncing from one team to another, never able to achieve stardom, or even first-string status.

While still in college, Frank Parkins had the great good luck to marry a social-work major who had no deep interest in fame or fanfare. Came that inevitable autumn when no NBA team picked him up—Lauren was still there. Unlike so many of his fellow faded jocks, Parkins had a goal and a plan. His goal was to coach at a major collegiate basketball power. His plan was to begin at a little-known high school, build winning programs at successively larger schools, and then break into the college ranks. What better place to start, he thought, than his own Pepper Mill?

Parkins's plan, though, hit a snag. He'd been approached early on by several high schools with stronger basketball programs, but he found coaching the mixed bag of kids at Pepper Mill so satisfying he kept deciding to stay on "a little longer." His wife, too, had found a niche, running a women's "crisis intervention center" not far from the school.

The presence of Coach Parkins and the absence of much else to do "was just perfect for Jason," according to Sharon. Parkins drove Jason beyond his self-imposed limitations, and he thrived as he never had before, first on the basketball court and then, inevitably, in the rest of his life. It was a struggle, but his behavior and his grades improved enough to keep him eligible for the team.

Jason led Pepper Mill to a winning season, and then an unbeaten season. Still, no college that offered national exposure would take a chance on him. He enrolled in a small college in a suburb that adjoined Chicago on the city's northwest side, intending to prove himself and get a chance with a major school.

Now, barely into his second year at Cragman College, Jason had vanished.

Sharon hadn't even known he was gone until the first phone call. The man had wanted to interview Jason for a newspaper article, but no one knew where Jason was. The man was polite but persistent, and Sharon reluctantly promised to find Jason for him. She had called Jason. There was no answer. In fact, she tried a dozen times, night and day. She went to his dorm and no one knew where he was. His basketball coach was fuming.

Three days later, when the man called back the fourth time, Sharon was "flustered," she said. "Mad at myself for agreeing to help, mad at Jason for being hard to find, and mad at that darn reporter for pestering me." Instead of admitting she didn't know where her brother was, she'd told the man, "Stop calling me. I can't help you."

The man accused her of being deliberately unhelpful. He claimed she could find Jason if she really tried. Frustrated, she lost her temper. "You're right," she lied. "Of *course* I could tell you where Jason is. I just don't want to." She hung up.

Minutes later, the phone rang again. It was the same man. In a voice at once patient but more ominous, he admitted there was no newspaper article. "I must speak with him, however." He paused. "I'll be frank with you, Miss Cooper. Jason has broken the law. Now, we don't want to destroy his future in basketball. We don't want to go to the police. We simply want to talk to him. Tell me where he is. You'll be doing him a big favor"—another pause—"and yourself a favor, too."

Sharon, recognizing the unmistakable threat, still refused to help. She remembered the caller's response with absolute clarity.

"I'm very sorry to hear that. I really am." He sighed like a father whose reasoning with his stubborn child has gotten nowhere. "And, if you don't change your mind, *Sharonella,* you'll be very sorry, too."

His use of her given name, a name she had abandoned in fifth grade, had sent a chill through her. She was shaking as she hung up the phone.

There'd been more calls, with messages left on her machine when she wouldn't pick up the phone. She had no choice but to help, the man told her. They knew where she lived. They knew where her parents lived, and that they were traveling out of the country just then.

Terrified now, Sharon had not gone to the police. She knew the caller wasn't a policeman, but was afraid he might be right about there being something Jason didn't want known to the police. She didn't know what to do, and so she did nothing.

Then, the last call. She'd be receiving a "package" very soon, the man said. She was to consider it a final request. "Tell us where Jason is, Sharonella. Learn a lesson from what's happened to the little friend we're giving you. You can't get away."

Late that afternoon she found the "package," the "little friend."

There'd been no sign her car was broken into. She'd taken her violin case out of the trunk and with her to a practice room she used at Northwestern. When she opened the case she'd "screamed and screamed and screamed" inside the soundproofed practice room.

She slammed the case shut, and fled with it to her car. She drove around all night in a daze. Midmorning the next day found her back on the campus, wandering aimlessly. Eventually, she ran into Cass, who'd been one of her professors as an undergraduate.

That's all I knew as I geared the BMW up and down through the Friday evening traffic. What I didn't know was who was looking for Jason, or why. But those were things Breaker Hanafan might know. And while I waited to hear from him, I could talk to someone else who might have at least a hint about where Jason was.

CHAPTER 5

"LET'S GO, get back . . . *back,* goddamn it! All right, keep moving . . . *move,* goddamn it!"

Alone, halfway up the empty bleachers at Cragman College, sucking lukewarm Pepsi from a can, I listened to the unconsciously rhythmic chant of Coach Harvey Cartwright, haranguing his team through its final full-court scrimmage of the evening.

A few third-stringers lolled on the bench, while a student manager gathered stray basketballs and stuffed them into a huge sack. The players on the floor looked exhausted—blowing hard, but otherwise nearly silent.

Closing my eyes, I rested my shoulders back on the bench behind me. The bounce of the ball and the sharp staccato squeals of basketball shoes against the waxed floor echoed around Harvey's frenetic shouts, as though some crazed animal trainer were driving a pack of panting, yelping dogs back and forth across an empty circus arena. My mind floated and I breathed deeply of fifty years of sweat and dust and floor wax.

"All right, that's it. Outta here. Just get outta here and go home."

The suddenly softened tone of Harvey's voice jarred me out of a doze. The players stood in a haphazard circle around him, some with hands on their hips, others bent over with their hands on their knees, breathing the deep, desperate sobs of athletes at the limit of their endurance.

"You guys look bad," Harvey said, his shoulders sagging, his voice dripping despondency. "Really bad. Get your butts back here tomorrow at ten A.M. sharp. Now go home and get some sleep, Friday night or not."

The players dragged themselves away.

"Me, I ain't gonna get no sleep," Harvey called out mournfully to their backs. "I gotta worry what am I gonna do with a bunch of mopes who look so bad."

As the last player banged the door behind him, Harvey turned and looked up at me. "Fuckin' guys look damn good, don't they?" he said, the familiar Cartwright grin spreading across his face.

I lifted my Pepsi in a toast, and clumped down the bleachers to the gym floor. "Yes they do, Harve. And you're looking good yourself."

His phony dejection gone, he grabbed my hand and shook it enthusiastically. "Playin' any ball?" That was hello for Harvey. He was on the far side of fifty, but the game was still the center of his life. He coached it, he talked it, and he even still played it—in any league that would fit his schedule.

Just about anyone in Chicago who knew basketball knew Harvey. I'd logged playing time with him myself, and some against him. He played like he coached, with a ferocity that almost compensated for what he, like most of his teams, lacked in physical talent. He had coached at Cragman since most people could remember, and he'd be there till they chased him away.

"Been a while," I said. "I just lost interest. Been playing the piano a lot."

"Christ, I'll never lose interest. If my number comes up while I'm playing ball, I'll die happy."

When I said nothing, Harvey snatched up a sweatshirt and three or four dog-eared spiral notebooks and stuffed them into his gym bag. "Anyway," he said, "you don't look like you come out here to shoot the shit about the old days. And you know what? I got a feeling I ain't gonna like why you did come. So why not wait and tell me over a coupl'a cold ones?"

I followed Harvey through the wooden double doors, out of the gym and into a damp, tiled hallway. The sounds and smells of the locker room floated up from the far end of the hall. The clanging of locker doors punctuated the whoops of laughter and the same shouted obscenities that must have been pouring out of locker rooms since the dawn of team sports, in Sparta or the Olmec Empire or wherever.

"Team sounds happy," I said.

He stopped by a door on the right side of the hall several yards short of the hilarity. The door was a windowless slab of dark wood. Glued to it at eye level were gold-colored squares with slanted black letters that spelled out:

COACH

COME ON IN

The letters were almost evenly spaced.

"Shoot, they oughta be happy." He fumbled through his gym bag for a ring of keys and unlocked the door. "Best damn six or seven ballplayers I ever had on one team. And the best ain't even here just now. When he gets back next week, we'll all be even happier."

Inside the office, Harvey swept the contents of a wooden chair onto the floor. I sat down and flipped my Pepsi can into a wastebasket positioned under a sign taped to the wall that said "Cans" and had an arrow pointing downward. Harvey went behind the desk to a small refrigerator and pulled out two cans of light beer. We popped the tops.

Harvey grinned. "Doesn't get any better than this, Mal."

The thing about Harvey Cartwright was, he really meant it. Sitting there in his ten-by-twelve-foot office, made even smaller by the clutter of notebooks and assorted papers, surrounded by snapshots and team photos, fading and curling around the thumbtacks that held them to the walls, he was at home. Air that smelled like sweat flowed in and out of the windowless office through vents set high in the walls. Harvey didn't ask for much and didn't have much. One of the lucky ones. There wasn't much anyone could take away from him.

"Next week?" I asked.

"Next week what?"

"Is he really coming back next week?"

Harvey took a long drink. "That's why you're here, isn't it? Jason Cooper?"

I nodded.

"Well, next week is what I said. You know anything different?"

"I don't know anything at all. That's why I'm here. I'm trying to find out where the kid is, and why."

"Shoot, I don't know where he is." He swallowed the last of his beer. "I just know he called and said he's coming back."

"Wisconsin, Harve?"

He crumpled his beer can and tossed it across the office, banking it expertly off the wall. "Wisconsin what?" he asked as the can dropped into the wastebasket.

His attempt to distract me came an instant too late. He knew I'd seen the acknowledgment flicker across his face like the flash of a strobe. And I thought maybe he wasn't sorry about that. But we both played out the game.

"All right," I said, "so you can't tell me where he is. But what *can* you tell me? I'm not the only one looking, and the other guys have a head start."

"Yeah," Harvey said, popping the top on another beer.

"They been here already. Two guys. Real polite. Cold as ice. Asking about the kid like they were cops or something. You know, 'Sir, this' and 'Sir, that.' Pressing real hard, though. That was before Jason called, and I told them the truth, that I didn't know nothin'. They never came back. Then, when Jason called, I figured the problem was over."

"Not hardly." I told him just a little about the phone calls to Sharon.

"Aw Christ, Mal, what the hell's going on?"

"I don't know. But I need to find Jason. And I got a feeling time's running out. What can you tell me about his call?"

"Well, it was a few days ago, after practice, about nine o'clock. He called here, said he was at . . . said he ran into some personal problems he had to work out and he'd be back next week. Maybe I shoulda asked him more about it, I don't know. I was just happy he was all right."

"Got any idea what personal problems? I mean, drugs, or something?"

"Jesus, I don't think so, Mal. I thought about that a little, but I . . . well, I guess I was just hoping it was woman trouble or something."

"No offense, Harve, but why would *you* be the one he'd call?"

"Far as I can tell, Jason's not tight with his parents. And I never even knew he *had* a sister. All this kid has is basketball. I mean, a lotta guys love basketball. With Jason, it's more. It's like the game's what holds him in one piece. You know, at six-five, he's small for the big time. But he's damn good, and getting better."

"And no hint what the trouble was, or *how* he'd work things out?"

"He didn't say, I didn't ask and"—Harvey twisted uneasily in his chair—"deep down I guess I didn't wanna know. I told myself it was nothing. Now *you* show up. And I know there must be trouble, 'cause I hear trouble and you been hand in hand lately. Me, I'd rather stay away from trouble. I want Jason to be all right, and playing ball. But I don't wanna know what's been going on if I don't have to."

He stood up, and so did I, and we added two more cans to his collection. I followed him out into the hallway, thinking it was lucky the cold, polite questioners had gotten to Harvey before he knew anything—lucky for Jason and lucky for Harvey.

Out in the hall, with the locker room nearly silent now, Harvey told me I ought to get back to playing some ball. I made him promise to call me if he heard anything. We shook hands and he turned back toward the locker room, to his life. I turned the other way, toward the double doors, to *my* life. At least Harvey had his life figured out.

Halfway across the darkened cavern of the gym, I stood motionless, feeling the silence and the emptiness. *Stay away from trouble,* Harvey had said. I kept hearing that. Sounded simple enough. But even the ones who said it—even Cass—sometimes made it impossible. Or maybe I made it impossible. But at least they helped.

Stay away from trouble. My dad always said that—though not often to me, because he never talked to me that much. My dad the cop, whose goal was to do his job and *stay away from trouble.* Bust ass to get to the scene when there's "shots fired"? Hell, leave that to those cowboys in the tactical units. Success finally came with permanent desk duty. Answer phones, talk to walk-ins, and *stay away from trouble.* But even then you could overhear things. Like maybe how some dicks got something going—a truckload of TV sets or whatever. Figuring you heard, they offer a sliver of their pie. You say no, you *stay away from trouble,* and you don't need anything.

They insist. So? You take it or maybe you got a different kind of trouble. The wife wouldn't understand, so you open a new account. Not that much money, really, but dirty. Maybe you'll just give it away . . . the Franciscans or someone. Then one day you wake up and your picture's in the fucking paper with the rest of them. You get probation, no jail time. But you lose the job, the pension, and what self-respect you had. Jesus, all you wanted was to *stay away from—*

The sudden banging of heat pipes somewhere under the bleachers pounded through the empty gym like gunfire. A wake-up call. It was Friday night. One part of me wanted to run to Miz Becky's—drink some beer, eat some pretzels, play some piano. But another part didn't feel all that bad about heading out to do what I'd rather not be doing.

CHAPTER

6

The BMW was waiting where I'd left it in the nearly deserted parking lot. But now it had company.

"Mick and me been waiting for you, fuckhead," the fat one said. Mick was silent. The two of them leaned against the side of a dark Ford sedan, Mick motionless and practicing his bored look, the fat man slapping a familiar piece of pipe lazily into his left palm.

"Jaguar in the shop?" I asked.

The fat man squinted his eyes and turned his head to Mick. "Man thinks he's funny. Whadda *you* think."

Mick started to clean his left thumbnail with his right forefinger. "Let's just get on with it, Wilbur."

"That your name, is it?" I asked. "Well look, Fat Wilbur, I gotta—"

"Shut up." Fat Wilbur heaved his body upright from the side of the Ford. "Mr. Hanafan wasn't happy when he seen his car," he said. "He wants to talk to you. We're taking you to see him."

"No," I said.

Fat Wilbur squinted and grinned and wiped his palm across the greasy hair over his left ear. Mick shifted his gaze from his thumbnail to me. The smaller man seemed somehow the bigger problem. I wondered if I could take them both. Maybe I could. Anyway, there wasn't much choice. I wanted to see Breaker, all right. I just didn't want to be *taken*.

"I dunno, Mick. Maybe my hearing's gone bad. Did the man say he don't wanna go see Mr. Hanafan?" Fat Wilbur leaned toward me and away from Mick as he spoke.

Mick spoke quietly, patiently, as though to a child. "He did. He said he don't wanna go see Mr. Hanafan."

I wanted to goad them into making the first move. "Aw, come on, Mick," I said. "I mean Wilbur here's probably got grease in his ears. But you, you're just not paying attention. I didn't say I don't want to go see Mr. Hanafan. What I said was a couple of broken-down half-wits like you two aren't taking me. When you don't listen—"

Fat Wilbur moved toward me, Mick a step behind him. I looked past the fat man, over his right shoulder. "Now, Mick!" I shouted.

The human reflexive system hasn't changed much over the last several hundred thousand years. Mick froze, startled. Fat Wilbur turned his head to his right and I hit him just under the left side of his chin with the heel of my right palm, bringing my hand up from my waist and following through well past impact. I felt his jaws click together and his head snap backward. The big man was dazed and off-balance for an instant. I lifted the pipe from his hand without resistance and rolled into him with my right shoulder. He toppled backward into Mick and the two of them went to the ground, Fat Wilbur on top.

I stood over them as they fumbled around on the pavement. With Mick still beneath him, Fat Wilbur got to his hands and knees. I tapped him on the back of the skull with the pipe—rather gently, I thought—but enough to drop him back on top of Mick, who by then seemed more interested in getting something out of his jacket pocket than in getting to his feet. I stepped behind Mick's left side as the fat man rolled off him to his right.

When Mick finally got his right hand out of his jacket pocket with the gun, I kicked him in his left side, just below the rib cage—hard. He exhaled a noise that sounded something like "Galooomf." But he held on to the gun. I kicked him in the same place—harder. I'm not sure what he said that time. But the gun fell to the pavement and I scooped it up. It was a .38-caliber revolver.

With a backhand toss, I sent the pipe clattering across the pavement, and switched the gun to my right hand. Then it was my turn to lean against the side of the Ford and practice looking bored.

The two tough guys gradually picked themselves up off the ground and stood staring at a point somewhere between their toes and the barrel of the .38 leveled at their bellies. They seemed to have lost their spark.

I made sure there were no more guns among us.

"Into the front seat," I said.

They climbed in, Fat Wilbur behind the wheel. I got in the back and held the gun lightly against Fat Wilbur's right shoulder.

"What now?" he asked.

"Now we go see Breaker," I said.

"Well, damn," Mick pouted. "What was all that shit for, then? We were taking you, anyway."

"All that shit was because you're *not* taking me," I said. "I'm taking you."

"Big fucking difference," Fat Wilbur muttered.

But there *was* a difference, of course. And they knew it.

"Drive on, Wilbur," I said, and settled back in the seat.

There really wasn't much backseat legroom, for a sedan. I would have preferred the Jaguar.

CHAPTER 7

As a driver, Fat Wilbur had far more enthusiasm than skill. Cursing with every yank on the wheel, he hurled us around corners and dove into traffic like a drunk into a crowded pool. We careened down the Kennedy Expressway toward the Loop, leaving a trail of bewildered drivers in our wake. Fat Wilbur had a great time. I worked on keeping my beer down. Mick slept like a baby.

Finally, on Randolph Street just west of the Loop, we slowed to a crawl. Randolph there is four lanes wide, plus the equivalent of a couple of extra lanes on each side to accommodate the convoys of refrigerated trucks that carry fresh meats, fruits, and vegetables in and out of the warehouses lining the street. At ten o'clock at night, there was little moving traffic and only an occasional produce truck sitting silently in the bright, eerie glow of the streetlights.

Mick woke up and tapped out a number on the car phone. "It's us," he said. "Open up."

Fat Wilbur pulled the Ford to the front of a metal roll-up door that would have handled a moving van. When the door stayed closed, he tapped the horn three times. Nothing happened.

Mick still had the phone to his ear. "Now what?" he growled. He listened, then laid the receiver in its cradle.

"Turn off the lights," he said.

"Christ," Fat Wilbur complained, but the lights went out.

A slow minute passed, then another. Finally, the metal

overhead door slid open. Fat Wilbur drove inside, into darkness. The door clanged down behind us and we sat there.

Fat Wilbur turned off the engine. "Uh, look, Foley," he said. I could barely see the outline of the back of his head in the front seat. "Mr. Hanafan ain't been too happy lately and, uh, you could do me and Mick a favor. It wouldn't cost you nothing."

"I know," I said, "I know." I emptied the gun and stuffed the live cartridges down behind the seat cushion.

Now that we were here, I had nothing to lose by Hanafan not knowing who brought whom. If he found out, they might be out of work, at best. Besides, you never know when doing someone a favor might prove helpful down the line. I passed the gun clumsily to Mick. More time went by as my eyes tried to accommodate to the darkness.

The howl of an air horn roared, suddenly, not two feet from the car window, and a blinding beam of light struck me full in the face. In the instant before my eyes snapped shut, I glimpsed Mick facing me over the back of the front seat, pointing the empty gun at my nose.

The car door was yanked open and I stumbled out, eyes clenched tight against the light. A pair of hands placed me in the position, feet spread wide and far enough out from the Ford so my weight was on my palms against the car window. The hands searched me, quickly and expertly, while the voice that belonged to the hands spoke in a rolling baritone. "Y'all been through this before, my man. I can tell."

Too often, I thought. I opened my eyes to darkness again.

"He's clean," the voice said. He would have found a sharp toothpick if I'd had one.

"Course he is, asshole," Fat Wilbur said. "Me an' Mick seen to that."

There was an audible sigh, then, "One thing 'bout you,

Wilbur, you a *consistent* motherfucker. Now you an' Mick see to keeping my man here under control. I'll get the light. You take him on up."

Footsteps receded into the darkness. A door opened and closed. In a moment, a single pale lightbulb went on in the ceiling three stories above our heads.

"Okay," Fat Wilbur said, "move your ass."

"Be nice, Wilbur," I said, "and you two can march me into Breaker's office and he'll never know Mick's gun is as empty as your head. Otherwise—"

"Jesus, forget that shit," Mick said, waving the gun in my face. "Let's just get moving before Breaker gets pissed at all of us."

We were in a huge indoor truck dock. To the left of the overhead door the building stretched away into darkness. About thirty feet to the right a metal stairway, like fire-escape stairs, led up the side of a brick wall about a story and a half to a platform and a steel door. To the right of the door, beyond reach from the platform, was a large reflecting-glass window. A person inside could view the length of the dock from that window. As we walked to the stairs in the dim light, it suddenly struck me that neither the stairs nor the platform at the top had a guardrail. What would OSHA say?

Fat Wilbur started up first, with me following, and Mick and his empty gun trailing behind. By the time we neared the top, Fat Wilbur was panting. He stopped one step short of the platform and had to stretch high above his head to press a button embedded in the bricks beside the door. We waited long enough for Fat Wilbur to caress the grease above his ears twice.

Finally, the steel door swung open across the tiny platform. If we'd been standing in front of the door instead of on the stairs, we would have been swept off onto the concrete floor below.

Fat Wilbur stepped up and through the open door. I followed, and then Mick, who pulled the door closed behind us.

"Well, well, well . . . c'mon in, Foley. Wilbur, clear off a chair for the man."

To the right of the door, Breaker Hanafan was parked in a gray metal swivel chair at a gray metal desk that faced the picture window overlooking the dock area. The desk was piled high with ancient papers, phone directories, and huge, bulging loose-leaf binders. A squat mug, with the face of Winston Churchill on the side and jammed full of wooden pencils and ballpoint pens, sat beneath a goosenecked lamp that had no lightbulb. In a semicircular clearing on the desk there were three half-full plastic foam cups, a hot plate with a glass carafe of coffee, and an old black telephone with a row of buttons below the dial. One of the buttons glowed.

The overhead fluorescent lights reflected off Hanafan's bald head. What hair he had was white and thick and ran in a ring from ear to ear around the back of his head. Also running around his head was a thin elastic band that held a patch over his right eye. He had the shape and face of a muscular monk going soft around the edges. He looked a lot like a one-eyed guy who bought and sold vegetables.

Holding the telephone's receiver hunched against his left ear with his shoulder, Breaker nodded to me and waved me in the general direction of the chair Fat Wilbur had unloaded. "Mick," he said, "get Foley a beer." He sipped coffee from one of the plastic foam cups.

I sat in the gray metal chair on its gray imitation leather seat cushion and rested my arms on its gray plastic armrests. Breaker Hanafan talked on the phone. He kept saying "Yeah" and "No" and it wasn't very interesting. I gazed around the room. The wall opposite the door from the dock area held a row of glass brick windows, with a door at one end of the row. Each of the other two walls also had a door. All four doors were steel, with panic bars; and all opened outward from the office. Each had a peephole in the center, about the height of my throat, which was about the height of Breaker's one working eyeball. The door in the side wall nearest his desk had two peepholes—in and out, I supposed. You can never be too careful.

Mick got me a bottled beer from one side of a double-doored, stainless-steel refrigerator. The beer was a Moretti. There was a clock on one wall and a calendar below it that said HANAFAN & CO., Purveyors of Fine Fruits and Vegetables.

Breaker was a purveyor, all right. But he didn't know a turnip from a begonia. What he was buying, selling, and shipping those days was vicarious sex. He was happy to leave the live hookers and pimps, the massage parlors and exotic dance clubs, to somebody else. For the time being at least, he'd carved his niche on the media side of the orgasm market—print, video, CD-ROM—something for every persuasion imaginable, and probably some unimaginable.

He'd been into other things through the years, of course. But whatever the endeavor, Breaker acted from only one motive—profit. If sometimes he resorted to breaking things, a more frequent occurrence in his younger days—he'd earned his name as a teenager out in Blue Island—it was never for mere honor, or loyalty, or what he called "the rest of that phony Italian bullshit." With him it was basic economics. "You never break a leg when a finger will do. But you always break whatever you have to." No one doubted his philosophy included breaking a back or a neck, if economics called for it.

Married to the same woman for over thirty years, Breaker had three adult children. "All of 'em bright enough not to live within eight hundred miles of their old man," he would explain, with a hint of pride in his voice.

Sitting there contemplating Breaker's complex value system and drinking Italian beer was interesting, but what I wanted was to tap into Breaker's information bank. I'd gone to a lot of trouble to get in to see him, and he had me cooling my heels. He continued to "yeah" and "no" into the phone. A power technique.

"I gotta hand it to you, Breaker," I said, between swallows of Moretti. "This almost looks like a place where someone ships peas and lettuce around the city."

He ignored me. Part of the technique.

I stood up and started walking around the room. Fat Wilbur and Mick stiffened and kept their eyes on me. Breaker ignored me. "But your authenticity is outdated," I said. "You need a fax machine, a computer, a couple of monitors, a modem—and maybe a laser printer."

"Quiet," Mick muttered. "Mr. Hanafan is on the phone."

Breaker ignored me. Taking my cue from him, I ignored Mick.

But I wasn't getting very far. I looked at the Moretti. It wasn't a bad beer and there was well over half left in the bottle. I felt bad about the waste, but . . . I poured the beer carefully in a wide circle on the concrete floor. When I ran out of beer I set the empty bottle in the center of the circle and started toward the refrigerator.

Breaker put the phone down. I had gotten his attention. "What the hell are you doing?" he said. Fat Wilbur and Mick were on their feet.

"Plus," I said, "your phone system is antiquated. What you need is a state-of-the-art telecommunications—"

"Foley, sit down." Breaker sounded tired.

I sat down. Fat Wilbur and Mick sat down.

For a while, no one said anything. Then Breaker ran with the ball. "So, Foley, we haven't even seen each other in two, three years maybe, right?"

"Right," I said.

"And we got no ongoing business with each other, right?"

"Right again."

"And then you fucking bust up every square inch of glass in my Jag, right?"

"I think I missed the dashboard glass, and the front passenger window."

"No glass in the dashboard," he said. "It's plastic."

"Well, anyway, pretty close to right again. And excessive, I admit."

"So," he said, "what's the deal? Why shouldn't I have Wilbur here stomp on your head for a while and then throw you out in the alley?"

"First," I said, leaning forward in my chair, "Wilbur already irritated me once, and all it got you was broken glass. Second—"

"Wait a minute, hold on," Breaker interrupted. "I don't need no phony huffin' and puffin'. I'm too old to listen to that shit. I already know you think you're tougher than you are. And I already know you act real strange sometimes. I mean, that's expensive beer you spilled on the floor."

"I didn't spill it," I said. "I poured it."

"Anyway, I didn't like your messing with my Jag, and I had you brought in. Now—"

"No, Breaker. I wanted to talk to you. So here I am. Whether Winnie and Piglet here could have brought me in otherwise is something you can ask them. Meanwhile, let's not waste each other's time."

I guess Fat Wilbur had finally gotten his breath back from climbing the stairs, because he spoke for the first time. "Mr. Hanafan don't like people talking to him like that, fuckhead."

"Shut up, Wilbur," Breaker said. "When I'm through with Mr. Mouth here, you and Mick and me can talk. Meanwhile"—he turned back to me—"what information you looking for?"

"I'm looking for a kid, a college kid. He disappeared and his family's worried about him."

"Come on, Foley. Must be a dozen guys looking for a dozen college kids in this city every day. What am I, a fucking missing-persons bureau? And if I did know something, why would I tell you?"

If somebody big was looking for Jason, Breaker knew it. But why he should tell me was a question I had no answer for.

"Kid I'm looking for is a black kid. Name is Jason Cooper."

Breaker drained his coffee cup and carefully set it back on the desk. "Wilbur," he said, "you and Mick go on downstairs. When Foley comes down, you take him back to wherever you got him from and then you meet me. I'll be at the Greek's."

When the two had gone, Breaker poured himself another cup of coffee. "Decaf," he said. "Not bad for decaf. But it still ain't coffee. 'No alcohol, no coffee,' the doc says. Triple bypass. Well, I go all day and do pretty good. But by nighttime, you know. Well, shit, you don't live forever whatever you do, right?"

As he was speaking, he got up, crossed to the refrigerator, and got out two bottles of Moretti. He handed one to me as he passed on his way back to his desk. He was talking without paying attention to what he was saying. I could almost feel his brain working.

By the time he got back to his chair, he'd made up his mind. "Let me ask you something, Foley. What makes you think I want to help you find this kid . . . uh . . . Cooper, is it?"

"Right. Cooper," I answered. "And I don't know what you want. I need answers, so I ask questions. That's the only way I know how to do it. Most people I ask couldn't care less about helping me. Some would rather get in my way than help. Meanwhile, all I do is ask questions. So, what do you know about Jason Cooper?"

"You don't wanna hear what I know."

"I'll decide that."

"I won't kid you, Foley. You're a pain in the ass, but I got no reason to see you dead, or maybe worse than that. Yeah, I heard of Jason Cooper. And I wouldn't touch him with gloves on. And if you got any sense left in that beat-up brain of yours you'll forget about him."

"I don't want to hear that."

"I told you a second ago you didn't wanna hear it."

"I didn't come here to be scared off. I'll find the kid, but I want him to be in one piece. I'm not sure just now what's in it for you for telling me what you know. But it can't hurt you. You know I can keep my mouth shut."

"I'm not talking about being scared off. I'm telling you, first, you aren't gonna find him—at least not alive. And second, if you keep on trying, you'll wish you didn't. Forget about the kid and go chase ambulances for your buddy Barney Green or something."

"I think you know where the kid is, Breaker, or at least who wants him, and why." I stood up and put my bottle on the desk. "You don't want to tell me, that's your business. But I'm going to find him and it won't be by sitting here drinking your beer."

I crossed to the door and pressed against the panic bar. It wouldn't budge. I turned and faced Breaker. "Open the door."

"You got in here, Foley, because I let you in. You'll get out when I let you out. Why don't you use your brain to think for once? You see the security I got here? Why do you think I got all this shit? Maybe I'm scared. Maybe I got good sense. Maybe those two are the same thing. You know what? I don't give a shit what the difference is."

I sat down.

He stood up and leaned to look through the window overlooking the warehouse floor. "So, we both know this fucking city's a battleground. It was that way before you and me were born, and it'll be that way when we're dead. Like right now, some people are—you heard about Izzy Bonagucci?"

"Of course."

"Well, just now there's a sort of struggle over who's gonna step up in line, what with Bonagucci going away for twenty. Me, I stay outta that shit. People always fighting over one thing or another. The little reasons come and go. But the big reason's always behind it—money, control—whatever you wanna call it, it's the same fucking thing. Word is your boy Cooper's a little reason that's big to somebody just now—somebody with muscle. If he ain't dead already, which he may be, he's walking around with information that's gonna get him dead . . . real soon."

"Who's the somebody?" I asked.

"I don't know if I'd tell you if I knew, but I don't. And I'm not about to poke my nose into it far enough to find out. You know why? Because I use my head. Guys like you, of course—"

"What information does the kid have?" I asked.

"I don't know that, either. But my guess is he either doesn't know himself what it is, or doesn't know what it means."

"But maybe—"

"Nope." Breaker sat back down at his desk. "That's the end of our conversation. Now get out of here. And Foley, if you do find the kid, do me a favor, will you?"

"What?"

"Don't tell me about it, okay?"

That wasn't all there was. Breaker wouldn't have thought so hard about what to say if that was all there was. But there was no need to press. He'd gone as far as he was going to.

"Not *if* I find him," I said, *"when."* I turned to the door. "Oh, by the way"—I tossed an envelope on his desk—"for the car."

I never did see how Breaker triggered the mechanism, but when I leaned on the panic bar this time the door swung open easily. As I went back down the stairs, I wondered if the ten hundred-dollar bills in the envelope would cover the cost of replacing the glass. It *was* a Jaguar, after all.

Maybe it would pay the deductible on his insurance.

CHAPTER

8

ON THE RIDE BACK to Cragman we didn't hit anything or run anyone over—clearly more a matter of chance than of concern on Fat Wilbur's part. Again Mick fell asleep almost immediately. In the backseat, I closed my eyes and actually dozed a little myself.

Back at the gym, the BMW stood alone under the harsh glow of the parking-lot lights. Fat Wilbur swung too close to the bike, but managed to stop without knocking it over. Outside the car, I leaned toward the open window. "Till next time, then," I said.

"Next time," Mick said in a flat voice, nodding, but not looking at me.

Fat Wilbur's mind was elsewhere, his eyes scanning the parking lot. "Got it!" he yelled, then put the Ford in gear. Careening across the lot, he skidded to a stop, opened the car door, and retrieved his trusty pipe before screeching off into the night.

Breaker hadn't completely leveled with me, but I believed him as far as he'd gone. Jason had something someone wanted, someone with muscle. Muscle and money go hand in hand, and that meant the ability to gather information—buy it, steal it, beat it out of people—far more quickly than I could. The chances of my finding Jason first dwindled by the minute. I cranked up the BMW and headed east.

The Edens Expressway runs straight north out of the city

past the North Shore suburbs, then joins up with the Tri-State Tollway that continues on up into Wisconsin, toward Milwaukee. Before climbing on the Edens I stopped at a doughnut shop and started the caffeine into my system. A trip home to trade the BMW for my car would take time I couldn't afford. Besides, there was a long night ahead, and riding out in the cold would keep me awake—maybe.

It was getting late, but the clerks where Cass and Sharon shopped might have stretched closing time a bit for two women with an obvious urge to buy. So maybe they'd still be at Juanito's when I got there.

They weren't.

Cass had left a note with the cashier. They had waited, then decided I wasn't going to make it. They were going back to my place for the violin, and then to Cass's parents' home. I could call them there. "Take care," the note said.

I ordered the taco-and-enchilada combination, feeling vaguely uneasy about their going back for the violin. But I decided missing Cass was what really bothered me. And the fact that the gap between us seemed to be widening. "Take care" seemed a long way from the "Luv ya" her notes always used to end with.

I'd never eaten at Juanito's except with Cass, and they'd always served the best Mexican food in the Midwest. That night it was like cilantro on wet cardboard.

On the way out, from the phone by the front door, I called my apartment and broke into the interminable recorded message to ask Cass if they were there. I didn't think they would be, and there was no answer. I hung up. I thought of calling Cass's parents' place. But it was very late.

I climbed on the BMW and set out for Wisconsin and Pepper Mill.

* * *

ABOUT FIVE in the morning my headlight picked the sign out of the black at the end of a long arc in the road:

KETTLEVILLE 4 MI
PEPPERTON MIL. ACAD. 5 MI

The halogen beam held the words frozen in its unblinking stare as I swept past, leaning around the bend at a moderate forty-five to fifty miles per hour.

Moments earlier I'd been sailing a deserted two-lane, on the crest of a high I later guessed came from too little sleep, too much coffee, and the sting of the cold night air. At the time, though, it seemed a hyperconscious awareness of the road, the bike, and the ride.

I'd started the trip angry about missing Cass and Sharon, anxious about Jason and how quickly I could get to him. But as the night and the miles passed, the race through the dark—the ride itself—became everything, apart from any rational need to hurry. Time compressed itself into an instant that held nothing but rider and ride. I might have been flying, for all the contact I felt with the asphalt rushing by.

The bike would do one hundred miles per without a shudder. So what my speed had been I have no idea, when suddenly a deer soared out of the woods ahead and to my right. It darted into the road and, when it froze halfway across, I should have been panicked. But I felt only a smooth easiness, as though the deer were expected somewhere in my psyche, a natural part of the moment. My body released the accelerator and began leaning to my right to let the animal pass to my left. Just then, though, the deer bolted again, reversing itself, and I had to tilt the big bike the other way to swerve back left, sweeping by as the terrified creature bounded back into the trees where it had come from. In what was maybe a two-second incident, I must have traveled fifty yards. It was all by reflex, the whole maneuver as unconscious as the blink of an eye at a grain of dust.

I came to my senses then and slowed down, trembling only after the fact, astonished at having avoided the collision. So by the time the road sign popped up I was down from the high—just a sore, tired rider on a dark country road four miles short of Kettleville, Wisconsin. What would I do at five o'-clock on a Saturday morning at a military academy in the middle of nowhere I'd ever been before? I didn't count on anyone stirring, even under a military regimen, until seven at the earliest.

Even at moderate speed, it took just seconds to roll through the tiny cluster of frame buildings that was Kettleville. Not long after that, I pulled up to an open iron gate between two massive fieldstone pillars. A bronze plaque set into one of the pillars announced *PEPPERTON MILITARY ACADEMY,* and below that: *Formatio militium futurae, pro Deo et Patria. A.D. MCMXLIX.* There was a wrought-iron arch that spanned the entrance and linked the two pillars. The whole effect was impressive enough, though I wasn't quite sure of the Latin grammar.

With my headlamp switched off, I started down a long, gently curving asphalt drive, lined on both sides with white-painted rocks like misshapen basketballs spaced about ten feet apart. Beyond the rocks, lawns rolled away to the right and the left. In the darkness the grass looked gray, and disappeared into black woods about a hundred feet off the drive on either side. They had either a hell of a landscaping bill, or plenty of future soldiers for God and country doing discipline duty.

The entrance drive ended in an empty parking lot, lighted by two dimly burning, old-fashioned streetlamps. Just beyond

that was a broad, three-story redbrick building with about seventy white-trimmed, small-paned windows. Shining in the light of autumn sunshine, the building probably soothed the doubts of parents delivering up their soldiers of the future. At night it might have been a debtor's prison, its windows dark and sullen.

Broad cement steps led up to the ancient glass doors of the entrance. Over the doors was a painted sign: "General Harmony Hall." It seemed strange to me, but who was I to say? I'd never been within fifty miles of a military school before. Maybe general harmony was the esprit they all aimed for.

Roads led out from each end of the parking lot and curved around the sides of the building. Little white street signs announced that the road to the right was Captain Highsmith Lane and the one to the left was Major Chapman Lane. I realized then that General Harmony was more likely a graduate than a communal state of mind.

Captain Highsmith Lane looked the less traveled road, and that was the way I went. It was an hour to sunrise and overcast at that, but I left the headlight off and rode slowly past the east side of General Harmony Hall, which must have housed most of the classrooms and administrative offices. Beyond it was a scattering of campus buildings, in what seemed a pretty haphazard layout. I thought I could pick out some student dormitories, a gymnasium, and some maintenance buildings.

Along the road ahead of me and to my right, four small brick bungalows sat in a row, imitating a tiny town. Each had a driveway leading to an attached garage, a sidewalk from the driveway to the front door, and flower boxes at the windows flanking the door. Each had a mailbox on a post near the entrance to the driveway. It was like a deserted film lot.

The first mailbox told me that a Major and Mrs. T. Richardson lived there. I could see curtains on the darkened windows and flowers in the window boxes. A low-watt bulb burned over the front stoop and illuminated a flowered wreath hanging on the closed front door. The next two mailboxes had no names. The houses had no curtains, no flowers, no bulbs burning.

I reached the last of the four houses. Stenciled carefully on the mailbox were the words Mr. and Mrs. Frank Parkins. There were curtains in the windows and flowers in the window boxes and a low-watt bulb burned over the front stoop. It looked a lot like the Richardsons' house. But there was something wrong about it.

The front door was standing open.

With the BMW leaning on its side kickstand, I unlocked the hinged seat and took the Beretta from the toolbox. Halfway across the yard, holding the gun pointed down beside my right leg, I stopped. Sweat broke fast and cold on the back of my neck. The front door wasn't simply standing open. A splintered hole was all that was left where once the doorknob and lock had been.

After a long slow breath, I moved forward again. A breeze I couldn't feel rustled fallen leaves in the darkness. A dog barked frantically miles away in a farmyard. Otherwise, silence. I wanted to be where the dog was, or back on the road scaring up deer, or playing semipro piano in a bar. I wanted to be anywhere but on Mr. and Mrs. Frank Parkins's doorstep.

A voice in my head told me to turn around, told me I shouldn't go inside.

"I know," I whispered back, and then stepped through the open door.

CHAPTER 9

It was a small living room, with a sofa and a couple of easy chairs, all facing the television set in the corner to my right. In the glow that leaked in from the bulb over the front stoop, the room looked undisturbed. Straight ahead was a hallway. I moved forward, listening to my own soft footsteps and inhaling the faint, mixed odors of bath soap and something else—maybe burnt toast.

A few steps down the hall was a door, an old-fashioned skeleton key sticking out of its lock. It opened onto a stairway leading up. I leaned in and listened. Nothing but silence, the top of the stairs shrouded in darkness. I closed and locked the door.

The hall continued on to a bathroom, then turned left and dead-ended just past two other open doors across from each other. I reached first inside the bathroom door and turned the light on. Nothing but a stronger smell of soap. Next to the tub was a shower stall. I pulled open the opaque shower door. Nothing. Back in the hall, the other two doors led into bedrooms. The larger one had a window that looked out on the front lawn. Leaving the bathroom light on, I went into that bedroom.

Other than a couple of dressers and an unmade bed with the covers tossed off onto the floor, there was nothing. No one was hiding under the bed. Lifting the gun in front of me, I opened a door I thought must be a closet. It was, and it held nothing but clothes. I crossed the hall to the smaller rear bedroom. It was just as vacant.

The house seemed empty and yet not empty, and I went more quickly back down the hall, through the living room, and into a formal dining room that looked like it was never used. The acrid odor of something burnt—maybe not toast, maybe something spilled in the oven—was stronger now.

Beyond the dining room, I switched on the overhead light of a large yellow-walled kitchen. At one end was a round oak table with four place mats and only three oak chairs. On a countertop that divided the eating and cooking areas was a small TV set that could be swiveled to face either way. Notes clung to the refrigerator under tiny magnetic apples and oranges, and snapshots and more notes were pinned to a bulletin board next to a yellow wall phone with an extra-long cord for walking around while you talked. The kitchen was the room in the house that looked most lived in. The kitchen was the room Frank Parkins died in.

The fourth oak chair had been placed against the wall beside the sink. It was a stiff-backed, uncomfortable-looking chair, and Parkins sat very straight in it. Except Parkins was dead, and the dead don't sit up straight, not unless they're tied to their chairs. It was heavy copper wire that held Frank Parkins in place. He was a big man and the back of the chair stopped just below his shoulders. His head was tilted back, leaning against the wall. One of his eyes was swollen shut. The other, wide open and staring, was as empty and hopeless as the eyes of the rat in Sharon's violin case.

The mahogany skin of his ears and upper face was bloated and bruised purple. Surprisingly, his mouth was closed. It may have been my imagination, but something in the lines around the mouth and the set of his jaw told me the information Parkins's killers—there must have been more than one—had

tried to pound out of him had stayed locked inside, finally frozen there forever by the bullets that had ripped his chest apart.

Coach Frank Parkins had been a large, handsome man with a dream, who'd kept putting the dream off until later. Now was as late as it would ever get for Frank, though, and now there was no dream. Now there was just a big dead man in blue flannel pajamas and imitation leather bedroom slippers.

My body sagged as if someone had dropped a lead shroud over me. I sat down at the oak table, my back to Frank Parkins's corpse. It would be light soon. I had to get out of there if I didn't want to report the murder and wait for the police. But I was drained, too tired to move, and not sure where I should go—or if I should stay. Needing a minute to think, I laid my forehead on my arms on the table in front of me.

I didn't hear anyone come into the room. But someone did.

"If you even twitch a muscle, I'll kill you," someone said.

I twitched, and then some. But she didn't kill me. That was a positive sign.

"I . . . I've got a gun," she said. "I'll shoot. I'm calling the police. Don't move."

I moved. I raised my hands, slowly, and clasped them on the top of my head. No shooting.

I stood up, facing away from her. Still no shooting.

"I swear I'll shoot you if you turn around." Her voice was rising in pitch and quavering. She was close to hysteria. But that didn't mean she didn't have a gun.

I remained standing, hands on my head. "I don't believe you, Mrs. Parkins." I forced an unfelt calmness into my voice. "I don't think you have a gun at all."

"Please," she said. "I do have a gun. Sit down. I don't want to shoot you."

"You're scared, Mrs. Parkins. But I don't think you'll shoot me. First, because I don't think you've really got a gun. Second, because I'm on your side. If I'd have gotten here a few hours sooner, Frank might still be alive."

"Frank? You know Frank? But . . . you don't know Frank." She kept repeating the name, as though that might bring him back.

I turned around, hands still on my head.

She had a gun. A 12-gauge San Marco, double-barreled, over and under. And she had as much idea what to do with a shotgun as I did with a crochet hook.

"No," I said, "I didn't know Frank. But I know about him. And everything I know is good. Frank was a fine man."

She dropped her chin and stared down at the shotgun, resting in her hands about waist high.

"*Was* a fine man," she said. "*Was*. That's how it sounds, is it?" She raised her eyes to me. They were red and puffy behind wire-rimmed glasses. She was tall and slim, her skin pale white. Beneath her unbuttoned raincoat was a rust-colored shirt, tucked into dark corduroy pants. The pants in turn were tucked into wide-cut leather boots. With her auburn hair, turned-up nose, and a mouth designed for smiling, she would have been a pretty woman. Just then, shock and grief had pulled the plug and drained the prettiness out of her.

I walked over to her and she gently handed me the shotgun. I broke it open and laid it on the counter. There were no shells in it.

"You didn't kill Frank," she said. It was a statement, not a question. "I thought you were the killer, come back. But that doesn't make any sense."

"That's right."

"I was hiding in the back hall, just outside the kitchen," she said. "When I heard you stop moving, I peeked in. You were asleep. I thought I'd smash you on the head with the gun.

But . . . I couldn't." She looked at the shotgun. "I don't even know how to load that thing. Frank leaves it on the shelf in the back hall. He loves to go hunting. Next weekend he's . . ." She stopped, suddenly aware of what she was saying.

"Frank?" she whispered, and started to turn back to the body. I grabbed her by the upper arms and held her facing me.

"No," I said. She couldn't twist away. Her body was without strength.

"Please," she pleaded. "Just once more. We had a song—sort of a theme song, to . . . to sort of encourage each other. I want to sing it to him . . . with him. That's all. Then it's over."

I let go of her.

She turned and I followed her across the room. She looked down at Frank. I stood to the side and watched the tears pour down her cheeks, her lips moving in a whisper through the words of an old, old song she'd never sing again. ". . . we ain't got a barrel of money," she sang. It was a song I'd played a thousand times—usually in ragtime. But I'd never play it again without hearing her slow, whispered words. ". . . singin' a song, side by side."

When it was over, she smiled a sad, sad smile. She placed the palm of her right hand against Frank's left cheek and held it there for a long moment. When she withdrew her hand, she turned to me. She wasn't smiling and she wasn't crying. She didn't look panic-stricken or hysterical, either. What she looked like was that most of her had died with Frank.

"We have to call the sheriff," she said, "and I guess my sister. She's the only nearby relative I have. There's another phone in the living room."

CHAPTER 10

I CALLED THE SHERIFF and while she called her sister I went out and put the Beretta under the hinged seat of the BMW and locked it closed. Then we sat on the couch in the living room as the darkness turned to daylight. She told me her name was Lauren, something I already knew from the newspaper archives. I told her Sharon Cooper had asked me to find Jason and that I had learned he might be staying with Frank and her.

"I rode all night, but . . . I should have called. I'm sorry, Lauren."

She didn't answer. She didn't move. We sat in silence for a few moments. "Say something," I pleaded. "Anything."

There was another long silence. Then, in a soft monotone, she told me what she knew about what had happened.

When he'd arrived unexpectedly several days earlier, Jason hadn't told them much, just that he needed some time away from Chicago, to "figure out a few things." They didn't press him. He said it was "no big deal." But they couldn't help worrying.

The previous afternoon the phone had rung and whoever it was hung up when Frank answered. About an hour later, the same thing happened again.

"We thought it was a wrong number, of course," Lauren said. "But Jason seemed to get more and more edgy. Finally, during supper, he blurted out that he was hiding from someone. He wouldn't say who, but the phone calls frightened him.

We decided he should go to my sister's and stay there awhile. Jason drove his car and I led the way in our car. Maureen—that's my sister—lives on a farm and Jason would never have found it alone. I was going to stay all night and come back today. Frank would have come with us, but on Friday nights he keeps the gym open late so the boys can play basketball and go swimming.

"After we got to Maureen's I was too nervous to sleep, and finally, about three o'clock this morning, I gave up and decided to drive home. I got here not too long before you did. I just pulled into the garage and . . . and came into the kitchen through the door from the garage. That's when I . . ." She stopped, her eyes filling again with tears.

I told her she didn't have to say any more. She said she wanted to go on, that it was better to keep on talking. With the heels of both hands she wiped the tears down her cheeks, away from her eyes. She started in again, in the same monotone, her head hanging down.

"When I found Frank. I . . . I just stood there for a while. I couldn't breathe. I don't think I was thinking anything. I ran through the whole house, in the dark, hoping whoever had killed Frank was still here. Maybe I thought I would kill them with my bare hands. Or maybe I thought they would kill me. I didn't care. I felt guilty and ashamed. But there was no one here. I saw that the front door was open and the lock was broken. Then I heard you coming on the motorcycle and I ran out into the back hall to hide."

"You came up behind me when I fell asleep."

"Right," she said. "I had it in my mind somehow that you had killed Frank. I wanted to smash you into pieces, but . . . I couldn't. I wasn't really thinking straight." She paused and looked up at me. "What am I going to do now?" It was a plea, made in a little girl's voice, as though I might have an answer.

"I don't know what you're going to do. I just know you're going to be very sad," I said, "maybe for a long, long time. But I know that after that, you're going to be all right. You'll discover, one day, that you actually feel pretty good. And then you're going to be all right."

She looked at me. "Thank you," she said softly. "I don't believe you."

"You don't have to believe me. Just try to remember what I said." She didn't look like she was even listening to me. I didn't know why she should.

The phone rang and Lauren answered. It was her sister calling back, saying she was just leaving the house. I told Lauren to tell her to bring Jason with her, but not to tell him Frank was dead.

It was too late. Maureen had already told Jason that Frank had been killed, and Jason was gone.

I grabbed the phone. "What do you mean, gone?" My voice came out too loud. "Where did he go?"

"Who is this?" Maureen shouted over the phone. "You put Lauren back on—right now! If you do anything—"

I put Lauren on the phone and she convinced Maureen to tell me about Jason. Maureen said when Jason heard Frank was dead he started "acting crazy." He kept saying it wasn't his fault and then ran out of the house. She didn't know where he went. She didn't think he was coming to Pepper Mill because he didn't ask the directions and he didn't know his way around.

As I gave the phone back to Lauren, sirens were screaming, far away at first, then drawing nearer. Lauren hung up and we sat and waited.

I couldn't get it out of my mind that if I had just made one phone call Frank Parkins wouldn't be dead. But he *was* dead. And on top of that, I'd let Jason get away. Despite his denials, he was blaming himself for the death of Frank Parkins, the one he had turned to for help. There was no telling what guilt and anger might lead him to do. I knew, because I felt the same guilt and anger.

In the meantime, I had to stay and deal with the sheriff's officers. It was too late to leave now. Even if I got away unnoticed, out some back road, they would know a man had put in the call. Lauren would have to tell them about me, and I'd be picked up before I got very far.

Squad cars came screeching off the road and roared down the drive toward General Harmony Hall, one after another. Doors started banging in the dormitories and students called out to each other.

"The cops are here," I said, needlessly. "It may be rough for a while. But they'll get things organized, and then they'll have a lot of questions to ask. Just tell them everything as well as you can remember." I paused, then added, "I . . . I'm not sure what they'll think of me."

"What do you mean?" she asked.

"Well, they're not going to buy my story easily. I look like a bum. I'm tired, I need a shave, and I'm a million miles from where they're going to think I ought to be."

Besides all that, I'd had nothing but bad luck with police for a long time. As the patrol cars screeched to a stop out front, their sirens winding down into a moan, I couldn't think why this might be an exception.

My spirits weren't lifted any when the first two came charging through the front door, guns drawn. They looked like football players gone to seed. Lauren and I stood up.

One of the two had a police radio in his left hand, a gun in his right. The little brass rectangle on his breast pocket said his name was Sorkiss. He waved the radio at me. "You and the little lady can sit down, pal. Where's the body?"

By then there were two more deputies inside, and a couple more out front to head off the platoon of future soldiers racing up to get in on the excitement.

I wanted to sit down, but somehow I just couldn't do it. "Pal?" I asked.

One of the second pair of deputies stepped forward. He was almost young enough to be my son, and he looked like he might have some sense. "Excuse me, sir," he said, "but—"

"Shut up, Zeman, I'm in charge here," Sorkiss said. He turned back to me. "Okay, *sir,*" he sneered, "sit down."

I sat on the couch.

"Now, like I said, where's the body?" He was unconsciously waving his gun in my face.

"In the kitchen," I said, pointing. "But careful with the gun, huh?"

"Bubba," Sorkiss said, turning to his partner, "keep an eye on this guy. He's a suspect in a homicide." He went through the door toward the kitchen.

Bubba grinned at me. His nameplate said Bubanovec. He unsnapped his holster and hitched up his belt. He looked about ten months pregnant, but otherwise mean and muscular.

Zeman's partner followed Sorkiss into the kitchen. We could hear their voices, and the scratching sounds of the police radio. In a few moments, they reentered the living room.

Sorkiss had the radio up to his face and was talking into it. "That nigger coach all right—wasted."

Lauren gasped and stiffened on the couch next to me. Zeman's eyes widened. The other deputies seemed not to have heard.

I stood up. Bubba took a step in my direction. I shoved my left palm toward him and he stopped, so he wasn't as aggressive as he looked. "Look, Deputy Sorkiss," I said, spreading my hands, "I don't mean to be any trouble. My name is Malachy Foley. And this is Coach Parkins's wife. She's been through a lot the last—"

"Shut up," Sorkiss said, his right hand reaching to his belt behind him and returning with a nightstick. "I know who the little lady is, and I know you think you're smart and you're a goddamn pain in the butt. I told you to sit down."

I was frustrated, drained, and angry for lots of reasons, none of them any good. I just didn't feel like backing down. I was as stupid as he was. "Couldn't you just try *thinking* before you talk, Sorkiss?"

He stepped toward me. I didn't move.

Zeman came between us, facing me. "Now take it easy, sir. We have a homicide investigation on our hands. Sheriff Jorgensen oughta be here any minute. In the meantime, you just relax and let us handle things, all right?" His calm, authoritative tone was good enough for me. I started to sit down.

But Sorkiss, enraged at the younger man's taking over, lost control. He swept Zeman aside from behind with his left arm, at the same time bringing the heavy nightstick in his right hand down toward the side of my head. I leaned to my right, and took the blow—hard—on the left shoulder and the side of my neck. Something exploded inside me and, while he set up to swing again, I charged head down and butted him across the room, driving him backward until his spine slammed into the wall.

I backed off then and left him pressed against the wall, gasping, the breath gone out of him. The collision left me dizzy and I stumbled backward, wanting only to collapse on the sofa. But he was fumbling at his holster with both hands, and there was a strange, savage gleam in his eyes. Out of fear this time, not anger, I reversed, lowered my head, and dove for him again. But by this time the others had come alive. They caught me and pulled me backward, a deputy on each arm. I didn't struggle with them. I was relieved, thankful that it was over.

But it wasn't over. Not yet.

His breathing came in deep, loud rasps, but Sorkiss had gotten his bearings and was moving slowly toward me. He held his service revolver, not by the grip, but flat in the palm of his right hand. As he took his last step forward, he brought the gun in a wide, roundhouse arc, roaring through the air toward the left side of my head. Whether instinctively or intentionally I'll never know, but the deputy at my side suddenly dropped my arm and stepped back out of the way. I froze.

"Sorkiss! No!"

Zeman's futile cry was the last sound I heard as my head exploded, shattering like a crystal ball struck by a hammer. Millions of slivers of glass scattered and whirled and floated around me as I tumbled into a deep and quiet darkness. If I ever hit the bottom, I didn't know about it.

CHAPTER 11

I STRUGGLED TO THE SURFACE ONCE, but couldn't get my eyes open. The whole pool was being carried along inside some moving, screaming vehicle, and how that could be seemed too complicated to figure out, so I let go and slid back down into the dark, quiet liquid.

Then I was out of the pool and lying on a hard cot. An impatient voice kept urging me to wake up. I winked one eye open, then shut—quickly—hoping that would be enough to make him go away. But it wasn't. So I opened both eyes. There was a man there, and behind him the bars of a jail cell.

"Thank you, Mr. Foley. Now sit up please."

"Can't. Wanna sleep."

When I started to roll over to face the wall, the man grabbed me by the shoulder. It was the shoulder that had taken the shot from the nightstick and I felt like I'd been hit by lightning. I let out a yowl and sat up.

"You see?" the man said. "Sometimes we *can* do things we thought we *couldn't* do." He peered at me through dark-framed glasses with thick lenses, perched high on a thin, sharp nose. As he spoke, he pulled up the upper lids of both my eyes with his thumbs and stared first into one, then the other.

"Some bedside manner you got," I said.

"Sorry. But, whatever it takes, right?"

He unbuttoned my shirt and rolled it back off my left shoulder. "Ah," he said, as though delighted at his discovery, "a nasty bruise." He squeezed the shoulder with his left hand and with his right hand grabbed my arm and rolled it around and up and down. The pain made my eyes water and my breath come in sharp gasps.

When he tired of this torture he dropped my arm. "Good, no real harm done."

"You mean by you?" I asked, "or by that cretin who clubbed me?"

"I mean it's a bad bruise and that's all it is. Now, that blow to the side of your head, that's different. That might prove more interesting."

"Interesting," I repeated. "What are you, the coroner?"

"Oh no," he smiled pleasantly. "Just a doctor. Name's Ronald Penney. I have a son at Pepper Mill. Graduated from there myself. Lauren Parkins's sister called me and asked me to meet her and Lauren here. She's in pretty bad shape. Lauren, I mean. But she's a tough woman. She'll be all right. Terrible thing about the coach. Anyway, the sheriff wanted to be sure you were okay. So, let's have a look at you."

He reached into the bag on the floor next to him and pulled out various instruments that he used as he peered into my eyes, ears, and throat. He thumped around on my chest and back, with the usual "breathe in" and "breathe out" routine. Then he asked a series of questions. Some of them made sense, some didn't. Maybe he thought the same about my answers, I don't know. There were wooden mallets pounding away inside my head and my heart just wasn't in it. When he finished, he scribbled for a while on a form on a clipboard, then looked up at me. He seemed as pleased with himself as he had when he'd found the bruise on my shoulder.

"You'll be fine," he said, "apart from a headache for a while. But I suppose you'll be out of here in a few days and if it's still bothering you I'll have the neuro people take a look at you. A blow like that could cause serious injury."

I started to stand up, but a sudden dizziness sat me back down.

"Won't hurt to rest. I'll check back tomorrow," he said. "I told the sheriff to take it easy on the questioning for a while."

After he left, I slept again. I don't know how much later it was that I woke up. A dull ache throbbed in my left upper arm and continued up through the shoulder, the side of my neck, and into my head. I sat up on the bunk. I was in a small holding area with four windowless cells along one wall. A walkway ran along the fronts of the cells, wide enough for two persons, and led to a steel door at one end of the room. Two small windows were cut high in the concrete wall opposite the cells. I was in the cell farthest from the door and was the only prisoner.

My shoulder was stiffening up, but I rotated the arm in every direction. The arm movement seemed to ease the pain in my head. Then I realized that the head pain wasn't less, only overshadowed by the increased shoulder pain. About the time I had that one figured out, the door swung open and a female deputy came in.

"Got some lunch for you," she said, shoving a grease-soaked paper bag through the bars. "I been waiting till you woke up."

I took the bag. "Thanks," I said. "Where am I?"

"Boxford County Jail. Lockup, actually," she said. "Part of the County Administration Building. Sheriff's police headquarters is here, and the courthouse, and some other county offices. Main jail's across the road." She was a pleasant, plump woman, near forty. Her body was stuffed into her deputy's uniform like a bunch of volleyballs stuffed tightly into a sack. "Actually, you're better off here. Cleaner, quieter, not so many bugs." She turned and headed back toward the door. As she left, she turned and said, "Course, food's better at the main jail. But you best eat your lunch now. Sheriff'll want to see you pretty soon."

Inside the bag were a hamburger, a batch of greasy french fries, and black coffee. All the same temperature—cold. I ate the burger and drank the coffee. I was still hungry and was considering whether to wring out the french fries one by one and eat them, when the deputy opened the door again. She held the door open and Deputy Zeman came through and continued down to my cell, a ring of keyes in his hand.

"Up and at 'em. Sheriff wants to talk to you." As he turned the key in the cell door, he spoke more softly. "Look, about what happened . . ."

"Forget it," I said, and followed him out of the lockup.

Sheriff Jorgensen was a shade under six feet, with close-cropped white hair. He looked like a man who ran a couple of miles every day, as straight and tough as a railroad spike. His mind was as rigid as his body, his language straight out of some official police manual. He was full of "Let me advise you" this and "Let me advise you" that. He advised me that I was not a suspect in the Parkins murder and he advised me that he wanted my statement about whatever I knew "in that regard."

He went on to advise me that I was, however, being charged with a crime, aggravated battery, and would remain in custody because of my attack on Deputy Sorkiss. Finally, he advised me that I had the right to remain silent as to the charges against me and the right to an attorney of my choice. The sheriff was tiring to listen to, but he was no fool. He knew he had about as much chance of finding out who killed Frank Parkins as he did of winning a Pulitzer Prize for poetry—or of finding out everything I knew, for that matter, which was far less than he supposed.

For my part, I told him I had a headache that wouldn't quit and that it had been caused by Deputy Sorkiss slapping me in the ear with his pistol while other deputies held my arms, that I knew what my rights were, and that I chose not to be represented in the bogus battery charge. I told him I'd file a lawsuit that would put the county into bankruptcy and embarrass both him and his department. Finally, I told him that he served lousy food in his lockup.

To his credit, Sheriff Jorgensen ignored my little speech and got on with his questioning. He kept at it for a couple of hours, on and off. A couple of Wisconsin State Police homicide investigators sat in and took their turns from time to time, and an assistant county DA added to the cast for a while. They all asked the same questions and they all got the same answers. I'd been hired to find Jason Cooper and, lacking any other leads, I rode up to see Frank Parkins because Jason was a former Pepper Mill student. They were curious as to why it was so urgent to see Parkins that I rode up at night. They had a point there. I didn't want to mention Breaker Hanafan or Harvey Cartwright. I told them I had a hunch Jason was in danger.

They called to check the status of my private investigator's license, but the State of Illinois offices were closed for the weekend. There were other ways to check on that, but they didn't ask me and I didn't tell them.

I wasn't in a volunteering frame of mind.

CHAPTER 12

About six that evening, I was back in the lockup washing down another hamburger, when Sheriff Jorgensen came in.

"Meals are getting better," I said.

"Uh-huh."

"Yeah. The burger and the coffee are as cold as ever. But at least no fries this time."

The sheriff wasn't interested in my diet. "Mrs. Parkins wants to talk to you. She's on her way."

"Why don't you just let me out of here?"

"Fractured ribs. I've got a deputy with a couple of fractured ribs. You'll remain in custody until you're brought before a judge to set bail. That'll be Tuesday morning, and I expect the bail to be substantial."

"Tuesday? Today's Saturday. What about Monday?"

"Monday's a court holiday—Cleanup Day."

"What? You can't—"

"Last Monday in October every year. Courts are closed, schools, everything. Been that way up here for years. It's so close to Halloween that folks usually—" His head turned as the lockup door opened. "Well, here's Mrs. Parkins now. You can have three minutes. Then you can make a couple of phone calls if you like."

The sheriff left and Lauren and I spoke through the bars. Dr. Penney hadn't let her be interviewed until she'd had time to rest, and she'd just finished giving a statement. Maureen was waiting to take her to the farm.

"I wanted to see you and . . . just say thanks, I guess." Her voice trailed off to a whisper. She was clenching the bars between us with both hands and staring straight at me, but not seeing me.

"Lauren," I said, "what about Jason?"

"Jason?"

"Jason."

"Oh . . . I'm sorry. I'm not thinking very straight."

"Have you heard from him?"

"No. He just ran out of Maureen's house and drove away." Suddenly her eyes filled with tears. "It was because of Jason wasn't it? I mean, they killed Frank because of Jason."

"Yes. I think they came for Jason and killed Frank because he wouldn't tell them where Jason was."

"Oh my God," she moaned.

"Lauren, are you sure Jason didn't tell you anything that might help me figure out who's after him, or why?"

"I . . . oh, I don't know. I shouldn't have left Frank alone. I feel so guilty and ashamed of—"

The lockup door banged open. It was Sheriff Jorgensen. "It's time."

"Just a few more minutes, please, Sheriff?" she asked.

"Okay, ma'am. A few minutes. But we're bringing in prisoners soon, and your sister's waiting." He left.

"I want to help," Lauren said, "but I . . . I don't know anything." Her voice was very soft, and she kept her eyes away from mine. "And . . . what about Maureen and her family? Do you think someone will come looking for Jason at the farm?"

"I don't think so," I said. "They'll know the sheriff's looking for him, too, and that a young black man can't stay invisible around here for very long. They'll expect him to do just what he did—get out fast." I gave her my card. "Meanwhile, if you think of something you haven't told me, you'll call me, won't you?"

"Yes. Yes, of course." She seemed far away, lost in some other time and place.

I believed it when I said they wouldn't be looking for Jason with Lauren or her family. But where would he go now? And what was he involved in that would lead to something as brutal as Frank Parkins's death?

"I'll find Jason," I said. "And Lauren, I'm going to find Frank's killers, too." The words sounded melodramatic and hollow. I wished I hadn't spoken them.

"Well," she said softly, "that won't bring Frank back, will it?" She looked at the floor, then back at me. "But"—and there was a slight spark of hope in her voice—"maybe you can help Jason. Frank would have wanted that."

The lockup door opened and the woman deputy came through, one hand wrapped around the upper arm of an old man in a plaid flannel shirt and bib overalls, straggly white hair down to his shoulders.

"Come on, Big Oley," she said, patiently tugging the man to the cell next to mine, "off to beddy-bye."

Big Oley was about six foot two, and weighed maybe 120 pounds. Jangling his bones like Ichabod Crane, he sat on the edge of his bunk and tried to focus on Lauren and me through the mist of too many whiskies over too many years. He waved his hand in a vague gesture of greeting, let out a bloodcurdling belch, and fell back on the bunk. He was snoring before his head hit the folded blanket.

The deputy locked his cell, then turned and unlocked mine. "Sheriff says you got to go now, Mrs. Parkins. Mr. Foley here's gonna make some phone calls and then come back and enjoy the Boxford County lockup's version of . . . *'Saturday Night*

Live, including Big Oley Olmerson and the rest of the usual Saturday night crowd.' " She chuckled, enjoying her little monologue as she led us out of the lockup.

Lauren's sister was waiting and they left together. The deputy took me to Sheriff Jorgensen's office.

He looked up from reading his reports and gestured to the phone that had been pushed to my side of the desk. "Let me advise you that you get three phone calls."

"From here? Right in front of you?"

"You want to call someone, you call them from here. Local calls, which I don't suppose you'll be making, are on the county. Long-distance are on you. I've examined the contents of your wallet and didn't find any credit cards. You'll have to make collect calls, or we'll keep some of your cash when you're released and the amount over the charges will be refunded to you by mail."

It had been years since I had a credit card. Telephone calls I charged to Barney Green, using his PIN. The sheriff returned to his reports while I started my calls.

I called my own number and immediately bypassed the answering message. No one picked up when I identified myself. Why should they? No one lived there but me.

I called Cass's parents' number. When there was no answer there, either, my gut tightened. Sharon and Cass should have been there, waiting for a call. They might have gone out for dinner, but the agreement was they'd lie low until they heard from me. Maybe I had misdialed.

I tried again. No answer. I tried Cass's number. No answer. My heart was racing now, and I made myself breathe slowly and deeply. I forced a grin at Sheriff Jorgensen. "I hope my three calls aren't used up when there's no answer," I managed to say.

"Uh-huh," he said.

I took that to mean he agreed, and called back to my own number. I tapped in the numbers that would read back my messages to me. There were two callers who hung up without saying anything. A third caller left a message—or part of a message. Just four words, "Mal, they . . . oh, please . . ." Then a click.

My hand trembled as I put the phone down. That third caller was Cass.

What can you read into four words? Maybe she'd started to leave a message and then changed her mind. Maybe Sharon had interrupted her. Maybe there was something wrong with the phone. Or the answering machine. Maybe anything except what I knew to be true from the sound of her voice. She had been calling for help—and something, or someone, had stopped her. Who? Where was she calling from?

"Hey, Foley. Foley!" the sheriff was saying. "Wake up, will ya? Jesus, maybe Sorkiss really did scramble your eggs."

"I have to get out of here, Sheriff. Something's come up."

"The hell something's come up. You haven't even gotten an answer out of six calls. I told you, no court and no judge to set bail until Tuesday morning. You attack an officer of the law, that's your problem. I want to go home to my supper. If you have someone to call that might actually talk to you, make it quick."

"The next call's to my lawyer, Sheriff. An accused has the right to consult with counsel in private. I haven't seen a newspaper in the last few days, but I don't think the Supreme Court's eliminated that one—not yet, anyway."

"Hell, you can have all the privacy you want." He gathered in his reports, got up, and went to the door. "Five minutes," he said, and closed the door behind him.

There was little hope of catching Barney Green at home on a Saturday night, but I called. Seth answered. At least there I had some luck. Seth was eleven years old and, though otherwise smart as a whip, he was the only person in the world who wanted to grow up and be just like me.

"Look, Seth," I said after he told me his mom and dad wouldn't be home until sometime after midnight, "I'm working on a case, and I need your help."

"Gee, Mr. Foley, you can count on me. Shoot."

I didn't think kids still talked like that, and wondered if he was playing with me. But not Seth.

"I want you to talk to your dad as soon as he comes home. I don't care how late it is. Tell him . . . Wait a minute, you better get something to write this down."

"Don't have to, Mr. Foley. I'm putting it into my computer while we talk. Shoot."

"Okay. Tell your dad to call the Lady as soon as he gets home."

"The Lady?" Seth asked.

"Yes," I said. "He knows who she is. Tell him she'll take the call no matter what time it is." I knew Barney would have the Lady's number, but I gave it to Seth anyway. "Look, your dad might say he'll call her in the morning. You've got to convince him it can't wait, that it's life or death."

"Don't worry, Mr. Foley. I'll bug him. That's my specialty. He won't get any sleep until he makes the call. But"—and his voice took on a conspiratorial tone—"who is this 'Lady'?"

"Look, Seth, I'd fill you in on the details, but there isn't time. Plus"—I paused, then added in a quiet voice that tried to match his tone—"plus, I can't talk on the phone, if you know what I mean."

"Sure, I get it. Like I said, you can count on me."

"Thanks, Seth. Good-bye."

"Bye, Mr. Foley."

I hung up, first picturing him sleeping in the breakfast nook with a string running from his toe to the door his dad would be coming through, then remembering that he'd use something more sophisticated, something electronic.

Meanwhile, I tried to focus on what had to be done, and not let my mind dwell on what might have happened to Cass and Sharon. The trouble was, I had no idea what had to be done. I only knew I couldn't wait until Tuesday morning to get out of Boxford County. I'd go crazy by then.

I called the Lady's number. It was about six-thirty and on the fifth ring a young woman answered.

"Michigan House, good evening."

"I'd like to speak to the Lady, please," I said.

"I'm very sorry, sir, but the Lady's at supper. May I take your name and a telephone number at which you can be reached?"

Among the wonders the Lady works is teaching at least some of the women who come to her for help how to talk like that on the telephone. Most of them have spent their formative years on the street, cursing and screeching and clawing at each other and at the men who abuse them.

"Go and tell her it's Malachy Foley," I said.

There was a pause, during which I could almost hear her neural relays putting together something like: *Look here, shitsucker, I said she can't come to the fucking phone!* What came out, though, was, "Very good, sir. Please hold on and I'll deliver your message."

I never doubted the Lady would come to the phone.

"Good evening, Malachy," she said. Always "Malachy," never "Mal." But it's just the way she was raised. You learned that, and you got used to it.

"Hello, Helene," I said. Everyone calls her "the Lady" or

"Lady Bower" when she isn't around. But she prefers "Helene" in person. Maybe trying to break through her own ingrained formality.

"It's good to hear your voice."

"Sorry to interrupt your supper, but—"

"Oh, that's no bother." She meant it. I doubt she ever says anything she doesn't mean. That makes her easy to talk to, somehow, even with her British accent and mannerisms. "We're all excited here, though," she said, "We're debating what to call the new home."

"New home?" I asked.

"Yes. We'll talk about it sometime. But you're worried about something. What is it?"

"It's Cass. I think she's been . . . I think someone's grabbed her . . . kidnapped her. I don't know who, but . . . I'm afraid."

The Lady didn't say a word. She loves Cass.

I told her where I was and what had happened, and that the sheriff planned to hold me over until bail was set. I told her Barney Green would be calling her later that night. "I can't stay here until Tuesday, Helene. I'll go crazy."

There was silence for a moment. "Malachy," she finally said, "you won't go crazy. You will simply use the time to its best purpose." Another pause. "However, we shall get you out of there as quickly as possible. I strongly suggest that in the interim you get some exercise, and then go to sleep."

Fat chance. "How do you plan to get me out?"

"I have no plan, Malachy," she said. "How could I? I'll finish my supper, then wait for Mr. Green to call. When he does, we'll formulate a goal, or a series of goals. Once one's goals are clearly in mind, plans tend to reveal themselves, don't they. In the meantime, you must use your time as well as you are able. And, Malachy, one more thing . . ."

"Yes?"

"Only that there are, as you know, never any guarantees."

It was clear she was talking about more than just getting me out of jail in a hurry.

CHAPTER 13

THE LADY'S NOT ALWAYS RIGHT, and I don't always follow her advice. But a workout was a good idea. I went back to my cell and stripped down to my shorts. There wasn't much room, but I started with a series of stretches and eventually even worked up a sweat. When I finished, I was hurting all over and physically exhausted, but the fears racing through my mind had slowed a bit.

A deputy came with a handful of aspirins, courtesy of Dr. Penney, and I slept well, with the cell to myself all night. I'd had worse accommodations by far, including Chicago's Cook County Jail, where I'd finally learned to sleep around the screams and curses of some of the world's truly frightening professional prisoners. The lockup at Boxford County, with its handful of drunks and brawlers in the cells near mine, was a piece of cake.

Shortly before nine o'clock Sunday morning, a deputy took me to Sheriff Jorgensen's office. The sheriff was there, and a small man in a checked sport coat, a crisp white shirt, and a red bow tie.

As I entered the room, the man jumped to his feet. One hand tugged at his lapel, the other smoothed his thin black hair. "Ah, yes," he said, "so this is Mr. Foley. How do you do, sir?"

I nodded to him, then looked at Jorgensen, who stayed put in his chair. The sheriff swept his right hand from my direction toward the standing man. "Meet Wyman Adams. Mr.

Adams is an attorney. In twenty years, I've never known him to represent a criminal defendant. But he tells me he's your lawyer. He wants to talk to you."

A deputy came in with a sheet of paper. "Five minutes to roll call, Sheriff," he said.

Jorgensen took the paper and waved the deputy out of the room. Turning to Adams, he said, "Go on back to Foley's cell and confer with your client, Counselor. Who knows, maybe you'll find out he wants to develop a shopping center, or buy someone's farm, something more in your line of work."

"Ah, yes, thank you very much, Sheriff. Thank you," Adams said. With his right forefinger he smoothed one of those little mustaches that look like they're applied with a felt-tip pen. "But"—and he smiled what would have seemed a shy smile if you missed the shrewdness in his eyes—"the cell wouldn't be very comfortable, I'm afraid. And as for privacy, I believe it would expedite things if Mr. Foley and I remained here. You could take care of reveille and by the time you return we might have reached a resolution of this whole matter."

"Wyman, you're pressing your luck a little," Jorgensen said.

"Well, whatever you think, Sheriff. But"—Adams smiled the same shrewd smile—"it might be more convenient for everyone."

"All right," Jorgensen said. "I'm going. But Wyman, it's roll call."

"Pardon, Sheriff?" the little man said.

"It's not *reveille*. It's *roll* call."

"Ah, yes, Sheriff, thank you very much."

The sheriff went out, leaving me with my lawyer. We sat looking at each other. He seemed to be waiting for me to say something. So I did. "You've talked to Barney Green?"

"Oh yes," he said. "A telephone conference call, in fact—myself, Mr. Green, and a Lady Helene Bower. Seemed a very nice person, Lady Bower did. Certainly very concerned about you. Very direct. Very persistent. Mr. Green and I have, ah, worked together before. He asked that I handle your matter personally, and of course I'm delighted to do so."

"You don't do much criminal work, I take it."

"Good gracious, no," he said. "I concentrate my efforts in the areas of commercial transactions and civil litigation. In fact, after, oh, thirty-four years in the practice, you're my first criminal—I should say *alleged* criminal—defendant. Actually, I'm rather enthusiastic about it."

"Well I'm not," I said. "Nothing personal, of course. It's not so much the criminal charges. They're going nowhere. What's important is I need someone tough enough to cut a deal and get me out of here—right away."

"Tough enough," he said. "An interesting way of putting it. However, I've done quite well, Mr. Foley, over the years. And I've learned two rules that make a lawyer, as you say, 'tough.' Only two rules, really. Rule one, always be meticulously prepared. Rule two, always maintain excellent relationships with the judges." He beamed his shy-but-not-shy smile again. "I can say in all candor that I am rarely excelled at rule one . . . and *never* at rule two."

His ego was starting to shine through, but I still wasn't convinced Barney had made the right choice. "So, when can you get me out?" I asked.

"Ah, yes. Well, rule one, preparation. We've been conducting preliminary interviews this morning and have determined how the various witnesses at the Parkins residence would testify. Mrs. Parkins will support your version of the incident. The other deputies will back Deputy Sorkiss, with the exception of Deputy Zeman, who has a problem. He wishes to be loyal to his comrades, yet does not wish to perjure himself. His problem has become Sheriff Jorgensen's problem. The sheriff has high hopes for the young deputy, and does not wish to wreak havoc with Zeman's conscience. To avoid that, the sheriff would agree to a dismissal of the charges."

"Good. When do I get out?"

"On the other hand," Adams continued, "the district attorney raises a good point. Should you later choose to sue the county, the fact that charges were not pressed against you would significantly improve your civil action."

"Adams," I said, "please. I'm not interested in suing the county. I'm only interested in getting out of here."

"I know that. But my responsibility, as I understand it, is to see that you are not only released, but that you need not return to face criminal charges. Now the district attorney must, as he says, 'cover all the bases' before disposing of the charges. I have proposed, therefore, that you agree to release any claim you have against the county, in exchange for the striking of all charges against you. That is acceptable to the district attorney, although the county prefers not to reduce such an agreement to writing. So, I have prepared a release for you to sign, which I will then hold in my safe. I have given my word that, should you later attempt to make a civil claim against the county, I will deliver the release to the district attorney."

I was starting to be impressed. The man had spent a busy morning, getting "meticulously prepared." I reached for the paper he removed from his briefcase. But he held up his hand. He wasn't finished.

"However," he said, "I must be certain that, in my representation of your best interests, I myself have, as the district attorney says, 'covered all the bases.' Dr. Penney, in whose opinion I place great confidence, assures me that the likelihood that you have sustained any serious neurological damage is virtually nonexistent. On the other hand, head injuries can be unpredictable, and you may decide it is not wise to release the county from any claim. In that case, the charges would remain against you, you would be released on bond, and a date would be set for your return to defend against the charges. Of course, I would be pleased to handle both the criminal case and any action for damages, and I am confident that we would prevail on all fronts."

"Look, Adams—," I started.

"Yes, you know all this already," he interrupted, "but it is my duty to remind you and ask you whether you are interested in following that course. It does, in fact, have considerable merit."

"Even if I were interested, I can't do it, because I'd have to sit in here until Tuesday to have a bond set," I said.

He gave me the smile again before he spoke. "Ordinarily, that might be true. But not in this case. You see, Mr. Green and the Lady were quite adamant that, whatever your choice, you must be set free at the earliest possible moment. Fortunately, I never forget rule two. So I've been able to make, ah, special provisions. All aboveboard, of course, though not easily arranged. At any rate, should you decide *not* to release your claim, there will be a prompt emergency hearing before Judge Harold Iverson, at which time a bond would be set. I would advance whatever funds you might need and you would be free to go."

"You mean the judge will hold a bond hearing before Tuesday?"

Adams looked at his watch. "Judge Iverson will have left home by now. I can reach him on his car phone. He generally attends the ten-thirty service at Emanuel Lutheran, near Kettleville. The courthouse is not far out of his way. So you see—whether you sign the release, or whether you choose to preserve your civil action and be set free on bond—you'll be on your way in a matter of hours."

I must have had a surprised look on my face.

Adams smiled. "Well, Mr. Foley . . . *tough* enough?"

I felt my face break into its first smile in forty-eight hours. "Tough enough," I agreed. "But call off the judge. I'll sign the release."

CHAPTER

14

On the ride home I had plenty of reasons to regret having accepted a used motorcycle as a fee. I had no rain suit, and the cold, relentless drizzle had me soaked to the skin and shivering within half an hour. I kept stopping for snacks and to try to get warm, but fear for Cass drove me on. I didn't know what I would do when I got home, but I felt compelled to get there. Maybe the Lady would have some ideas.

It surprised me that the Lady had opened another home. That made three now, if you included the Evanston house. She dreaded being consumed by administrative duties, and routinely rejected the impulse to expand her program—if you could call what she did a program, which she refused to do. She'd ask for help sometimes, but hated fund-raising. All she wanted was to live well, but simply, and to provide the same comfortable, frugal way of life for the women she temporarily sheltered. She accepted donations to supplement her own resources. Those resources, though hardly unlimited, were considerable, thanks to a little foresight and a lot of bad luck on the part of her husband, the late Sir Richard Bower.

They'd come from London to the United States some years ago for a six-month stay. Sir Richard, a renowned surgeon, was giving a series of lectures at medical centers across the country, and they'd chosen Chicago as their home base. On a dreary November Saturday evening, Sir Richard's chartered jet, having been battered by unusual turbulence all the way from a Lake Tahoe conference, was into its approach at O'Hare when it nearly collided with a jumbo jet headed for Disney World. Contact was avoided, but the small plane plunged five hundred feet to the ground. Very little was found of Sir Richard amid the charred wreckage.

At the time, I'd just been admitted to the bar and was working for Art Green, Barney's father, a personal-injury lawyer. Turned out I didn't much like the practice of law—with its long hours and meticulous details—but the opportunity to be around the legendary Art Green was invaluable. Some people called him an ambulance chaser, but no one denied his legal ability. He had a sharp, creative mind—and a heart condition he never told anyone about.

Art heard about Sir Richard's crash and had Lady Helene Bower signed up as a client before his office opened Monday morning. It was a tragic accident, but a great lawsuit. Art made Barney and me his co-counsel, filed suit within a week, and worked on the case as though it would be his last one, with Barney and me tagging along.

The Lady was childless, with no known talents back then beyond being gracious at black-tie dinners and charity balls. There wasn't much for her to go home to, so she stayed in Chicago.

The lawsuit included a large number of defendants, all of them well insured. They got together and made a settlement offer six months after suit was filed, a seven-figure offer structured as an annuity over the Lady's lifetime. We were all taken aback except Art, who said to be patient and wait for a higher offer. There was one, too. And a few days later Art dropped dead of a heart attack.

The Lady approved the settlement and ended up with a guaranteed income for life, more than adequate when added to Sir Richard's insurance annuities. Cass and I spent a great summer helping the Lady find just the right mansion on the lakefront in Evanston, virtually surrounded by Northwestern University's campus. It was Cass, in fact, who brought her the first of what would eventually be scores of battered women, many of the later arrivals running from pimps.

Meanwhile, my half of the attorney's fee went into a trust fund I couldn't touch, but which paid me the income earned by the money each month. Not enough to live on, but enough so I gave up working on anything I wasn't interested in. I leased the space above the Lady's garage and we called it our coach house. I spent a lot more time at the piano, and took a criminal case when I felt like it or needed the money. Then, after my law license got yanked, I drifted back into the investigative work that had led me to law school in the first place. Small as it was, the trust income was the psychological push I needed to set me free from a career that held no reward for me other than money.

So here I was—free enough to get myself locked up because I couldn't keep my mouth shut, and then free to ride a BMW home from Wisconsin flirting with hypothermia and a fear in my belly that was colder than the pellets of rain whipping through to my bones.

It was late afternoon when I got home. With my left shoulder stiff and throbbing, I continued to shake even after I was inside and had punched the digital thermostat up to seventy-five.

Sharon's violin was still on the shelf at the top of the back stairs. The note Cass left at the restaurant said they were going to pick it up. They hadn't made it.

I poured a tall tumbler of red wine and took it into the bathroom. I hadn't shaved for a couple days, but I wouldn't have liked the anxious, guilty look on the face in the mirror even if it had been clean-shaven. With the shower set as hot as I could stand, I let the water pour over my aching muscles. I didn't know where Cass and Sharon were, or where Jason was. They were all in danger—or worse—but I didn't know the source of the danger. I didn't even know *why* they were in danger. What I didn't know was just about everything that would have been of any help.

All I knew was that whoever was looking for Jason was willing to kill to find him, and had taken Cass and Sharon—and maybe Jason by now, too.

While I shaved I struggled to come up with some plan, but drew a blank. I swallowed a handful of aspirins with the rest of my wine. In the kitchen, I sat down with the telephone and called Cass's apartment, her parents' home, and Sharon's apartment. There was no answer anywhere, not even a machine. I called Barney Green and left a message on his machine. I called the Lady and she was out. By that time, a second glass of wine had disappeared. I started to pour a third, told myself that was foolish, and started a pot of coffee instead. I congratulated myself for that, but I still didn't have a shadow of a plan.

Maybe I was using the wrong side of my brain. Maybe I needed to relax, put the creative side to work. I lit a fire in the fireplace, set the kitchen timer for two hours, and looked in the freezer. The package of dead rat was as solid as a brick. There was also a quart-sized carton of peach ice cream that I told myself was half-full, not half-empty. I took a mug of coffee and the ice cream to the couch in front of the fire. When I finished the ice cream, I still didn't have a plan.

To change my point of view, I lay down on the couch and looked at the fire from that angle. When the kitchen timer went off, I woke up. I didn't have a plan. As far as I knew, I hadn't even had a dream of a plan.

Back in the kitchen, I poured more coffee and went to the windows. Lake Michigan through the trees didn't look like it was shining from shook foil at all—or like it ever had, or ever would. It looked like both sides of my brain, sullen and dreary and without hope.

Just the night before I had been desperate to get out of the Boxford County lockup. Now, unless I did *something,* I might as well be back there. I recalled what the Lady had said about a plan appearing once you have your goal clearly in mind. I went back to the couch and tried that approach. The phone beeped just as I was about to declare the Lady wrong. Not that *she* would have cared. But it would have bothered *me.*

I picked up and said hello.

"Mr. Foley." It was a declaration, not a question, and I didn't like the tone of his voice.

"Hold on a minute," I said. Then, not covering the mouthpiece, I yelled, "Hey, Foley!" Not very bright, but I wanted time to pull myself together. After a pause, I said, "Foley here."

"Please, Mr. Foley." He sighed. "No games." If this wasn't the same father struggling with a stubborn child whom Sharon had described, I'd eat my sheet music. "We believe you have information we want," he said.

"And who is we?" That didn't sound right. "Or is it who *are* we?"

Silence. Then he said, "We think you know where Jason Cooper is."

"Why should I care what you think?"

"Because if you decide not to cooperate, you will regret that decision . . . very, very much." He'd moved on to his ominous tone.

"Hold on again," I said, and set the receiver down loud enough so he could hear that's what I had done.

I didn't know where Jason was. But I was going to find out. And then? If I had to choose between saving Cass and giving up Jason? They had the best leverage possible.

I picked up the phone. "Me again."

"Mr. Foley, my patience is wearing thin."

"Mine, too. If you've got a deal to discuss, tell me. Otherwise, I'm going out for Thai food."

"There is no deal, and no discussion. What I have to say is simple. Give us Jason Cooper and your reward will be handsome. I need not discuss alternatives. You have seen what we can do."

A handsome reward could mean anything.

"You listen to me." My voice was shaking with fear and anger. "I don't want 'handsome' anything. I want both women."

"Hold on a min—"

"No. You hold on. My wife and the kid's sister, both of them, alive and well."

There was a long moment of silence. "Thank you," he finally said. "That's exactly what I was waiting to hear. Now, where is Jason Cooper?"

"I don't know yet, but I'm very close," I lied. "Let me talk to my wife."

"You think I'd have her here with me? She's safe, as long as you don't contact the police. But you better produce. Time is short and who knows what, ah, *interesting* things could happen to the women if you don't deliver."

The delivery bothered me, too. "If I give up the kid what happens to him?"

"You need not concern yourself with that. And besides, there is no *if,* Mr. Foley. Only *when*. Because otherwise, what will happen is something you don't even want to think about."

"I need time. Give me a name and a number where I can reach you."

"You can't reach me. But as for a name, why not just think of me as, oh, Mr. Troublesome. You'll hear from me soon."

"How soon is soon, Mr. Troublesome?" I asked. But I was talking into a dead phone.

I didn't know who they were, I didn't know why they wanted Jason Cooper, and I didn't know what they'd do with him if they got him. That was a lot of ignorance, even for me. But I did know one thing he'd said was accurate. What might happen to Cass was something I didn't even want to think about. I brewed decaf and poured some, trying to focus only on whether it was the mug hand or the pot hand that was shaking.

By ten o'clock, I was pacing the floor with my decaf and had pretty well calmed myself down. The phone beeped again and coffee slopped everywhere. I don't suppose calm people jump when their phone rings. I let the machine answer and the caller pressed seven, bypassing the recorded messages.

"Malachy?"

I grabbed the phone. "Helene, I didn't hear you drive in. I need to talk to you. Are you at the house?" The house was thirty yards down from where I stood.

"Certainly, Malachy," she said. "You can come immediately." She paused. "However, on my way in a few moments ago I noticed a car parked on the street about a half block south of the driveway, a tan four-door something-or-other. The same car was parked there hours ago, when I went out. But the two men sitting in the car now aren't the same two who were in it then. That's curious, isn't it?"

"Curious," I agreed. "I'm on my way over, Helene. But give me about a half hour."

"Very good, Malachy. I'll be here."

At least now I had something to do.

Just a few hours earlier, I'd decided to mothball the BMW for the winter, maybe for the rest of my life. Now it would come in handy. I unlocked the seat and took the Beretta from the tool kit. With the gun in my jacket pocket, I fired up the bike and rolled down the drive. The tan car was a Buick Electra. When I pulled onto the street it slid into traffic several cars behind me. I didn't know what I'd be doing later that night or the next morning, but whatever it was, I wanted to do it without company.

Traffic was light, and the Buick dropped back. I headed west. They wanted to tail me unobserved and I wanted them to think I hadn't seen them. In the wide-angle view of the bike's convex rearview mirrors, everything on the street behind seemed about three times farther away than it was, making it hard to keep track of the Buick's headlights behind me. But when I emerged from a twenty-four-hour convenience store with a budget-sized bottle of aspirins and climbed back on the bike, they picked me up again. I went back east and turned onto Sheridan Road.

At the south end of Evanston, approaching Chicago's city limits, Sheridan leaves the vintage apartment buildings behind and winds along the lakefront, separated from the water to the east only by massive boulders and chunks of concrete stacked up against the pounding waves. As I reached that stretch I was in a southbound lane, with Calvary Cemetery spreading westward to my right. The road right-angles to the west just south of the cemetery as Evanston becomes Chicago, and then, about a hundred yards farther, veers south again. Between the two turns is a self-service gas station.

I accelerated past the cemetery, the Buick the equivalent of a block and a half behind me and losing ground. I swung around the first turn. But instead of continuing on, I applied front and rear brakes and skidded into the gas station lot to my right. At the coin-operated air machine I positioned the bike to face the street, my headlamp switched off. Leaving the engine running, I dismounted and knelt by the front tire with the air hose in my hand.

If the boys in the Buick missed me, fine. But with nowhere to park on Sheridan Road, if they did spot me they had only two choices—either join me at the gas station or continue on west, then south, and take their chances on picking me up again.

They saw me all right. I was sure of that. And they kept on going. As soon as they disappeared around the turn southward, I was back on the bike and northbound on Sheridan. There was no reason for them to think I'd seen them. I'd simply gone out for aspirin and gotten air in my tire. Having lost me, they'd head back to the coach house. I sped back home, taking the Fat Wilbur approach to the traffic code.

At the coach house, I left the BMW in its usual spot under the eaves and backed my beat-up Chevy Cavalier out of its garage stall. I was out of the driveway and about a block away in the other direction when I picked up the returning Buick in my rearview mirror. They must have seen the parked bike, because they repositioned themselves several car lengths from the entrance to the drive and settled in again.

A couple of blocks to the north, I left the Cavalier on a residential street. In a few minutes, via the "back way"—mostly alleys and a backyard or two—I was at the Lady's. I twisted the old-fashioned metal key in the middle of the front door and heard the bell sound on the other side. It always reminded me of a bicycle bell.

CHAPTER 15

The woman who opened the door looked Mexican and was new to me. She was short and stout like the teapot in the nursery rhyme, but she didn't look easily tipped over. Her dress went down to her ankles, full of green leaves and bright red and yellow flowers and birds. She could have been twenty-four or forty-two. Her smile, although missing a few significant teeth, was as wide and hopeful as her eyes.

"Good evening," she said. "Will you become Mr. Foley?"

"I will," I said, "if I keep working on it."

Her English was probably better than my Spanish ever would be. But if the stupid crack bothered her, she kept it to herself. She said, "I am so happy. Come in please. The Lady waits upon you."

I followed her down the hall and into what the Lady calls her front parlor.

She was seated in one of two uncomfortable wing chairs that faced each other across a low table in front of the fireplace opposite the entrance to the parlor. There had been only one fire in the fireplace since the Lady had moved in. That was the previous Christmas, when I started one as a surprise for her. It was long after New Year's before they'd finally gotten rid of the smell of the smoke that billowed through the house. This Christmas, I'd give her a chimney cleaning.

As I entered the room, she had already set her book down on the table—she reads a lot—and was rising to greet me. The Lady is a powerful woman, and it startles many people to discover how ordinary she looks. Neither tall nor short, medium build, dark hair streaked with gray and cut like a grandmother's—she doesn't draw much attention standing in a checkout line at Wal-Mart or at the water fountain at the Lyric Opera. It doesn't take long, though, to notice a certain aristocratic manner about her. It's a manner that rubs a lot of people the wrong way. But they can take it or leave it. It's there to stay.

She stepped toward me, stretching out both her hands, palms down. "It's so good to see you, Malachy," she said, with that trace of Britain still in her voice.

I took her hands and kissed her lightly on the cheek. "Hello, Helene," I said.

She turned to the woman who had met me at the front door. "Thank you so much, Consuela," she said with a gentle smile. "I think you should go to bed now. You have a big day tomorrow."

"Okay, Helene. Good night," the woman said. "I will see you soon in the tomorrow." As she closed the door behind her, she flashed her wide, gap-toothed grin that almost made even me feel good, and I felt rotten.

"Sit down, Malachy," the Lady said.

I sat in the chair opposite hers. From a cabinet across the room she came back with about a thimble's worth of brandy in a huge round bowl of a glass. She handed it to me.

"You've heard nothing from Cass?" she asked.

Until she said that, I'd thought I was handling things pretty well. But then the bottom dropped out. "They've got her, Helene. They'll kill her, and Sharon. Or . . . or something worse."

"Who?" She was still standing.

"I don't know who, and I don't know where. I don't even really know that she's still alive. And if she is, I have to give them someone else to kill to get her back. How can I do that?

I can't. There's nothing I can do. It's hopeless."

"Hopeless," she repeated. She went across the room, came back with her own thimble's worth of brandy, and sat down. She took a tiny sip, barely enough to survive evaporation before it got into her system. I looked down at my own empty glass.

She gestured toward the table across the room. "Help yourself, as always. But under the circumstances . . ."

The Lady knows I overdo things on occasion. "Thanks. I guess you're right."

I wondered how often I'd said that to her in the past few years. Not that she hadn't said it to me as well. Neither of us is always right, but I'd say the Lady has the edge—and then some.

"And what would you do if it weren't hopeless?" she asked.

"I don't know," I said. "That's the point. There isn't anything to do."

"Well," she said, "is it hopeless because you can think of nothing to do? Or is there nothing to do because it's hopeless?"

"Helene, I'm just not in the mood for . . ."

"I suppose not," she said. She took another imaginary sip of brandy and returned her glass to the table. Standing up, she turned her back to me and took a couple of steps in the direction of the brandy. I hoped she was going for the bottle. But she stopped and turned to face me.

"Does Consuela look like a hooker to you?" she asked.

The sharp turn in the conversation was a jolt. "Not much, not to me," I said.

"No," she said. "Not to you, and not to anyone else. Not anymore. But that's the only job she's ever had since she was maybe eight or nine years old. She doesn't know exactly. She doesn't even know how old she is, maybe in her late twenties. Her family was very poor and . . . well, they sold her. She was a pretty child and she was put to work first in Mexico City and later across the border, in El Paso. She never thought much about it. It's just what she did. She lasted quite a long time in the business. Eventually, though, when she no longer had any value, her employers abandoned her on the street. That was about six months ago. She was overweight, sickly, and absolutely without resources. She never learned much English. She'd been beaten so many times her brain should have been mush. But, surprisingly, it wasn't. She learned that a cousin was leaving for Chicago and she demanded that he take her with him. When he refused, she waved a knife and threatened to stab him. Whether she would have done it, she's not sure. She thinks she would have. Anyway, he brought her along."

The Lady was sitting down again and looking at me while she talked. I turned away and looked into the empty fireplace. I didn't really want to hear the life story of a Mexican whore.

"Look, I—"

"No," she said. "Listen to me. When Consuela arrived in Chicago, she had no idea what she would do. She lived mostly in parks and on the street—sometimes in shelters. One day, the police found her unconscious in some bushes somewhere along Lake Shore Drive. She had pneumonia and was lying in her own feces and urine. They tossed her into a patrol wagon and carted her to a hospital. The nurses had to wash her and clean away the lice, and even maggots, before they could treat her sores and infections. She was dehydrated and malnourished. She didn't even talk for days. They thought she was retarded. But she got better, and when it came time to discharge her, the social workers asked her where she would go, what she would do. 'I don't have nowhere. I can't do nothing,' she told them. 'But I want to go somewhere. I want to learn to do something. Help me.'

"They couldn't think of anything else to do with her, so they called me. It's taken her a long while to adjust. I swear it seemed hopeless at first. But Malachy, guess what? Tomorrow Consuela is starting a job. A terrible, merciless, backbreaking job, actually, in a huge, steaming-hot laundry. But it's a start, isn't it? And she's so excited about it she can't sleep."

She picked up her glass then. "So . . . hopeless?" This time she actually drank some brandy before, very gently, she said, "Now, tell me about your situation."

She wanted to hear the whole story, and I told her in as much detail as I could—from Sharon and the phone calls, to the rat, to Fat Wilbur and Mick and Breaker Hanafan, to Harvey Cartwright, to Frank and Lauren Parkins, to my stupid macho heroics with Deputy Sorkiss, to Cass's aborted message on my answering machine, to Mr. Troublesome. She knew, of course, about the intervention of Barney Green and Wyman Adams in Wisconsin.

"Such an interesting man, that Mr. Adams," the Lady said. "He sounded so, oh, so *competent* somehow. Oh, by the way, Malachy, what about that car out on the street?"

"They think I might lead them to Jason. They didn't see me come here."

"There was something Lauren told you," she said, taking one of her frequent sharp mental turns, "that she felt 'guilty and ashamed' about her husband's death. Why would she feel that way?"

"I don't know. She was upset. Everyone says guilt is a common reaction to the death of a loved one."

"Yes, everyone says that, don't they." She frowned. "Anyway, let's see. You have three things to do. Find Jason and put him in a safe place. Find Cass and Sharon also. Figure out out who it is that's looking for Jason and why. And finally, resolve Jason's problem so he can go back to pursuing his dream."

She sat back with a satisfied smile. You'd have thought she'd taken care of everything and there was nothing to worry about.

"Helene," I said, "that's more than three things."

"Well, any realistic plan should be open to modification as you go along. Plus, I'm not sure I put everything in the proper order. But it's a start, isn't it?"

I gave in. "I suppose it is."

"Now," she said, "you'll need a base of operations other than the coach house, don't you agree? Especially after you find Jason. Did I tell you we have two neighborhood homes now? We've a new one in Hyde Park. And the one in Uptown has a name now, 'Happiness Haven.' Absolutely atrocious, but the women voted, you know. Anyway, that one will be more convenient for you. We've always had a room there behind the kitchen for a janitor. They come and they go. But no one's using it now, and I've asked Mrs. McDaniels to get it ready for you. Here are the keys. The fancy one with the little curlicues is for the front door. The hall leads straight down past the kitchen to your room. The plain round key opens that door. There's a little bathroom and a door out to the alley. The plain key fits the back door, too. The room's not very luxurious, but there's a telephone. And guess what? They have a piano in the parlor. Although, come to think of it, I'd rather you keep Jason out of the parlor. Now, here's a card with the address."

"I know the address. I was there before it had that . . . name, the day you first opened it."

"Oh? Anyway, it's all set then. Mrs. McDaniels is expecting you any time and you can come and go as you like." She stifled a very prim yawn. "Well, then, is there anything else you need? You have enough money, I suppose?"

"Yes, I have enough money for now. But I don't know that I'll use Happiness Haven. There's something I need to do first, and depending on how that turns out, I might or might not need to use the room."

"That's fine. Take the keys anyway. But Malachy, did you hear what you just said?"

She'd caught me off guard again. "Well, I—"

"You just said there's something you need to do first. A few moments ago there was nothing to do, nothing that *could* be done. Now there's something, and that, whatever it is, will lead to another something. And from there . . . well, what's that old saying about a journey of a thousand miles? Or climbing a mountain?"

"Helene," I said, "could I have a little more brandy?"

She smiled. "Help yourself. Me, I'm going to bed. It's past midnight."

We both stood. I took my glass to the table, poured out several thimbles of brandy, and swallowed it. The Lady walked me to the front door. I took her hands again and kissed her on the cheek.

I opened the door, then turned back to her. "Helene," I said, "you know, maybe this will help. I mean I'm going to get Cass back, and maybe it'll help heal things. . . ." Even as the words came out, I was ashamed of the thought they revealed.

She lowered her head for a moment, then looked up. "You and Cass, you've been drifting apart. It will take far more than a bold rescue to bridge that gap."

"I'm scared, Helene. I mean for Cass."

"I'm frightened for her also . . . and for the boy and his sister." She lowered her head. "And for you, too."

As she pushed the door closed, she looked at me again and her eyes were filled with tears.

The route from the Lady's front door to the rear of the coach house can't be seen from the street. I went up the back stairs and entered through the kitchen. Leaving the lights out, I checked my machine for calls. Maybe Mr. Troublesome had called back. Maybe Breaker Hanafan had called with some information. Maybe someone wanted me to play the piano at a bar mitzvah.

But there was only one message. "It's Harvey Cartwright, Mal. I just heard about Frank Parkins. Gimme a call for Crissake, will ya? I wanna know what the fuck is going on."

That made at least two of us.

CHAPTER 16

I POKED THE ALARM OFF at six o'clock and when I did I thought about Cass. I always thought about her in the morning. How she'd groan and pull the covers up over her head if I got up before she did. How she'd pretend to be asleep when I brought her coffee in. Those things I always thought about—and more. Sometimes, then, I'd call her and ask her to come back home. It didn't work very often, but there was always the hope.

Now, though, hope was running low.

By seven I was jogging to my car, the back way again, in running shoes, loose-fitting jeans, and a leather jacket zipped up over a Lyric Opera of Chicago Radiothon sweatshirt the Lady bought at a rummage sale. Besides the Beretta in my jacket pocket, I carried my NAM, a nifty little North American minirevolver, in a holster strapped to my left ankle. In a gym bag slung over my shoulder I had extra clothes, extra rounds of ammunition, a toothbrush, and a little package that just might come in handy if I ever found out what was going on and why. I wore heavy socks to keep the NAM from chafing the skin off my ankle.

I tossed the gym bag into the trunk of the Cavalier and got behind the wheel. It was still unusually cold, close to freezing. Circling around a few blocks, I came up behind my watchers, still in place. It wouldn't take them forever to wonder whether the BMW was parked outside an empty nest, and to call in for new instructions.

Heading west toward the Edens, I knew I'd accept the Lady's offer of a room if I had to, but I didn't like the idea. The battered, abused women who used the Lady's places for shelter were a tough breed, but they had enough trouble without me. One man had died so far, and I didn't need any more innocent victims added to my list of regrets.

On the back of a snapshot of Jason she'd given me, Sharon had written his address, a room in a student residence near Cragman College. I wouldn't be the first to go through his room since he ran, and I didn't expect to find much, but it was somewhere to start. So, just after nine o'clock, I parked the Cavalier and walked a couple of blocks back to the building. It was one of three four-story, tan brick rectangles standing in a row. They looked like a public housing project. They'd been cheaply built in the seventies and they'd be lucky to survive the turn of the century.

I turned up the walk to the center building. Inside the front door was a small lobby with cement-block walls, painted light green. The wall to the left held a huge bulletin board, covered with flyers, posters, and messages to and from students in mostly illegible handwriting. To the right there was a single elevator and a steel door with a small square window about head high, through which I saw a set of stairs leading up. Straight ahead was a desk with a small printed sign that said Security: All Visitors MUST Sign In. Below that admonition someone had written with a felt-tip pen: This Means You! There was a book lying open on the desk which I supposed was a ledger for visitors' signatures.

A uniformed security guard stood with his back to me, looking out the window behind the desk and chuckling softly into the telephone tucked under his left ear. His right hand slapped gently against his thigh in time with the rhythm pulsing from a pocket-sized radio on the desk. I turned and went through the door to the stairway. The guard never even turned my way. Maybe he thought I'd sign in on my way out.

On the fourth floor, the smell of stale beer and popcorn hovered in the air of the otherwise empty hallway. The same rock tune that had been playing on the tinny little radio in the lobby boomed out from behind the door to D-5. The next room, D-7, was Jason's, and the door had a spring lock even I could pick. It was a typical two-person dormitory room, with built-in cabinets and shelves covering every available inch of space. Even for a student's room, it was an extraordinary mess. No book was left unturned, no cushion unslashed. All the drawers were emptied, the shelves swept vacant. Their contents were tossed on the stripped beds.

I took a pass at the room, but my heart wasn't in it. If there'd ever been something of value there, it had gone out the door with the professionals ahead of me. The books had Jason's name in them, and there was no sign that he had a roommate. I sat down on one of the beds. It felt like the bunk in the Boxford County Jail.

The bass from the speakers in the room next door made the walls throb. It was lucky I had no homework to do, because thinking was out of the question. My brain vibrated with the music. I went out in the hall and was headed for the stairway when my fatherly instincts must have kicked in. I turned back and pounded on the door to D-5 and walked in.

"Hey," I yelled at the back of the skinny kid hunched over the tiny student's desk, "knock it off!"

He jumped and spun around in his chair. His ears were buried beneath the huge earpieces of a headset clamped over his frizzy blond hair. His eyes bulged when he saw me, and he yanked the headset from his head. At that, he looked even more surprised, then broke out into a grin and turned off the power switch of the amplifier on the desk.

He was still grinning when he said, "Sorry about that. I was listening through the phones, and forgot to cut the speakers out." Then he stopped grinning. "Hey, what are you doing here anyway?"

"I'm looking for Jason Cooper. I . . . I do some scouting for, uh, Ohio State and just happened to be nearby. Is he in class somewhere?"

"I don't know where Jason is. Seems like everyone's looking for him. Two guys were here the other day. Said they were from Notre Dame or Purdue or someplace."

"Yeah, well, we can offer him a better deal. . . . I mean a better all-around program. Doesn't he have a roommate? Maybe his roommate knows where he is."

"He doesn't have a roommate anymore. He used to, Scott Strelecki. He was a gymnast."

"Was?"

"Yeah. He's dead. Him and his girlfriend went flying off the Outer Drive. Sploosh! Right into the lagoon in Lincoln Park. Not really that deep, but they sank like a rock to the bottom. Had their seat belts on. Makes you wonder about seat belts, you know? Anyway, it was all over the news. Looked like a suicide, people said. I don't know. Scott seemed pretty stable to me. But the girl *was* kinda spacey, I guess."

"I remember that," I said. "Couple weeks ago."

"Yeah. And I mean Jason was *really* shook up about it. Not long after that he just took off. I didn't think it would hit him that hard. I mean, him and Scott got along okay, but they didn't seem like close friends or anything. I mean, a black guy and a Polack, you know? But he sure hasn't been back yet." He paused and looked at his watch. "Uh, look, I got a test coming up, you know?"

"Yeah, I should be on my way. But do me a favor will you?" I took one of Barney Green's business cards from my wallet.

"This is a friend of mine who's a lawyer downtown. If Cooper shows up, or you hear anything about him, give my friend a call, would you? He'll let me know."

"Sure." He took the card and dropped it on the desk. "Take it easy, huh?"

He jammed the headphones back on and, when he flicked a couple of switches on the amp, his body started to jerk and sway. His eardrums must have been worn through years ago. Now, the pounding booms that barely leaked out around the headphones could beat directly on his brain.

Closing the door on his bouncing body, I went back along the hallway and trotted down the stairs. Through the window in the lobby door I saw two students waiting for the elevator and the back of an older, larger man talking to the security guard. I skipped the lobby and left through a door marked: Emergency Exit Only! Alarm Will Sound! If it sounded, I didn't hear it.

Back at my car, I sat behind the wheel awhile. Maybe the death of his roommate had nothing to do with the hunt for Jason Cooper, but that was about as likely as my being invited to play at the Newport Jazz Festival, or even at a club with a cover charge. Besides, if I accepted that hypothesis, I'd have nothing to do but go home and practice the piano until some other lead turned up.

I don't read the papers often or see much television news. But I remembered the deaths of Scott Strelecki and Amy Radcliffe, mostly because I'd once known Amy's father. I hadn't paid attention to what school Scott attended. I did recall it had been about three o'clock in the morning, with the weather clear and dry and virtually no traffic. Amy Radcliffe's little red Mercedes jumped the curb of the southbound lanes of Lake Shore Drive where a damaged section of guardrail had been removed and not yet replaced. The car, with Amy and Scott inside, bounced across the grassy turf and into a lagoon in Lincoln Park, along the lakefront north of downtown.

An unidentified man called 911 from a roadside phone and said he'd seen a car go off the road. Police department divers pulled the bodies from the Mercedes as it rested on the bottom of the lagoon. Accident reconstruction experts estimated Amy's speed at eighty miles an hour or more when the car left the road.

The story certainly had the elements of drama: Nice kid from hardworking Polish family on the southwest side meets vaguely troubled Highland Park debutante at a "March against Hunger." Although culturally worlds apart, their shared ideals draw them together, until friendship blossoms into romance. Surely, a match designed for disaster. Then that mysterious predawn ride . . . and young love turns into tragedy.

"A Tragic Accident? Or a Lovers' Leap?" was one headline I recalled.

I started the car and, crossing back into the city, found a local branch of the public library. It was a storefront, filled mostly with well-worn children's books. The lone librarian seemed amazed that anyone at all was coming in before noon, and especially someone over ten years old. I told her I was interested in recent back issues of the *Tribune* and the *Sun-Times.* She knew I had to be some kind of weirdo, and wasn't enthusiastic about the search. Finally, waving a pen and a small spiral notebook, I told her I was a freelance writer doing an article for *Chicago* magazine on the value to the city of its branch libraries. A little weak, sure, but the writer-on-a-story line had failed me only once before. That was six months earlier, when I'd fed it to a nun who had part of the answer to the mayhem circling Happy Mallory's son. The nun, with eighty years' experience with truth and its absence—and with maybe an angel by her side—soon showed me the door. This time, though, the librarian swallowed it and produced a stack of newspapers.

The papers had been full of the case for a few days. Scott's father, Gerry, was a supervisor on a trucking dock; his mother a checkout clerk at a Kmart. Scott graduated from De La Salle, a Catholic high school boasting dozens of prominent Chicagoans, past and present, among its alumni. The principal, Brother Something-or-Other, praised Scott as a student-athlete whose interest in social issues like world hunger and racial justice made him a "credit to his family and his school." Gerry Strelecki, though, had a different view. "If the brothers would stick to teaching religion instead of politics, maybe kids like my son wouldn't get mixed up with people who got more money than sense, and nothing to do but tear around in the middle of the night and kill themselves."

Amy grew up on the North Shore, and hadn't been in school at the time of her death. She'd started at some New England college too exclusive for me to have heard of, but lasted just a few weeks. She was the only child of Calvin W. Radcliffe, a partner at Haskinson & Craw, a Chicago law firm with offices around the world. "Cal" Radcliffe handled mostly high-profile, high-profit white-collar criminal-defense cases. He was a pretty good trial tactician, as well as a workaholic, with only one interest beyond his law practice. That was his devotion to Amy, who'd been born the year Cal passed the bar and started as a federal prosecutor in the office of the United States attorney for the Northern District of Illinois, in Chicago.

Amy was eight years old when her mother, driving alone late one night, plowed headlong into a concrete viaduct on Skokie Highway, several miles from the Radcliffe home. Blood tests showed twice the alcohol to qualify her as legally intoxicated at the time of her death. Cal never remarried, devoting himself to his career and to Amy, with the help of a succession of live-in maids and nannies. A year after his wife's death, he left the U.S. attorney's office to graze in greener pastures at Haskinson & Craw.

Unlike Scott's father, Cal hadn't spoken to the media. Instead, a spokesperson released a prepared statement. I read it now, printed in full in the *Tribune.*

> Mr. Radcliffe is deeply saddened at the shocking accident that has taken his only child from him. He expresses his most sincere sympathy to the parents of Scott Strelecki. As you know, Mr. Radcliffe is a possible nominee as United States attorney for the Northern District of Illinois. He will issue a statement soon as to whether he will continue to hold himself available for that position. Mr. Radcliffe is thankful for your expressions of sympathy and asks that the press and his many friends understand and respect his need for privacy during this difficult time.

The funerals came and went. I never heard any public statement from Radcliffe that he still wanted to be chief federal prosecutor for one of the most important districts in the country. But he must have told someone, because the president selected him and he was awaiting Senate confirmation. No one doubted he'd be confirmed. He was considered cleaner than a plastic whistle in a shrink-wrapped package.

I made photocopies of the *Tribune* article, with its pictures of Scott and Amy. I didn't know that I'd have any use for them. But it seemed like the investigative thing to do. On my way out of the library, I paused to look around for a moment, trying to appear critically pleased. I thanked the librarian and carefully wrote her name in my notebook, reminding her to watch for the upcoming article.

Outside, I sat in the Cavalier to think again. There had to be a connection between Jason Cooper and the deaths of Amy and Scott. But how could Cal Radcliffe be involved? I reminded myself that my own belief that Radcliffe was a man of no recognizable redeeming social qualities shouldn't get in the way of my thinking. The times I'd met him, after all, he'd been prosecuting clients of mine who were invariably guilty. He had done what prosecutors do, alternating dire threats with promises that might or might not be kept, depending on whether the government could be forced to keep them. My own opinion was that the truthful, fair prosecutors I ran into must have concealed their true colors during their job interviews. Maybe I'm biased. Anyway, Cal wasn't that much worse than the majority, professionally speaking. But there was something about him. . . .

Radcliffe was tall, broad shouldered, and square of jaw, and his rugged good looks and impeccable taste in clothes seemed especially suited for public display, whether in a courtroom or before a wider audience, such as on television. Face-to-face, though, something was missing. He had a deep-seated attitude of superiority that he tried hard to camouflage with false congeniality. But even though his artificial manner couldn't quite conceal his overriding arrogance, that hadn't seemed to hurt his career so far.

Pulling away from the curb, I recalled once telling the Lady about my aversion to Radcliffe. Her response was that people she disliked often reflected qualities she didn't approve of in herself. That had seemed a little off base to me, and I dropped the subject.

There was construction on the Kennedy Expressway—as

there always is—and it was nearly noon when I took the exit ramp at Ohio Street, about a half mile north of the Loop. A few blocks east, I parked in the lot of what they call the Rock 'n' Roll McDonald's. I took my gym bag inside and ordered coffee. Music poured out of wall speakers. When my cup was empty, I took the gym bag into a stall in the men's room and changed into a sport shirt, gray slacks, and cordovan loafers. My leather jacket was in pretty good shape, but I probably still didn't look much like the typical Haskinson & Craw client.

CHAPTER 17

PEOPLE STILL SHOPPED IN THE THE LOOP, peering in the windows of Marshall Field's, Carsons, and a few other stores. But, despite the best efforts of the State Street Council, most of the "downtown" shopping action in the city happened along the "Magnificent Mile," on Michigan Avenue north of the river. Meanwhile, the Loop's high-rise office buildings just sucked people inside every morning and spit them out every night to run home.

Haskinson & Craw occupied several floors toward the top of a monolith recently risen along the Chicago River, the Loop's new north boundary. In the lobby, along with a faintly disapproving look, I got directions to the elevators that would take me to the law firm's "main reception area, thank you sir."

From a nearby pay phone, I got through to Cal Radcliffe's secretary and asked for an appointment later that afternoon, identifying myself again as a writer on a rush assignment for *Chicago* magazine. She put me on hold, then came back. "Mr. Radcliffe is tied up in meetings all afternoon. But he can see you tomorrow morning if that's convenient."

I told her I'd try to change another commitment and call her back. In an hour or less, they'd have inquired and discovered there was no magazine assignment.

The elevator sped me up in elegant solitude. I stepped off and, to my left, a tall, wide entrance opened into the law firm's reception area. It had about three times the square footage of my coach house. Opposite me was a glass-walled panorama of Lake Michigan, with the city spreading north and south along its shore. The walls that weren't glass were marble and polished wood. Clusters of sofas and chairs around low tables were placed throughout the area, on Oriental carpets that looked right at home on the polished parquet floor. Ornate chandeliers hung from a ceiling two stories high. All in all, the room was designed to make a person—me, for instance—who entered the sanctuary of Haskinson & Craw feel small and surrounded by power. It was the effect the pharaohs of ancient Egypt had been after, with their vaulted antechambers. It works, too. On the other hand, though, even the mighty pharaohs are dead now, and you don't get much smaller or less powerful than that.

At both ends of the room, hallways led off into offices where the firm's lawyers sat around making the rough ways smooth for their clients. Hiking the gym bag over my shoulder, I made the long walk toward the only other two persons in the reception area. They smiled, looking delighted to see me. Both were in their thirties, both gorgeous, both with hair, clothes, and makeup that looked a little expensive for receptionists. Brass nameplates on the wide desk announced the black woman as Charlotte Payne and the white woman as Melanie Kotlarz. I smiled back at them.

Charlotte spoke first. "Good afternoon, sir. May I help you please?"

"Sure," I said. "Malachy Foley to see Mr. Radcliffe."

"Very good. And did you have an appointment, sir?" Charlotte spoke, while Melanie scanned a printout that would prove I had no appointment.

"Yes, certainly," I said. No need to give up yet.

Still smiling, Melanie said, "I'm afraid we don't have you down, sir."

I was ready to dislike everything about Haskinson & Craw.

But these two made it tough. They must have been genuinely warm even before they were trained to treat every visitor as a potential moneymaker for the firm. You hate to lie to nice people like that.

"Well, darn," I said. "How can that be? I'm sure it was for today."

Charlotte was undaunted. "Maybe they just didn't enter it properly."

"That's possible," Melanie added. "Let me call Mr. Radcliffe's secretary for you."

"Thank you, Miss Kotlarz," I said. "Just have her tell Mr. Radcliffe I'm the one wants to talk to him about Jason Cooper."

"Very good, sir," Melanie said. "And that was Malachy Foley, right? You just have a seat and I'll check for you."

At a nearby conversation pit, I tossed my gym bag on the sofa and sat down beside it. Either I'd be ejected in a hurry, or I'd sit there a long time. My bet was I'd sit there.

Melanie spoke softly into the phone. I couldn't hear what she said, but the conversation went on for some time, long enough for Charlotte to disappear through the doorway behind her, and then to reappear and sit down again.

Finally, Melanie put the phone down. "Mr. Foley?" she called.

I got up and went to the desk. I tried to look sincere and hopeful.

"I'm terribly sorry," she said, "but there must be some mix-up. Mr. Radcliffe will be tied up for some time, and you don't seem to have an appointment."

"Well," I said, "I tell you what. I'm in no hurry. I'll just sit here and read magazines and wait until he can see me. How's that?"

"Really, sir," Charlotte said, "that's not possible. I'm afraid you'll have to leave now and call Mr. Radcliffe's office sometime for an appointment."

They were still, I thought, honestly trying to be helpful, but also starting to get a little confused. They'd be more confused before this was over.

"Look, ladies," I said, "you just tell Cal I'll wait right here until he decides he wants to talk to me." I went and sat down. "I may order out if it gets to be suppertime," I called back, "maybe Thai food."

Picking a magazine off the table, I thumbed through it. It was all about fine wines and gourmet foods and the single issue cost more than a lot of my meals.

Radcliffe was tied to Jason Cooper somehow, but it wasn't necessarily a tie he knew about. If he did know, he wouldn't be likely to call the police. So, if he did call them, I'd have learned something important, although I wasn't looking forward to being rousted in possession of two firearms, licensed and registered or not. On the other hand, I might just sit there all afternoon while Radcliffe left by another door. What I'd do at closing time I hadn't figured out.

From time to time people came in. They'd go to the receptionists' desk, then go and sit down—never very close to me. Eventually, a secretary would come out, greet the visitors, and spirit them off into the inner sanctum. Meanwhile, I paged through the upscale food magazine for a while, but it only made me hungry. I switched to an upscale men's fashion magazine. That depressed me and I wasn't sure why, so I switched to an upscale travel magazine.

Looking at pictures of faraway places made me wonder how long I'd been sitting in the same chair. I looked at my watch. Long enough, I thought.

Besides, by then two young men had appeared, one at each

end of the reception area near the entrances to the hallways. Both filled out their blue blazers and tan slacks like health club instructors. One had wavy blond hair, the other a blond crew cut. Both sat in chairs near their respective halls, striking identical relaxed "in charge" poses—legs crossed, hands resting lightly on the arms of their chairs. They were both very large young men, even sitting down.

Looking at my watch again, I stood up, yawned, and stretched. The young men uncrossed their legs, then recrossed them the other way. I continued to stretch, bending this way, then that, gradually breaking into a pattern I'd learned from my sixth-grade basketball coach, one which still seems to serve best before any athletic activity. It felt good.

When I started bouncing, then jumping lightly on the balls of my feet, the bodybuilders simultaneously stood up and leaned casually against their respective walls, arms crossed. They had to be wondering, behind those blank expressions.

The leather loafers weren't very comfortable. I stopped jumping and leaned over my gym bag on the sofa. The room was very quiet just then, and I swear when I unzipped the bag the sound echoed off the walls. I rummaged around a little for effect, and came up with my running shoes. Sitting back down, I removed my loafers and tossed them into the bag, then pulled on the running shoes and stood up. There was a sturdy, expensive-looking end table next to the sofa. I lifted my right foot, slapped it on the edge of the table, and laced up the shoe. I did the same with my left foot, being careful to keep my pant leg over the ankle holster.

I stuffed my leather jacket, with the gun in the pocket, into the gym bag, then carried the bag across the room to the center of the wall of windows and placed it on the floor, as far from the two young men as possible.

Then I started doing jumping jacks, arms and legs scissoring out and together, out and together, out and together.

I counted loudly. "One-*two,* two-*two,* three-*two* . . ."

My back was to the windows and I watched Melanie pick up the phone, tap out two digits, speak a few sentences, and hang up.

"Thirty-three–*two,* thirty-four–*two,* thirty-five–*two* . . ."

Charlotte started to stand, then leaned and whispered to Melanie. They glanced toward the two young men, then smiled at each other and settled back. Thoroughly modern women or not, if there was going to be a battle of the bulls, they both wanted to be there.

I was hoping to disappoint them. "Seventy-nine–*two,* eighty–*two,* eighty-one–*two* . . ." The two bodybuilders were intimidating enough for me, and I didn't want to test their professional status. Besides, who knew what might be lurking offstage?

"Ninety-nine–*two,* one hundred–*two.*" I stopped the jumping jacks.

A fight was not what I wanted. My goal was Calvin Radcliffe's attention. I had no interest in him or his ambitions. I didn't care if he became U.S. attorney, or governor of Illinois, or president, or pope. I had little interest in any of those people and the things they said and did. I wanted Radcliffe's attention. I wanted someone to steer me in the right direction. I didn't want to mix with the two Golden Glovers who by now were rolling their shoulder muscles around and flexing their fingers.

I started a slow jogging circle around the reception area, first along the windows, then a sharp left along the wood-paneled wall. As I passed the first young man, he couldn't keep quiet. "Very funny," he said.

I winked at him as I turned left again and continued along the wall opposite the windows. As I came to the wide doorway from the elevator area, two men were entering, both with gray suits, gray hair, and gray skin. I stopped, and jogged in place to let them pass. They gaped at me.

"Great exercise, running," I said, pumping away in my wool slacks and sport shirt. "Addictive though. You get nervous if you miss a day."

They headed toward Charlotte and Melanie, watching me over their shoulders as I continued my loop. As I passed the second young man, he shook his head as though he felt sorry for me. I gave him thumbs-up with my right hand and kept going.

Approaching the first young man on my second round, I stretched my right hand out. He almost slapped my palm, I thought, catching himself just in time. I made another circuit of the room. It was actually kind of fun.

I was passing across the elevator area for the third time when a voice called from behind me, "Mr. Foley, what do you want?"

I didn't turn toward him, or break stride, but swiveled and trotted straight across the middle of the room to the windows. Hoisting the gym bag over my shoulder, I swung around to face Radcliffe striding across the room toward me, his two musclemen behind him. Whether the Lady was right, and I saw something of myself in him, I don't know. But I didn't like him any better that day than I ever had before.

I grinned and stuck out my hand. "Hey, Cal," I said, a little too loudly. "How they hangin', pal?"

Charlotte and Melanie giggled at each other, covering their mouths with their hands. Some things don't change—like how their reaction made me feel good. I let myself enjoy the feeling. You have to take what satisfaction you can get.

CHAPTER 18

Calvin Radcliffe looked a little harried, not even up to his usual phony smile. He ignored my outstretched hand. "I don't have much time," he said. "But if you insist on talking to me today, let's go back to my office."

"Good idea. I'm in a bit of a hurry myself."

We walked together, Cal and I and the bodybuilders, through the reception area and on into a carpeted hallway. Along one side were offices, many with open doors and shirt-sleeved lawyers talking earnestly into telephones or tiny dictating machines. Secretaries' stations lined the hall opposite the attorneys' offices. People came and went along the way, some of them laughing and chatting. There was nothing sinister in the air at all. It was a suite of offices in a prosperous law firm. I might have been there for advice about pushing cigarettes or soft drinks to Asian kids, or dropping an oil rig off the Florida Keys, or any other respectable business.

We turned this way and that, until my sense of direction was hopelessly confused. Finally, Radcliffe ushered me into a large corner office. The blue blazers walked in behind us—too closely for my comfort. I started across the room, then stopped abruptly. The crew cut bumped into me. He didn't apologize. Radcliffe turned, and the four of us stood there, looking at each other.

"Cal," I said, "why not send these two boys off to sniff steroids or whatever they do to grow those bulges? I mean, they're kind of cute, dressed alike and blond hair and all—"

It must have been something I said. The crew cut took a step toward me, reaching with his left hand to grab my shirt just below my throat—a classic bully's move. He was about two inches taller than I, and would have lifted me to my toes by my shirt, if he had made contact.

Dr. Sato, my *sensei,* constantly chides me. "You are not devoted sufficiently to the art," he says, "so you remain always short of excellence." And he's right. But a few routines I practice over and over, endlessly, and they've become second nature. As the crew cut reached toward my throat, there was no need for thought.

Pivoting back on my right foot I turned sideways to my left, grabbing his left wrist with my right hand and pulling him around with me in the same direction he was moving, taking advantage of his momentum. As his body passed mine, I swung his wrist upward and back over his head in a circular motion. He flipped over backward just like they do in practice—only he fell a lot harder. I stepped over and across him, releasing his wrist and grasping his hand and thumb in a hold that would have brought tears of pain to anyone's eyes. Like it did to his, as he twisted his head to look up at me.

It was over before it started, which is the whole idea. Because my knee between his shoulder blades pressed him to the floor, and because of the pain, I could control him with just one hand. I thought his arm was bent just short of dislocation, his thumb just short of breaking. I couldn't be sure because I'd never tried to go any further. In fact, I wasn't sure I could bring myself to go any further. But how could the crew cut know that? All he knew was that I was a person who acted a little crazy.

The hold requires so little physical effort that I was able to speak evenly and wave the other bodyguard back. "If I were you," I said, "I wouldn't even breathe heavy."

Neither was a street fighter; neither was acquainted with serious pain. The one on the floor was gasping, unable to speak. He was hurting, and he was afraid. His friend wasn't anxious to join him.

So we all stayed put—except Radcliffe. He sat down behind his desk, leaned back in his executive's chair, and clasped his hands behind his head. I had to hand it to him. He sure didn't *look* impressed. The tic in his left eyelid might have betrayed some nervousness. But maybe he was just tired.

After a few seconds, Radcliffe spoke. "You two can leave now."

When they were gone, I sat in an armed leather client's chair, facing Radcliffe.

He leaned forward, resting his hands on the desktop. "I have only a vague recollection of you, Foley. You've been disbarred, haven't you?"

"Suspended," I corrected. "I remember you very clearly. I never liked you."

There was silence, then finally, "What is it you want?"

"Jason Cooper. I want to talk about Jason Cooper."

He looked straight at me, nothing in his handsome gray eyes but weariness. "I'm afraid I don't know any Jason Cooper," he said.

"You know *about* him, though," I said.

"I don't," he answered, rising to his feet. "Now, that should terminate this conversation." He'd returned to the intimidating, arrogant tone I remembered from years ago. The same anger and frustration I'd always felt back then rose in my chest and tightened my throat muscles.

"You're lying," I said. "Sit down or I'll sit you down." I tried to imitate his tone, not too successfully. But it did add a strange edge to my voice.

"You're insane," he said. But he sat down.

Until then I might have been talked out of his knowing of some tie between him and Jason. Once he sat down, though, any lingering doubt vanished. He knew something, all right. But if I'd had any hope he might open up to me, he'd have been right about my sanity. I understood that, but I wasn't ready to leave yet. I wanted to let him know I wasn't just guessing.

"Nice office you've got here," I said.

Actually, it wasn't very nice. It had lots of space, expensive furniture, and a great view of the city, if you didn't mind looking northwest from downtown. But with its off-white plasterboard walls, the room had a vacant air despite the papers and books piled everywhere. None of the clutter was personal—no photographs on the walls or the desk, no little statuettes of golfers or tennis players. Even the coffee mug was plastic foam. I thought of Harvey Cartwright's office, equally untidy, but unmistakably Harvey's. This could have been anybody's office, or nobody's office.

"Someone is looking for Jason Cooper, Cal. I think you know who it is, and why. I just want you to tell me what's going on, why he's so important. I'm not interested in you, or your career hopes."

"You're wasting your energy. I told you I don't know anything about any kid named Hooper, or Cooper, or whatever. I don't know what you're talking about. Now why don't you get out of here so I don't have to call the police to have you hauled out? *My* time, at least, is valuable."

That's about as far as I was going to get. "Well, that's that. I might as well be going."

"I'll show you out."

We both stood, but as I reached down for my gym bag, I noticed I still had my running shoes on.

"Hold on a minute," I said. I sat back down and, more deliberately than necessary, took a few moments to change my shoes. He was used to getting his way, and his growing frustration would help him remember this moment.

When I had changed shoes and put my jacket on, we retraced our steps to the reception area. Charlotte and Melanie were still there. "So long, ladies," I said. "Thanks for your help." They smiled the same smiles they had given me when I came in. As far as you could tell from their faces, they didn't think I was crazy at all.

Radcliffe walked me to the elevators. When the doors slid back, I stepped inside. Holding the doors open, I said, "I guess if you don't know Jason Cooper, you don't. But one thing I *did* find interesting, Cal."

He bit. "Oh? And what's that?"

"Just that you're the one back there who called Jason a *kid,* not me."

I let the doors slide silently closed and rode down.

CHAPTER

19

THE ELEVATOR WAS A LOCAL to the twenty-third floor, then express to the lobby. It was late afternoon, and the car soon filled up, mostly with secretarial types headed for home or some watering hole. With the gym bag as a bumper, I managed to get out unharmed on twenty-three. A bank of elevators at the opposite end of the building served the first twenty-three floors, and I rode down from there, part of a different cluster of people anxious to be on their way.

An ex-cop I know manages security for a department store chain and claims his trainees learn to detect even expert shoplifters in just a few days. "There's no magic to it. Just practice looking for the signs. Pretty soon you're spotting the grabbers before they even lift anything."

There's no magic to spotting a tail, either. Just takes practice. I stepped off the elevator and scanned the large, now bustling, lobby. Off to my right, two men watched the other bank of elevators, waiting for me. I turned left, clutching the gym bag to my chest, out of their sight if they turned my way. I joined the stream of people pouring through the revolving doors. Outside, I walked quickly south for a couple of blocks, stopping abruptly now and then to window shop. Anyone tailing me was quicker than I am.

I stood on the curb for a while looking for an empty cab. When there weren't any, I decided I could use the walk back to McDonald's and my car. I headed for La Salle Street. To the south it runs past city hall and finally, several blocks of office buildings and financial institutions farther, dead-ends at the Board of Trade Building topped by its statue of Ceres, goddess of agriculture. I turned north.

By the time I reached the LaSalle Street Bridge over the Chicago River, my pace had unconsciously quickened, almost to a trot. Maybe I was running away from La Salle Street's political and commercial power, or maybe compensating for my slow-motion progress in finding Jason. Anyway, I forced myself to slow down. I didn't need to hurry. I needed to figure out where I was going.

Halfway across the bridge, I stopped and stared down at the dark river. I imagined Scott Strelecki and Amy Radcliffe, trapped in their snappy little Mercedes, sinking slowly through the black water to the bottom. Jason's flight was linked, somehow, to their deaths. Was their plunge an accident? a double suicide? or something more sinister? What about Cal Radcliffe? Surely he couldn't have been involved in his own daughter's death. But then why not just throw me out of his office? His denial that he knew anything about Jason was false. And that he was about to be appointed to the highest federal law enforcement office in the state couldn't have been mere coincidence.

The trick to tying everything together was to be methodical, gather information, place one piece next to another, follow up each lead, gather more pieces. Slow and steady wins the race. Eventually the pieces fall together into a pattern. It's the only way.

So far it wasn't working.

Traffic passed back and forth behind me on the bridge. As hard as I peered down into the water, I couldn't see any pattern. All I could see was a car with two people in it, drifting lazily back and forth and downward through the water. I kept watching, staring at it, and as I did I saw that what should have been a Mercedes wasn't a Mercedes at all. It was a Toyota. And that wasn't Scott and Amy trapped inside, but two women. They were struggling with the door handles and banging their fists against the windows. I leaned far over the railing and, though the water was swirling and murky and thick with urban grease, I could see through it clearly. I saw the faces of the women. Cass and Sharon. Their mouths open, screaming soundlessly at me.

All at once, the world exploded in a frenzied clanging of dissonant bells. Bloodred lights flashed on and off through the darkness that had fallen, and a huge male voice bellowed from high above and all around me.

"You are in danger," the voice from the multiple loudspeakers boomed. *"This bridge is about to be raised. Clear this bridge."*

I lifted my head. A small freighter was passing under the open Clark Street bridge to the east, headed our way. Vehicular traffic had already been cleared from our bridge and I ran to catch up with the last pedestrians scurrying to the other side before the bridge split in the middle and its two halves were raised to let the freighter pass. The bells and the lights and the bridge tender's voice chased us across.

Standing in the dark with four or five strangers at the railing north of the bridge, I listened to the groaning and whirring of the gigantic machinery that picked up La Salle Street—with its four traffic lanes and two sidewalks—and stood it on its end while the little ship passed through. As it did, the bells kept clanging and the red lights flashed, and from the dimly lighted deck of the freighter one of the deckhands waved silently at us. We all waved back together, like a family to a departing brother. Then we turned and went our separate ways.

I left the river and continued past the square brick building that houses traffic court, and into an area that had—just yesterday, it seemed—been run-down factories and warehouses. Now it held some of the hottest properties in town. The developers christened it "River North"—and suddenly the art galleries were followed by designers' boutiques and specialty shops, and restaurants and clubs kept sprouting up quicker than the dandelions that only recently grew in the cracks of the sidewalks.

Suddenly, I was hungry. And even though it wouldn't erase that picture of Cass and Sharon in despair, I wanted something more than just a quick meal. I headed for Overbury's. It was a bit above my ordinary price range, but what decent restaurant wasn't?

I needed a telephone, too. And Overbury's, catering to its large business trade, has some of my favorite phone booths. Actually, each booth is a glass-doored roomette where you sit at a writing desk and talk on the phone. When Overbury's first put them in, the cocaine and heroin dealers monopolized them, taking their drinks from the bar to the booths to set up their transactions by phone. But Overbury's owners apparently had friends somewhere who put the word out. So now the booths are available again to businesspeople, tourists, and your occasional stalled private investigator.

It was early for dinner and the dining room was empty except for a table of three women, thirtyish, attractive, and all in their power outfits. As I was ushered in, their heads simultaneously turned my way. I grinned at them and nodded. In perfect unison, they turned back to their cocktails and their conversation. They didn't look like they were talking about me.

I was taken to a table against the wall as far from the ladies as possible, and ordered a glass of red wine. When the wine arrived I told the waiter I needed a few minutes and took the wine to a vacant phone roomette. Retrieving the messages from my answering machine yielded calls from the Lady, from Barney Green, and from Harvey Cartwright.

There was also a message from Mr. Troublesome. "Sorry we missed you yesterday. The women are sorry, too. Your absence has been, well, hard on them. It's a shame, really. But it's up to you. You better surface."

How long I sat there, frozen, I don't know. But the Lady's advice came back to me. Hopeless or not, I had to keep plodding forward.

First, Barney. A personal-injury lawyer, he has investigators who photograph accident scenes, take witness statements, gather evidence. And if they hustle up a case for him now and then you won't hear about it from me. Maybe one of them could start checking on Cass and Sharon.

Barney was still at his office and his evening receptionist put me through. We talked first about what a genius he was for finding Wyman Adams.

"But look, Barney, now I need something else. I wonder if one of your investigators—"

"Jesus, you think you need to ask me something like that? When it's Cass, for Crissake? I've had people out checking all fucking day—hospitals, police department, newspapers. There's not a goddamn thing about Cass, or Sharon Cooper. The Cooper girl doesn't have a job and Cass didn't have any classes today, so no one's missed either of them yet, as far as we can tell. Anyway, no news is good news. At least we know nothing bad could have happened, right?"

"Yeah, Barney, right." But we both knew something bad could have happened, bad and so far unknown.

"Plus," he went on, "I don't know if the cops are looking for this Jason Cooper or not. But we did learn one thing. The kid's car. It was found abandoned on the street and towed to a police auto pound about five o'clock this morning."

It was the first hard piece of information I'd learned all day. My breath got caught somewhere south of my wishbone and sat there, expanding.

"Mal? You still there? Don't you want to hear about the car?"

Finally, I exhaled in a rush of air and managed to speak. "Where was it?"

"Right downtown, in a cab stand on Wacker, near State Street."

"So he came back to Chicago."

"And either he had enough smarts to ditch the car, or else somebody—"

"They haven't got him, or I wouldn't still be getting calls from Mr. Troublesome."

"Mr. Troublesome? That's his name? Come *on,* Mal."

"That's what he called himself. He may lack imagination, but he sure frightened Sharon Cooper. And he scares the hell out of me." I hesitated. "Something else, Barney. What do you hear about Calvin Radcliffe?"

"Radcliffe? You mean other than that he's a shoo-in for U.S. attorney? What's he got to do with anything?"

"His name came up, is all. Is there any hint he won't be confirmed?"

"Hell, Mal, they can background check Cal Radcliffe all they want. All they'll find out is what anyone knows who's gotten behind that photogenic face. He's as straight and clean as an ice pick, and just as nice to be near. He'll be confirmed all right. And as soon as he is, he'll find some high-profile pol with his hands in too many pockets, make a big deal out of sending the poor mope to prison camp for a few years, hold a lot of press conferences, and try to springboard himself into the governor's mansion—and then maybe Washington, for all I know." He paused, then asked, "Uh, Mal, you got something on Radcliffe?"

"Like I said, I don't know. But the kid who drowned with Radcliffe's daughter was Jason Cooper's roommate. And Jason took off about the same time. I just don't know. Anyway, I'd appreciate it if you'd have your people keep their eyes and ears open, mostly for Cass and Sharon, but for anything else that might turn up, too."

"No problem. You okay otherwise? I mean money and all?"

"Yeah, I'm all set. Thanks. I'll be in touch. And, Barney, tell Seth to stay alert. Who knows when I might need him again."

"Sure will, Mal. You know, you got a big fan there."

"Yeah, well, don't fret, he'll grow out of it. Anyway, I gotta run."

"I'll leave a message if I hear anything." Barney hung up.

My waiter came to the booth and refilled my wineglass while I tapped out the Lady's number. She answered the phone herself.

"I called earlier," she said, "to see what progress you've made. I understand you haven't gone to Happiness Haven."

"I've learned a few things. But I don't know whether I've made any progress or not. I might still use the Haven, but I don't know when. Barney's had people checking and nothing's turned up on Cass or Sharon. So that's good news."

"Yes. Although we have to face the fact that something might have happened that hasn't come to light yet." The Lady was good at facing facts. Sometimes it helps to hear someone else say what you know, but thought you didn't want to hear.

Before I could respond, she continued. "I've been thinking about this. Of course, I can't say I'm having much success, either. But the key is Jason. You surely won't find Cass and Sharon without finding Jason first. Barney told me about his car being left downtown. But with credit cards and cash machines, you know, Jason could be anywhere in the world."

"He could be," I said, "but I think he's nearby. If he wanted to take off, he'd have left from Wisconsin." I went on to tell her about my visit to Jason's room, the drowning of Scott and Amy, and my conversation with Cal Radcliffe.

"So then, let's see. First, what makes Jason important is information he has, either in his head or possibly written down."

"Or information someone *thinks* he has," I said.

"Of course. He either has it or he doesn't. And if he has it, he might not even know what it is." She was silent for a few seconds. "And . . . if Jason has information, where did he get it? He must have gotten it from Scott. Where did Scott get the information? From Amy."

"But what's the information? Why is it so important?"

"Well," she said, "we don't know yet what it is. But it's important, certainly, because it's about some person."

"Cal Radcliffe."

"Of course," she answered. "Jason has information about Mr. Radcliffe. And, whether it's written down or just in his head, whoever is looking for Jason either doesn't know what the information is, and wants to find out and possibly use it, or—"

"Or does know what it is, and certainly wants to use it."

"Or wants to ensure that it doesn't become public. Or"—she spoke slowly as she thought things through—"possibly some combination of those alternatives."

"I guess so, Helene," I said. "But at least they either know or they don't know."

"Or both, Malachy?" she suggested.

"That doesn't make sense." I reached for my wineglass, but it was empty. "Whoever's after Jason can't know and not know at the same time."

"But we're talking about possibilities. You have to keep an open mind."

"Helene, I hate to say it, but sometimes you can be a little irritating."

"Yes. Well, we all do the best we can, don't we? Now I suppose I ought to go and help with dinner or something."

"Wait a minute, Helene. I almost forgot. How did Consuela's first day go?"

"Oh, you should *see* her! She's so excited, running on about everything that happened all day. You'd think she'd been off doing microscopic surgery or something. Of course, doing laundry isn't going to satisfy her for long. But other jobs will come along, and—who knows—maybe school or something. Anyway, it's very satisfying. But I have to go now. Good-bye, Malachy. And . . . be careful."

The waiter was at the door of my booth. His expression suggested I might be a little irritating myself. I gave in and followed him. To his dismay, I insisted on carrying my empty wineglass with me back to the dining room. I guess wandering the premises with an empty glass just isn't done at Overbury's. As I arrived back at my table, the three budding power brokers were preparing to leave, busily dividing the bill among them and digging around in their purses for lipstick and money.

The other tables were filling steadily. The waiter whisked my old glass away and filled the new one sitting on the table. I opened the menu—and suddenly wanted Cass there with me. I missed her. I always miss her in restaurants. Airports are the worst. But restaurants are bad.

Besides, Cass could have filled me in about Sir Thomas Overbury. Apparently, he'd been a real person. The menu said he lived from 1581 to 1613, a pretty short life span. But someone still thought about him enough to name a restaurant after him, more than 350 years after he died. Quotations from his writings were scattered here and there throughout the four-page menu. The one that first caught me off guard was stuck in between "Salads" and "Sea Food" and went like this:

> *Absence doth sharpen love, presence strengthens it; the one brings fuel, the other blowes it till it burnes cleare.*

Cass might even have told me which of old Tom's works that was taken from. But she wasn't there. So I ordered something, and ate it, and it was probably delicious. But it was absence that marked the meal, absence that kept on bringing fuel to the fire. Absence is what Cass and I shared most with each other. There'd been so little presence for so long that I wondered if even when I found her, and this was over, there'd be strength enough to what we once had to ever keep us together again.

I kept the menu, and while I ate I tried to distract myself with more of the wisdom of Thomas Overbury. Some of it was pretty sexist by today's standards, like:

> *Wit and women are two frail things.*

But some of it hit home—especially the final quote. With what the meal was costing, I felt no guilt at all about quietly tearing a strip off the bottom of the menu's last page. It held Sir Thomas's final admonition to the restaurant's patrons:

> *Falsehood playes a larger part in the world than truth.*

I folded that one carefully and put it in my shirt pocket, close to my heart.

CHAPTER 20

I HAD ONE MORE CALL TO RETURN, but the booths were all in use as I left Overbury's. I walked the half mile to McDonald's and was happy to find the Cavalier hadn't been towed. My fuel gauge read empty and at a nearby gas station there were two empty phone booths standing outside the cashier's kiosk. One of them even had a working phone. I was on a roll.

I called Harvey Cartwright's office. No answer. I called his home. No answer. Probably an evening practice. I remembered a row of pay phones in the lobby outside the gym. With some persuading, directory assistance finally got me the number to one of the phones. I tapped it out and waited while the phone rang . . . and rang. It was one of those times when you're afraid to hang up because you *know* someone will pick up just as you do. I persisted. After all, I was on a roll.

"Yeah?" The kid who answered was breathing hard, like he'd just run from the practice floor to the phone. But even so, his voice had that "don't mess with me" tone ghetto kids learn at their mothers' knees, an unconscious survival tactic. Not that it works all that well.

"Coach Cartwright there?" I shot back.

"Yeah, he here. But he busy kickin' ass right now."

"Well, ask him to take a break for a minute. I need to talk to him."

"All right," he said. I heard him put the phone on the ledge, but he picked it up again right away. "Coach'll wanna know who it is."

"Just tell him I'm returning his call. He'll figure it out."

I waited, watching the rust spots grow around the wheel wells of my car.

"Hello?"

"Harve. It's me, Mal."

"Man, am I glad you called. I, uh, I think I got a little problem here." He spoke casually, but something in his tone told me both of those statements were far more true than he would have liked.

"Can somebody hear you talking, Harve?"

"Just a few players hanging around. But listen . . . I've got that package you've been looking for."

My brain reeled. "You mean Jason?"

"You got it."

"Is he all right, Harve?"

"Oh yeah, yeah, no problem there. All wrapped up and out of sight. Thing is, I don't know what the hell to do with it."

"I'll be there as soon as I can." Not that I knew, either. "Listen, Harve, have you noticed anyone hanging around, maybe keeping an eye on you?"

"Jesus, I don't know. You think so?"

"It's just . . . anything's possible, Harve. Anyway, I'm on my way."

"Well, hurry up, will you? Practice'll be over in a half hour. I'll have someone watch the door to let you in. See you." He hung up.

I was in the Cavalier and headed across the gas station lot toward the street, at about twenty-five miles an hour, when I remembered I hadn't gotten gas. I screeched to a stop and then, as I backed up to the row of pumps, convinced myself to calm down. I filled the tank, paid cash, and headed toward Cragman College.

The evening traffic was light, and I made good time. It was

hard to believe Harvey wasn't being watched, but Jason must have somehow slipped by unseen. How he did, and how Harvey was hiding him, I couldn't imagine. As I approached the gym, all I knew was that I had to get him away from there, and keep Harvey out of this.

The gym and its parking lot took up the better part of an entire block. I got a pair of sunglasses out of the glove compartment and put them on. Rummaging around beneath me under the seat, I came up with a White Sox baseball cap and a huge empty 7-Eleven soft drink cup. I jammed the cap on my head, pulling the visor low over my eyes, and held the cup in one hand and the steering wheel in the other. Was it Sherlock Holmes who said the best disguise is the simplest one? If it wasn't, it was someone else. Anyway, sporting *my* best disguise, I drove the streets around the gym in an eccentric circle, watching for watchers.

Bingo! A blue Dodge sedan. One man. Unusual. The Dodge sat facing north, on a residential street that dead-ended at the east-west street running along the gym parking lot. It was at the head of a row of parked cars stretching backward the entire block. When I spotted him, I was westbound, with the parking lot on my right. I had to pass directly in front of him. As I did, I took a swig of air from the empty cup and kept my face half-turned toward the gym. I made another run, but couldn't see any partner anywhere. Maybe it was a sign of a failing economy.

I didn't get much of a look at the driver, but the Dodge was parked directly across the pedestrian crosswalk, its front bumper jutting just slightly past the corner, its rear bumper close against the car behind it. From where he sat he had a view of the team van and the handful of other cars clustered near the door of the gym, and he could pull out and follow in either direction, as needed.

I continued for a couple of blocks and parked at a place called In'n'Out, a gas station and convenience store. Among the debris crammed into the trunk of the Cavalier was a flat, square delivery box that had once held a pizza—a "Fiesta," with sausage, mushrooms, green peppers, anchovies, and onions. I broke open a bundle of *National Geographic* magazines the Lady had given me long ago to deliver somewhere, and put as many volumes as I could into the box. It probably weighed ten times as much as a pizza—even a Fiesta—and I put it on the front seat next to me.

The Dodge was still there when I got back. I drove eastbound slowly, peering about like a deliveryman looking for an address. As I drove by the corner, I swerved to the right and stopped suddenly, the right side of the Cavalier not quite scraping the front of the Dodge and pinning it tightly into its spot. As I did, the Dodge's lights went on, and its motor roared to life.

I left my own motor running and jumped out of the car, balancing the pizza box on my left hand, like a waiter carrying a tray just above his shoulder. I walked in the street, heading past the open window of the Dodge. The driver was glaring at me. His head was as round as the globe, with cauliflower ears set on either side at the equator, and a black knit cap pulled tightly over the Northern Hemisphere. A thick black beard covered most of South America. A two-inch stub of cigar was bobbing up and down out of the beard. I didn't recognize him.

"Gotta make a delivery, man," I said, pulling down on the bill of the White Sox cap and jerking around like I might be on something. "Gotta make a delivery. Just be a minute, man."

"What the fuck you talking about, delivery? You can't hardly even walk straight. Can't you see you got me pinned in? Move your fucking car or I'll ram into the side of it." He talked through the teeth that clenched the cigar.

"Hey, pizza delivery, you know? But hey, man, go ahead, do your thing. Feel free, Jack. Ram away." I was bouncing and weaving a little, as though there were a tune playing in my head that only I could hear. "It's a free country, right? Ain't my car, anyway. Company car."

I dance-stepped right up to the side of the Dodge. Suddenly, I stood dead still, leaned forward, and stared at him through the sunglasses. "Hey, man, don't I know you?" I said. "Yeah, I know you. I seen you once in the shit house. The County, man, right?"

He was confused. So far, he had no idea who I was, but I couldn't believe he hadn't been told to watch for me. Through the car window, I could see a cellular phone between the bucket seats. I needed him away from the phone. I needed him out of his car. But most of all, I needed him out of the way between me and Jason.

"Anyway," I said, "you think I give a shit what you do, you melon-headed pus bag?" Unable to think of anything else creative to call him, I went into the bounce-and-weave routine again, staying close to his car. The pizza box weighed heavy in my left hand and and my shoulder started to throb again with pain left over from Wisconsin. But I needed my right hand free.

Finally, he opened the car door, forcing me to step back. Once he was on his feet, I saw that he was built like I'd been afraid he might be, tough and compact, wide and low to the ground. I stepped back farther, hoping to draw him to me. But he wasn't interested in me. He wanted the Cavalier out of his way, and started toward it.

"Goddamn dopeheads . . . screw up the whole fuckin' country," he muttered, not to me, but to himself.

I hurried after him. "Hey, man, stay away from the car," I said.

He didn't even look my way, and he didn't intend to.

As I followed him past the trunk of the Cavalier, I snatched the cap off his head. He still didn't turn around. I had to admire his singleness of purpose. But when the palm of my right hand slapped against the side of his shaven skull with a crack that reverberated up and down the street, he had taken all he was going to. He swung around to face me—and he caught a pizza box full of *National Geographics* flat and square in the face.

It felt as though I'd slammed the box into a brick wall. While my left arm disintegrated into a thousand pieces of pain, all the bald man did was stumble backward a step. The cigar, crumpled a bit, still stuck out through the beard. But when he caught his balance and started toward me, he found himself facing the barrel of the Beretta, about three inches in front of the cigar.

"On your face," I said.

He didn't move. He still wasn't sure I wasn't high on something.

"You're as tough as they come," I said. "I'll give you that. But if you're not crazy you'll go facedown on the pavement. I'm as sober as a judge, and not nearly as law-abiding."

He was convinced.

As he lay facedown, with his legs spread wide apart and his hands locked behind his head, I transferred a nickel-plated revolver from the holster over his right hip pocket to my belt. Then I stepped back to the Dodge, reached in and turned off the motor, and took the keys from the ignition. The Dodge's trunk wasn't very big, and there wasn't a thing in it but a spare tire and a canvas packet containing a jack and tools for changing a tire. I tossed the tool kit under the car behind the Dodge.

"Okay," I said, "up on your feet and into the trunk."

He stood up. He didn't say anything, but the ideas in his head were clear in his face. I didn't like them.

"Let me tell you something," I said, jerking the gun from side to side. "Whether you run at me, or run the other way, I'm not going to miss you with this thing. You might survive, but you'll be short a leg, or a kidney, or a lung—whatever. You'll find out when you wake up."

It was a very unhappy thug who curled up in the trunk. When I closed the lid, it sounded solid. I wondered how long it would take him to kick his way out. I found the Dodge's fuse panel, removed all the fuses, and put them in my pocket. I stuffed the car keys, the cellular phone, and the bald man's gun deep under the front seat of the Dodge. Then I drove across the street and through the parking lot, parked next to the team van, and pounded on the gym door.

It was Harvey who let me in. He had the players running laps around the gym.

"Jesus Christ, Mal, it took you long enough. What's with the shades?"

I'd forgotten I had them on. Stuffing them in my pocket, I said, "They had a man on you, Harve. But we're okay for a while, I think. Where's Jason?"

"Ya know," he said, "I drive my car back and forth from home. But during the day if I need to go somewhere I been using the team van. Thing's really a piece of shit, and the battery isn't so hot, so I like to run it around once in a while to make sure it's still alive."

"Uh, Harve . . ."

"I'm gettin' to it. I'm gettin' to it. Anyway, I go out this afternoon to get something to eat, crank her up, and I'm pulling outta the lot when I hear this voice behind me. 'Hey Coach,' it says. Almost gives me a heart attack or something. It's Jason, lying on the floor in the back of the van. I don't know when the hell he got in there. Van's been broken into so many times we never lock the damn thing anymore."

"You mean he's still out there? In the van?" I asked.

"Hell *yes,* he's still there. At least, I think he is. I got him a sandwich and told him I was going to get you. Told him your name. Told him you were a genius. Plus, I told him he better not lift his head to look out the window, or both him and me might be shootin' the pill with Saint Peter. I always keep a bunch of old blankets in the van because the heater doesn't work so well. He's warm enough, I think."

"Harve," I said, "how much longer will practice go?"

He looked at his watch. "Oughta be over now."

"All right. But just keep 'em busy till I'm outta here with Jason." I pointed through the door window across the parking lot. "You see that Dodge parked in the crosswalk?" I asked.

"Yeah, I see it." He stared. "Jesus, damn thing looks like it's shaking."

"There's a very angry man locked in the trunk. I'll call the cops about him when I leave. I don't think this'll be a problem for you. Whatever happens, just do everything like you normally would, okay? Anybody asks, just tell them I came in, acting kind of crazy and looking for Jason. You told me you haven't heard anything from him, and I left. You didn't see my car."

"Okay, Okay. I can handle that. But just hurry up, will you?" He glared at me. "I don't want any of these kids gettin' hurt."

CHAPTER

21

THE VAN HAD a sliding side door.

"Jason," I said softly, "I'm going to help you."

A pile of blankets stirred slightly on the floor in front of the bench seat at the back of the extended van. "What's your name, man?" came from beneath the blankets.

"Foley," I said. "Mal Foley. Don't get up. You got any clothes or anything?"

"Just what I got on."

"I want you to crawl to this door, and then into the floor of the backseat of my car. Bring any paper cups and whatever's back there from your sandwich."

He poked his head out and started sliding slowly toward me, dragging the blankets with him.

"Come on, Jason. Hurry up." I was getting nervous.

"Man, I'm so stiff I can hardly move." But he got to his hands and knees, crawled to the door, and then out and into the Cavalier. He didn't fit well on the floor behind the front seat.

"Shit, man, this here's even worse." There was a whining tone to his complaint, his deep voice notwithstanding.

I tossed the blankets back in the van and the remains of his lunch on my backseat. "Next time I'll rent a bus," I said, sliding behind the wheel. "Just stay down for a while, will you?"

I drove out of the lot and past the Dodge. It was still rocking. Fortunately, the trunk was too small to give the bald man much room to kick. I went back to the In'n'Out and parked at the corner of the lot, by a public phone.

"We gettin' out now, man?" Jason asked.

"Not yet. Just sit tight, or lie tight, or something."

"Yeah, well, for Crissake hurry it up, will you?" I hadn't expected him to be in a real good mood, but a rescuee with an attitude was something I didn't need.

I went to the phone and called 911. "I just saw a drug sale," I said, "right in my own neighborhood."

"What is your name, sir?"

"My name? Are you crazy? My family and I live around here. I'm looking out my window and I see a couple guys by this car, a Dodge I think, right at the corner. One of 'em's talking into a portable phone. One guy gives the other guy some money out of his pocket, and the other one hands him a package. It's gotta be drugs. Then they start arguing, and the first one pulls a gun. Right on my street, for God's sake."

"Sir—"

"Then the guy with the gun makes the other guy get in the trunk of the car. Then he runs off. I'm calling from a pay phone because I don't wanna get involved. But you oughta get someone over there right away. The one guy's still locked in the trunk."

"Sir, we can't send someone unless you tell me where the car is parked."

"Oh, sorry. I guess you're right." I gave the intersection.

"Thank you sir. Police officers will be there shortly. But it would help if you gave me your name."

"Not me," I said. "I pay my taxes, but I'm not giving my name. Heck, if you people were out patrolling the streets like you're supposed to, I wouldn't even have to call." I hung up.

Back in the Cavalier, I parked a block from the Dodge, facing away from it, my lights off and motor running. Sure enough, a suburban squad car pulled up beside the Dodge, then another.

"Jason," I said, "you can peek out the back window. But keep your head low."

"Hey man," he said, "you don't have to keep telling me what to do. I'm not stupid, you know?"

And this was the *post*–Frank Parkins version of Jason Cooper. No wonder no school wanted to take a chance on him. But I held my tongue.

He raised his head carefully and we watched. Four police officers climbed out of the two patrol cars. Two stood looking down at the trunk, as though talking to it. One, a woman, began to search inside the Dodge. On the driver's side, she reached under the front seat. She backed out of the car, stood up, and tossed a set of keys to one of the officers near the trunk. Then she reached back under the seat. This time she must have found the gun, because she called out something and one of the officers behind the car drew his own gun and held it pointed toward the trunk.

There was more talking at the trunk. Finally, one of the cops unlocked it and stepped quickly aside as the lid flipped open. The bald man sat up, his hands in front of him, palms facing out. In a matter of moments the police had him in custody and inside one of their cars. Several more patrol cars arrived, including some Chicago cops. I didn't stick around to watch them try to start the Dodge's engine.

"Who was that?" Jason asked as I drove away. "How'd he get into the trunk?"

"He was someone looking for you, and I put him in the trunk. Now let's find a safe place and talk."

"Yeah? Well, I don't know about talking, but I need some food—fast. And even before that, you gotta get me to a washroom somewhere."

So far, he hadn't said thank you.

After a return to the In'n'Out, this time for the washroom

and some supplies, we were back in the Cavalier, Jason in the front seat.

"Where we going?" he asked, dropping a crumbled potato-chip bag on the floor between his feet. Although the seat was back as far as it would go, his knees stuck up in front of him.

"Happiness Haven."

"Oh, man," was all he said.

On the way, neither one of us had anything to say for a long while. He didn't trust me, and I wasn't comfortable with him. Hell, I didn't *like* him. He was big, strong looking, and had the young athlete's veneer of self-confidence—call it arrogance—that comes from knowing you're better than most people at something everyone, at least everyone *you* know, thinks is a big deal.

Finally, Jason said, "You must be the dude was with Coach Parkins's wife when she called her sister, right?"

"That's right," I answered.

He was silent for a moment, and I saw him shaking his head. Then he said, "Man, I don't know. . . . I don't know. That wasn't my fault, you know?"

"No, it wasn't."

"Shoot, I didn't think something like *that* would happen," he said. Sounding like he was talking more to himself than to me. "How could somebody *do* that? I mean, Coach Parkins, he never did anything but good for no . . . for anybody. Anyway, it wasn't my fault."

Then we were silent again. He had enough sense to feel some responsibility for Frank Parkins's death, and enough sense to fight the guilt. The fact that he had fled to Chicago, and not some other direction, said something, too.

He deserved to know what I knew, so I summarized everything, from my first talk with Sharon to my meeting with Calvin Radcliffe. Well, *almost* everything. He didn't need more guilt to wrestle with just now. I didn't tell him about Cass starting to leave a message on my answering machine. He asked where Sharon was and I said I told Cass and Sharon to disappear and I hadn't heard from them since.

"But they're all right," I said.

"That doesn't make sense, though, them not saying where they are. Why wouldn't they just leave a message on your machine?"

He was bright enough, all right. Luckily, by then we were pulling up in front of Happiness Haven. All I could think of was, "I don't know. But that's not important right now." Even saying the words was difficult, because finding Cass was exactly the most important thing of all. I kept wondering what I would do if it came down to a choice between Cass and Jason. Like Jason with his guilt, I preferred to shut that problem out of my mind.

Surprisingly, I found a parking spot less than half a block away from Happiness Haven, right behind the burned-out hulk of a 1970s-vintage Cadillac, resting on its axles and waiting for the city tow truck that might be there any month now.

"Home at last," I said.

Jason looked around at the dismal surroundings and rundown buildings, many of them boarded up. "You mean . . . here?"

"This is it. Let's go."

He took the bags of groceries from the In'n'Out and I took my gym bag from the trunk, and we walked back to Happiness Haven. When the Lady had taken over the gray stone building, the bronze letters attached to the masonry above the front door were removed. If you looked closely, you could still make out the lighter outline of the word CONVENT on the soot-darkened stone. There was a church just around the corner, but it was long closed.

No sign announced what Happiness Haven was now. As we went up the steps, the front door opened and two young ladies came out. Both were nearly as tall as I. Both were black, one very light skinned with hair dyed red, one dark and with a brightly colored scarf wrapped around her head. They were attractive, but looked like they'd been around the block a few too many times. I wondered how long they'd been with the Lady's program. Or if they were just visiting old friends.

When the two of them saw Jason and me on our way up the steps, they stopped, then looked at each other and said simultaneously something that sounded like "Ooooo-*eeeee!*" They weren't referring to me.

We passed between them as we went up and they went down the steps. "City health inspectors," I said, "can't fraternize."

Of course they knew better, especially when I opened the front door with a key.

"Mus' be the new *night*time division," one of them drawled. But they went on their way.

Jason and I went inside, straight ahead down a long hallway, past the kitchen, then through another solid door that unlocked with the Lady's second key, through a tiny hall and into the janitor's room at the back of the first floor.

As the Lady said, it wasn't luxurious. You could have called it a studio apartment, with a tiny alcove of a kitchen. The first word that came to my mind as I stepped inside was *clean*. It looked clean, it smelled clean, it felt clean. There was a small table with two chairs on a linoleum-tiled square of floor near the kitchen. The rest of the room was carpeted. The other furniture consisted of a massive old chest of drawers, a television set, a full-size sofa that had seen better days, an almost new, inexpensive love seat that opened into a bed, and a small table with a lamp and a telephone. Opposite the door we entered was another door, leading to a sort of vestibule that doubled as a closet and held a door to the alley and a door to a bathroom with a shower.

The door to the outside was heavy and metal plated, with a peephole for security. I turned the dead-bolt lock and stepped outside. There was a concrete stoop, about five feet above the ground, with a metal railing. From high above the door, a security light bathed the entire back of the building in a bright blue-white glow. The stairs, and even the alley itself, appeared to have been swept. Two huge green garbage containers nestled against the back wall of the building.

I went back inside. Jason had left the groceries in their bags on the kitchen counter. He was on the sofa with the television on, tuned to what must have been the final moments of *Monday Night Football.*

I plopped my gym bag on the kitchen floor. In the kitchen cabinets and drawers were the usual pots and pans, dishes and utensils. I emptied the grocery bags and checked the refrigerator. It was working, with ice cubes frozen solid in the freezer compartment. I loaded things in the otherwise empty refrigerator and freezer. Jason paid no attention.

"Who's winning?" I asked, after I'd stowed everything away.

"How do I know?" Jason said. "I just turned it on."

"Good," I said, and turned it off. "You know how to make tomato soup?"

"No."

"The instructions are on the can. Better make two cans. Use milk instead of water. And boil some water for instant coffee, would you?"

He didn't stir. "So what am I?" he asked. "The cook? Or your servant or something?" There was a sullen tone in his voice.

I felt the blood running up my neck toward my face. I sat

down on one of the kitchen chairs and breathed a slow, patient breath.

"Jason," I said, "since I promised your sister I'd find you, I've been pipe-whipped and pistol-whipped, and ridden through enough cold, rain, and sleet to qualify for a mail carrier's pension. I've played the fool just to get to *talk* to people I wouldn't ordinarily bother to raise my head to look at. I've thrown up in the gutter and cleaned up rat diarrhea in my kitchen. I've . . . well, anyway, I'm a little tired."

He stared at me, his mouth slightly open. At least I had his attention.

"And you know what?" I continued. "If the time comes when you're busy doing something, I'll heat us up some soup, and you won't have to say please. Right now, though, I have to make some phone calls." I couldn't keep my voice from rising a notch. "So you can get up off your ass and make us some tomato soup. And I don't *fucking* have to say *please,* goddamn—"

"All right. All right. Take it easy, man." He got to his feet, giving me the same look Breaker Hanafan gave me when I poured Italian beer on his office floor. "I mean, you don't have to get all upset or give a speech or something."

As I watched him try to figure out how to work the old-fashioned can opener, I told myself I'd have made a wonderful father.

CHAPTER 22

My machine held a call from Mr. Troublesome, who must have decided that if he didn't leave me a number to call he wasn't going to talk to me. The name and address service told me the number was a pay phone at Union Station. Exactly *which* pay phone was asking a bit too much.

For our late-night supper we had a couple of bowls of tomato soup spiked with herb-flavored croutons. Jason added three bologna sandwiches on rye bread, potato chips, and a couple of cans of orange soda. I had coffee and one small sandwich. I was surprised I was hungry again at all. Probably came from watching Jason.

There was no sense trying to talk to him during the meal. He ate with single-minded concentration. I watched in awe. It wasn't only the amount. He was about six and a half feet tall, after all. But I began to see in him the same fluidity of motion, the same unconscious grace, I had seen in Sharon. His height wasn't outstanding for someone who hoped to make real the dream Frank Parkins had fostered in him, and he hadn't fully broadened and filled out his frame. But more height might still be on its way even now, and more weight certainly was—assuming he lived long enough.

Sharon was a beautiful woman and Jason had his share of the same genes. He had her coloration, and a stubble of curly black beard. His haircut was close and conservative, something Harvey Cartwright required. He was handsome, all right, and he exuded arrogant masculinity. But although he looked like a man and was bigger than most, he really wasn't grown up yet. I had to remember that.

He watched as I cleared off the table and ran water over the dishes in the sink. I made a mental note that we needed dishwashing detergent, hoping we wouldn't be there long enough to bother. I sat back down. "Now let's get down to business."

"Like what?" Like he didn't know.

"Like telling me about Amy Radcliffe and Scott Strelecki, and what they had to do with you, and why you disappeared, and who's after you, and why they want you so bad that they killed Coach Parkins to get at you, and—I don't know—whatever else you can think of."

We sat there a moment at the kitchen table, me worrying a mug half full of instant coffee, Jason fiddling with an empty soda can.

"Well," he said, "I can answer most of those easy. I don't know."

"How about the ones you do know?"

"Scott was my roommate. Tell you the truth, I hardly even knew the dude. He was all right, I guess. Some people had a lot of trouble with their roommates, but we got along okay. So we both put down to give us the same roommate this year, so they did." He looked at the can in his hands. "So, that's that."

He held the can at its ends, spinning it horizontally with the tips of his fingers.

"What made you run?"

He looked up. "Why should I tell you, man?"

"Because Coach Cartwright told you you could trust me. Because I put the man looking for you in the trunk of his car. And because, Jason, there's no one else to tell. You're stuck with me. So tell me what made you run."

"Yeah. Well . . ." He took a deep breath, then made the decision to talk. "The first time I knew something was up was the time the dudes searched me and Scott's room. I was supposed to be in class, you know, and usually I don't miss class that much. But that day I slept in. When I woke up it was eleven o'clock already. The bathroom's only a couple of doors from our room and I went down to take a shower and all. Then, I'm going back to the room and I see the door's open. I know I locked it. At first I figure someone's ripping us off. So I listen to see if I can tell how many it is. Then I hear them talking, and I know they're not just stealing things. They're looking for something."

"What did they say?"

"I don't know. Just like 'Look under there,' and 'We gotta find it,' and stuff like that. And anyway, they didn't find whatever it was and they start talking about leaving. So I ducked back in the bathroom. I heard 'em going down the hall and they left."

"You mean you didn't even see them?"

"Well, I did, a little, but just from behind, from out my window when they left the building. It got to me, the way they looked, you know? Plus the way they were talking and the way they were searching."

"What do you mean?"

"I mean these dudes were *serious,* man, dead serious. Not just kind of poking around for something. They musta went over every possible inch in that room. And they *talked* serious, too, man. I mean their voices were bad, you know?" He paused and twirled the can some more. "Just before they were leaving, one dude says, 'Well, if it wasn't in the goddamn car when they pulled it out, and it's not here, where the hell is it?' And the other one says, 'Don't worry about it. We'll get it.' The he laughed . . . chuckled like, you know? And said something like, 'Or else somebody's gonna lose his fuckin' face.' And it wasn't like watching a flick, you know? It was like he really meant it. I mean it was business, man.

"And I'm thinking there's gotta be a mistake here. They're in the wrong place or something and then the first one says, 'Let's go eat and then come back. That Cooper kid'll be outta class around noon. Fuckin' nigger wants to play ball anymore, he'll cooperate.' That's what he said, something like that.

"Then they left, and I looked out the window and even just from behind they looked bad. One of 'em was kind of average size and all, with black hair and a black raincoat. The other one was kinda short, but a wide dude, looked like a lumberjack or something, with a cap pulled down over his head. I said to myself these dudes are like *mob* people or something, you know? Then they got in their car—"

"A dark blue Dodge, right?"

"Yeah, right. How'd you know that?"

"That's the car we saw tonight."

"Oh man, that's right! Musta been the same guy! So anyway, man, that was it. Took some clothes and stuff and got in my car and I was outta there. First I went out to O'Hare, you know? Figured there'd be a lot of people around there and I could park the car and wander around awhile and figure out what to do. So I'm there a couple hours and I'm getting something to eat and I pick up the newspaper and—wham—I see Scott and his lady are dead, man. Drove off the Drive and drowned. And I read how the car was pulled out of the lagoon. And then it hits me, man. That's the car the two dudes were talking about in my room. I ask myself how do *they* know what's in the car when the cops pull it out."

"That's what I'm asking, too," I said.

"So anyway, I get some cash from the cash machine and I split outta there. Spent the night in this cheap motel, not too far from the airport. I didn't know where to go. My parents are off . . . I don't know . . . somewhere. I couldn't go to their house because I figured the dudes be watching it. I mean, these people seem *connected,* you know? Then I thought of Coach Parkins. So that's when I went up to Pepper Mill and . . ." He stopped.

"And . . . ?"

"You *know* what happened there, man. That was real bad. It was just crazy. So I came back to Chicago. I guess I was thinking I could *do* something, you know, retaliate. Then I got here and I *still* had no place to go. I kept trying to call Sharon and no answer, no answer. After . . . after what they did at Pepper Mill, I knew I shouldn't get Coach Cartwright into this, but . . . I didn't know what else to do. So I ditched my car downtown and I rode some buses and els and cabs. Finally, in the dark this morning I crawled into the team van and went to sleep. And . . . anyway, here I am."

Somewhere along the line, he had set the can down on the table. Now he picked it up and began to twirl it again.

"Yeah," I said, "and here I am. Now we have to figure out what to do."

"I figured maybe I'd just lie low for a while, till they lose interest or something."

"Or something?" I said. "Like *what,* do you think?"

"Yeah, well, how do I know what to do? Coach Cartwright told me *you'd* know what to do." The can was spinning again.

"Listen to me, son. I don't expect you to know what to do. But you left a little something out of your story."

He kept his eyes away from mine. "A little something like what, man?"

"A little something like what the hell is this all about? What are these people looking for? And where is it?"

He looked at me and something flickered across his face. It was gone in a nanosecond, but whatever it was, it wasn't candor. Then he dropped his eyes and looked at the table. The can stopped moving. He held it up in front of him with one hand and stared at it for a long moment, as though studying the list of ingredients.

"This kinda stuff's not good for you, you know?" he finally said. "Basically water and sugar and probably caffeine and a lotta artificial shit. Rots the mind *and* the body."

"I know," I said. "I drink it all the time."

He kept his eyes on the can.

"Look at me," I said. "What is it? What are they looking for?"

"What you asking me for, man? How would I know?"

"Come on, Jason. Scott Strelecki and Amy Radcliffe are dead. Maybe an accident, maybe suicide, maybe something else. Frank Parkins is dead. Not an accident, not suicide. Somebody's been chasing you all over the goddamn country." I paused. "And then there's Sharon and Cass," I said.

He looked up at me. "What do you mean?"

"I mean they're . . . gone. Someone's grabbed them."

He was silent. Then, very softly, "I knew it, man. I just knew it, somehow."

"Jason, Scott gave you something to keep for him. What was it?"

He looked straight at me. "There wasn't anything, man. Nothing."

I sighed. I really did.

Then I looked at my watch. "I have a call to make. I think you should listen."

I tapped out a number from memory. In less than half a ring, a familiar voice answered with a growl. "Who is this?"

"Hello, Breaker," I said, "it's me. Foley."

"What the hell *is* this?" Hanafan demanded. "How did you get this number? Nobody calls this number. I don't give it out."

"Don't worry," I said, "I won't tell anybody your secret number."

"Well, how did *you* get it? It's supposed to be a private number, for Crissake."

"Honest to God, Breaker, you sound like you're pouting. But I'll give you a hint. Look in the center of the dial on that old phone of yours. What's printed there?"

There was a silence of about a second, then, "Yeah. All right, smart-ass. But anyway, what are you calling me for? I told you I got nothing more to say to you."

"I got him, Breaker."

"What are you talking about?"

"Jason Cooper. I got him."

Jason was staring at me, his mouth open. I tapped myself lightly on the chest, mouthing the words "Trust me" to him and trying to look like I knew what I was doing.

"Look," Breaker Hanafan was saying, "I remember telling you if you found that kid I didn't want to hear about it. So what are you calling me for?"

"And I remember telling *you* it was 'when,' not 'if.' So, now is when. Jason Cooper. He's right here with me. I thought you'd like to know."

"Well, I don't like to know. So—"

"Hold on, Breaker, don't hang up, I want to ask you something."

He didn't say anything. But he didn't hang up, either.

"Breaker, who is it wants Jason?"

"You know, Foley, you got what they call a selective memory. I told you I didn't know who it was."

"I know what you told me. But maybe you were lying. Or maybe you didn't know then and you do know now. Or maybe . . . whatever. Never hurts to ask, right?"

"You're wrong. Some people get hurt real bad asking too many questions about things they oughta know enough to stay out of."

"So I don't know enough. Anyway, I thought maybe you might have something new for me. Something to do with . . . Calvin Radcliffe, maybe?"

"Calvin Radcliffe?" I couldn't see his face, of course, but he sounded surprised. "What's *he* got to do with this?"

"I don't know. His name came up, is all," I said.

"Maybe I'm getting as crazy as you, Foley. I don't know a goddamn thing about Calvin Radcliffe. But I *am* gonna tell you something. And if I ever hear from anyone that you heard this something from me, you're gonna have personal experience about how I got my name, you understand that?"

"I understand."

"All right. I still don't *know* who's looking for the kid. But I been hearing rumors, rumors that make me think it might be Josey Creole. That's all they are, just rumors, and that's all I got to say. Except I wonder why I even tell you anything at all. Maybe it's because I think you're a great guy. Or maybe it's because I'm losing my mind."

I would have said thanks, but he hung up on me. As I put the phone down, I was wondering why he told me, too. Not because he thought I was a great guy. And I didn't think he was losing his mind, either.

But there were bigger things to think about just then. Like Josey Creole. That sure fit the rat in the violin case. That was a Josey Creole thing, all right. I looked over at Jason, still gaping at me from across the room. "Well," I said, "as they say in the movies, we have a major-league problem here."

"What do you mean?"

"I mean Josey Creole. It's Josey Creole that's looking for you." If Breaker thought it *might* be Josey, then it was.

"I never heard of any Josey Creole."

"Not that many people have, not yet, anyway. But Josey's a very weird man, and very bad. Also very ambitious. Started out as a run-of-the-mill enforcer, in Cleveland or somewhere. You know, a bill collector for people who lend money at superhigh interest rates. Outgrew that pretty fast. Developed a reputation—in a rather restricted circle, of course—as a top-grade hit man, and willing to travel to do a job. He came to Chicago a few times, and now he seems to have found a home here.

"A little while back, the feds put one of the Chicago boys away, not a real top-level guy, you know, but big enough to convince the public they're still on the job. Since then, there's been a bit of a scramble to fill that empty slot. A couple of the top candidates got cut pretty quickly. Lacked the proper survival skills. One of them, a guy called Slammin' Sammy D, exploded on the fourth of July, pulling a club out of his bag on some golf course out in Oak Brook."

Twisting the cap off a bottle of Miller from the refrigerator, I continued, "Another finalist was 'IQ' Calcagno. Claimed a verified IQ of two hundred five. He was so smart he managed to fall ten floors from the balcony of his condo in Florida. He was partying with a couple of whores on the balcony in a rainstorm, when he went over the railing with one of the girls. He landed on top. She was the lucky one. She died. IQ is alive and as sharp as ever, mentally. He's learned how to eat and breathe through plastic tubes and he can flutter his eyelids if he really concentrates."

I lifted my Miller. "Here's to the candidate who might prevail," I said. "Can you guess who?"

"I got it, man."

"Right," I said. "The same Joey Creole who's taken such an interest in you. Now, if we only knew why, we might have just a little bit of a chance of figuring out what to do about it." I drank some beer. "If we only knew why."

Jason sailed the soft drink can through the air and it clattered into the kitchen sink. "Yeah," he said. "But I told you I don't know."

"That's right. That's what you told me. Well, it's late and we need some sleep. You take the Hide-A-Bed. I'll fit better on the sofa than you. Tomorrow's a big day."

"It is?"

"Sure it is. Tomorrow we try to find out why Josey Creole wants to talk to you."

"I don't think I want to find out, man."

"Me too. But remember what Shakespeare said: 'Knowledge is power.' "

An hour later, I was still trying to get comfortable on the sofa. Lying there, fighting anger and fear and depression, I was amazed at how soundly Jason slept. I knew he had to be afraid, although he wouldn't admit it. Of course, he'd been *alone* and afraid for days. Now he had me to stay awake and worry for him. I remembered one night, coming home from a camping trip in the Rockies, driving just this side of panic through a raging, endless snowstorm across the state of Nebraska. I was alone, except for Seth Green and a friend of his, both sleeping peacefully in the backseat. I wanted to holler at them, "Wake up, damn it! Help me see where I'm going! Be scared with me!" But they were eight years old, and I just kept driving.

Now Jason slept, and I just kept tossing from side to side, thinking: Knowledge is power. That wasn't from Shakespeare at all. Was it Alexander Pope? Ben Franklin? Maybe Aristotle.

Cass would have known.

CHAPTER

23

THINGS GOT NO BETTER as the night wore on. Whether it was the coffee or the beer or the bologna sandwich, I slept only fitfully, and then with variations of the same dream over and over. Alone and abandoned, I ran down unidentifiable city streets in a desperate hurry, my feet made of lead and getting heavier. I'd rotate my arms, as though swimming, to gain speed. It never worked. Except once, when I took off and flew above the street, swerving around trees and utility poles, up to the window of a tall building. Inside, a man without a face sat straight up and perfectly still. Lauren Parkins smiled at the man and sang "Shine On Harvest Moon." Then she saw me and started to cry, and it wasn't Lauren at all. It was Cass. She called and I wanted to answer, but instead I turned away. I was on the ground again, running, my feet getting heavier and heavier. . . .

Most of the time, though, I didn't sleep at all, and the waking visions were worse. I kept seeing Cass in my apartment, standing in the dark, looking out the window at the lake. I saw her rinsing her mug in the kitchen sink, stuffing a tennis ball in her pocket and running out the door. I even saw her in my arms. But I couldn't feel her.

I wanted to wake up Jason and slap him silly until he told me the whole story, but I didn't. Finally, I was rescued by the roar of a garbage truck in the alley outside as it picked up one of the refuse containers and tipped the contents into its belly.

Dim light was coming through the windows—and there was someone moving in the room.

I sat up fast, scrambling for the gun in the jacket under my head.

Jason turned and looked at me. He was putting water on the stove for coffee. He shook his head. "Man," he said, "you must have ice in your veins."

"What are you talking about?"

"How can you sleep so hard? I mean, I couldn't sleep all night. And you just lying there, snoring away like some little kid or something."

"Yeah. Well," I said, "you have to learn it doesn't do any good to worry about what might happen tomorrow or the next day, you know? You just take each day, each minute, and live in it."

It was the kind of thing the Lady was always saying to me. But when she said it, the words sounded better—more *sincere,* or something.

Not that it mattered much. Jason wasn't listening. He'd turned on the TV and was switching back and forth between channels. "Damn," he said. "They don't even have cable."

I dropped some bread in the toaster and put milk in my instant coffee. "Doesn't matter," I said. "You won't be here to watch it, anyway."

"We going somewhere?"

"Of course. That's what I said last night. No way I'm going to leave you here with a house full of women, many of them of doubtful repute."

"Doubtful repute?" That sparked his interest.

The toast popped up, and I opened a jar of peanut butter. "We'll talk about it sometime when you're a little older. Meanwhile, eat some breakfast, would you? This could be a long day."

If I had a plan at all, it was to figure out what it was that Josey Creole was after. Maybe then I could trade whatever it was for Jason's life, and for the release of Cass and Sharon. Maybe even for *my* life. Mr. Troublesome was apparently Josey's agent, but there was no sense calling the number he left until I knew what the big prize was, who had it, where, and how I could get my hands on it—for starters.

Meanwhile, I wanted Jason with me. If they found him, they'd find me with him, for better or for worse. Besides that, there was always the chance he'd break down and tell me the rest of what he knew.

After breakfast, we left Happiness Haven. I handed Jason the gym bag and locked the doors behind us. The morning air was bright and crisp, and cold enough to see your breath. If there had been clouds, I'd have been looking for snow, and it was still October.

"You take this bag everywhere?" Jason asked, talking around a piece of toast he'd carried out with him.

"Pretty much everywhere. It's got stuff in it I need."

He tossed the bag on the backseat, but I took it out and locked it in the trunk.

"Oh," he said. "Scared someone'll steal it, right?"

"Right. But it's colder in the trunk, too."

"Huh?"

"Forget it." I got behind the wheel.

Pulling the Cavalier out of its spot behind the Cadillac's rusting corpse, I started my pitch. "Some people think Josey Creole is a genius. Myself, I think he's crazy as a loon. But nobody thinks he's stupid. If he wants you it's because you have some value to him. So we ask ourselves, What could that value be? Is it because you're bright, good-looking, and a terrific basketball player?"

"It's not *me,* man. You know that. The dude's looking for

something and he thinks I got it. But I don't. And I don't know who has it, or what it is."

"Well, if you don't know and I don't know, maybe Josey's man knows. Let's go ask him."

"Great idea, man. Really great."

Is it just me or is there really an epidemic of sarcasm in the world?

We rode the rest of the way downtown in silence. I parked west of the Loop and we walked to Union Station.

Besides being the terminal for Amtrak trains from various cities around the country, Union Station is also the Chicago end of five Metra trains—commuter rail lines that carry thousands of people back and forth between the city and the suburbs every day. We'd be just two more travelers. Except, by the time we were arriving, the morning rush would be thinning out, and this pair of travelers included one white guy big enough to notice if you were watching, and one black guy three or four inches taller.

At the entrance to the huge structure, I gave Jason the keys to the car and to Happiness Haven. I told him to keep me in sight, but to stay far enough away so it didn't look as though we were together.

"If anything goes wrong, get out of here."

"Like if what goes wrong?" he asked.

"I don't know. But you'll be able to tell. Just take the car and go back to the Haven and wait for me to call."

"What if you don't call?"

"Well then, you won't be any worse off than you have been, will you?"

The entrance led into a hallway—more like a tunnel—about thirty yards long that opened at the other end into the cavernous main waiting room of the oldest part of the station. It was maybe four stories high, with marble floors, marble walls, and row after row of huge oak back-to-back benches. We separated and became part of a two-way stream of people passing through the waiting room. Only a few people waited on the benches. None of them sat near the clusters of public phones, or looked ready to answer one.

I continued on, assuming Jason was behind me somewhere, past little shops and take-out food stands in the more modern, less stately part of the station. There were banks of phones scattered here and there throughout the station. Occasionally catching Jason in the corner of my eye, I walked purposefully, as though on my way somewhere, working the shopping area systematically. I gave scant attention to the commuter areas. Anyone hanging around those phones for an extended time would soon draw the attention of railroad security.

I passed Chico's Chicken ("New Spicy Herb or Old-time Recipe"), the Pretzel Cart, the entrance to a men's rest room, and Dr. Sole's ("Shines and Repairs While-U-Wait"). I studied T-shirts at Mrs. Tease, and teddy bears wearing Chicago Cubs jerseys at the Gift Emporium.

"We have some with White Sox jerseys, sir," the clerk said, "and Bears, Bulls, Blackhawks. We even have Blue Demons. You know, De Paul."

"Any Wildcats?" I asked. "You know, Northwestern?"

"Nope. Can't keep 'em in stock since they went to the Rose Bowl. Sorry."

"That's all right. I just saw what I'm looking for somewhere else." At least I was pretty sure I had. "But I'll take one of those packages of rubber bands."

"Very good, sir. Thank you."

I walked back to Chico's, bought a cup of coffee with a lid on it, and took it into a glass-walled newsstand. I studied the magazines.

"How long we gonna hang around here, man?" Jason said.

He paged listlessly through a *Sports Illustrated* as I returned my *Business Week,* unopened, to the rack.

"Not long," I said, not looking at him. "Keep your eye on Dr. Sole's."

I scanned the rows of magazines and selected *Good Housekeeping*. I'd never seen the inside of a *Good Housekeeping,* but it had about the right number of pages and it looked sturdily put together. At the cash register I put my coffee down in front of the sign that said No Food or Drinks Allowed. I paid for the *Good Housekeeping* and rolled it tightly, wrapping a bunch of rubber bands around it. Leaving the cup where it was, I walked back to the row of five telephones that lined the wall between the men's room and Dr. Sole's, the rolled *Good Housekeeping* under my arm.

It was my third trip that way, and the receiver of the phone closest to the shoeshine stand was still off the hook and dangling at the end of its cord. The handwritten sign was still taped over the face of the phone and apologized: Sorry, Out of Order. The man in the Dr. Sole's chair closest to the phones was still concentrating carefully on the same page of the same sports section. And the door to the men's room was still propped open by a maintenance cart full of cleaning materials barring entrance.

I went to the phone farthest in the line from Dr. Sole's and called 911.

"Chicago Police."

"Yes," I said, "I'm near the men's room by Chico's Chicken, at Union Station? I mean I'm just in town on vacation, you know? But something's going on and you should do something about it."

"Yes sir. Can I help you?"

"Well, uh, there's this woman. She's in the men's room. And there's a man in there, too. And they're, uh, *doing* it, you know? I mean having, uh, relations. And there's some other people in there, too, standing around, uh, doing things, you know. I just thought . . ."

"Thank you, sir. We'll get someone over there right away."

I hung up and went down the row to the "out of order" phone. Removing the sign revealed a piece of tape holding the receiver hook down. I laid the sign on the ledge under the phone.

"Hey, you!" It was the man with the sports section. He was laying the paper aside and climbing down clumsily from the shoeshine stand. "Can't you read? That phone's out of order."

"Oh, no," I said. "It's just this piece of tape here. See? It's holding this thing down."

I tore off the tape, dropped some coins in the slot, and started to tap out a number. Who knows what number? I didn't get to finish before the man was at my side, pushing the hook back down. As he did, I dropped the receiver and, holding the rolled *Good Housekeeping* in two hands, drove the end of it, as hard as I could, deep into his gut. He bent to his knees.

I was congratulating myself on my choice of magazine when a voice spoke, very softly, very close to my ear. "Relax, Foley. Set your magazine on the shelf there, and hang up the phone."

I did both of those things. Very carefully, in fact. There was something poking me in the small of my back and I didn't care to experience firsthand whether it was really a gun or just a trick.

But I *did* ask. "Is that really a gun, or—"

"Walk ahead of me into the men's washroom, and I'll show you," he said.

Ah yes, the men's washroom. I wanted to say: "Oh, please, Br'er Fox, don't throw me in dat dere washroom. Anything but de washroom!" But I didn't say anything, just walked ahead of him. I had to push the maintenance cart out of the way to get inside.

"Why, there's no one cleaning in here, after all," I said. "Surprise!"

"Yeah, surprise, smart guy."

I turned to face Jason's little Lumberjack. He had a new cap pulled down to his ears, and no cigar. It sure hadn't taken him long to go from the trunk of the Dodge, to police custody, to Union Station. He looked as though he could use some sleep. His friend with the dark, curly hair was with us, too, a little pale beneath his olive skin and still a bit short of breath, but armed with my trusty *Good Housekeeping*. He stepped toward me.

"Hey, thanks," I said, reaching for the magazine.

He whopped me on the left side of my head, the same left side Deputy Sorkiss had softened up a couple of days ago. "Where's the kid?" he said.

"Kid?"

He switched hands and whopped me on the other side of the head. "Where is he?"

So they hadn't spotted Jason. I could scarcely hear over the chimes clanging between my ears, much less think of an intelligent answer. I spread my hands, palms up. "So you're ambidextrous," I managed. "Big—"

Unfortunately, just then Jason burst into the washroom, nearly knocking over the man with my *Good Housekeeping*. The kid had guts. But I'd have done better without him.

We all stared at each other, temporarily speechless, until I was able to blurt out, "Go on! Get outta here!"

He opened his mouth, thought better of it, and turned and left. The two men seemed riveted to the floor for an instant; then the Lumberjack came to his wits. He raced to the door after Jason—and came face-to-face with the police.

They were two city cops, a male and a female, and the Lumberjack had to stop and backpedal to let them in. They scanned the room and poked into the stalls, looking disappointed, I thought, at having missed the performance I'd phoned in about. The Lumberjack's gun was nowhere to be seen.

Someone had to take the initiative. "Thank God you're here, Officers," I said. "I'm the one who called nine-one-one. It's disgusting. These men were in this very wash—"

Then, just when I thought I might be home free, for the second time Jason broke into the party, but this time dragged in by two uniformed railroad security officers. "We seen this kid runnin' outta here," one of the security guards said.

The Lumberjack turned to his partner. "That's him. It's the kid!"

"What's he mean, 'It's the kid'?" the female city cop asked, directing the question to me, of all people.

"Well, uh, Officer, these men here, uh, these men are absolutely right. It *was* him." I pointed at Jason. "He's the one was in here with the lady when they were, you know, doing those things like I said on the phone. These men here were just part of the crowd, watching. I don't think they had their, uh, you know."

"What are you talking about, man?" Jason could barely speak above a whisper.

"I'm talking decency, son, plain old American decency." I turned to the cops. "Officers. I want that . . . that . . . perpetrator arrested. I'll swear out a citation, or whatever you call it. These two men, I don't know. I s'pose I can't blame them. They didn't do anything wrong, I guess. But this colored guy ought to be taught a lesson. It's just disgusting. No wonder this city has a bad name."

"Okay, okay," the female's partner said. "Relax, sir." He didn't believe a word I said, but he wasn't able to sort things out. So he decided to punt. "Since this happened on railroad property, these railroad police officers will take the young man into custody. You can go with them and give a statement."

"No way," I said. "This is a matter for the *real* police. I'm from downstate, and I was regional chairman for the governor's campaign committee, and let me tell you—"

"He's right." One of the railroad officers broke in. "We seen the kid peeking into the washroom and brought him back in, but we don't have authority over something like this, other than to turn the offender over to you guys." He and his partner didn't want any part of this mess, either. They were out the door.

The female officer turned to me. "Sir, why don't you just forget about it? There's no harm. . . ."

They'd missed the show they rushed over for, and even if they'd been certain I was telling the truth, they wouldn't have wanted to do the paperwork. A misdemeanor arrest for indecent exposure and lewd behavior just wasn't worth it. But I needed to get Jason out of there, and with protection. The two hoods knew what I was trying to do. They weren't about to go anywhere.

". . . sure the young man has learned his lesson," the officer was saying.

"Forget about it?" I was indignant. "I'll give you forget about. Let me tell you something. He's gone on to the hotel, now, with his mother, but I had my little boy with me when I came in here. You call that no harm? A young boy like that? What am I gonna tell him? You don't arrest this punk, somebody's gonna hear about it. I can tell you that. I got your names and badge numbers, and somebody's gonna hear about it."

She gave in. "All right. All right. Come on, young man. You too, sir. We'll take care of this at the station."

"Thank you, Officers. Oh I almost forgot." I plucked my *Good Housekeeping* from under the arm of the man with the curly hair. "Thanks."

CHAPTER 24

THE COPS HUSTLED US OUT to their patrol car through a series of doors and corridors not open to the public. Outside, with the two goons left behind, I told them I'd had a change of heart and decided not to make a complaint. They knew there was something funny going on, and they didn't like it very well. But why create work for themselves? They never even asked our names before they drove off.

The two of us raced back to the Cavalier, and I drove quickly out of the area, one eye on the rearview mirror. No one was following.

Jason's charging into the washroom said a lot about his character and was consistent with his heading back to Chicago after Frank Parkins's murder. I suppose I should have told him that, but I didn't. What I said was, "You know, you don't follow instructions very well. If anything went wrong, you were to go back and wait for me to call."

"Yeah. Well, I thought you could use some help, you know? They could've beat the crap out of you in there."

"They could have," I agreed. "Except it's you they want, so it was a pretty stupid thing to do, come running in there like that."

"Maybe it *was* stupid," Jason said, "but shoot, I thought you might at least say thank you or something."

Touché.

With no destination in mind, I drove through the littered, hopeless streets of the West Side. In cold vacant lots by liquor stores, clusters of black men stood around fires in metal drums and listened to each other tell big lies. Inside the crumbling apartment buildings, their women and babies warmed themselves by gas fires on kitchen stoves and listened to their televisions tell even bigger lies. Used automobile-tire stores boasted 1/2 OFF on crude, hand-painted signs. Grocery stores crouched in fear behind heavy metal grates and hawked wine and lottery tickets. All in all, the passing scene didn't inspire conversation.

Jason stared out the window. After a while he asked, "Where we going, man?"

The truth was I had no idea. I didn't say the truth. What I said was, "It all depends."

"On what?"

"On when you decide to tell me the truth."

That sure didn't break the ice. We rode on in more silence.

The sadness of the West Side seemed endless. It occurred to me that one reason we invented expressways must have been to divide all those seas of sadness so we can pass through their middles and not have to look at the leftover people piled up on the sides.

I was finally rescued from those musings when Jason spoke. "Okay, man, okay. Maybe I got something to tell you."

"Yes," I said, "maybe you do."

"Well, I . . . I guess I know why someone's after me. Or *maybe* I know, anyway." When I said nothing, he continued. "She told me not to tell *anyone* about it. 'Nobody, no matter what,' she said. I promised, you know? Gave my word. But now I think maybe I should tell you. I think maybe she's wrong. I don't know, man, I think—"

"Jason," I said, "stop *thinking* so much and just get on with it. Who told you not to tell anybody?"

"Coach Parkins's wife, man, she told me."

"Mrs. Parkins? Lauren Parkins?"

"Yeah. I told her about the envelope, and she told me I shouldn't tell anyone about it. 'Not anyone,' she said."

"What envelope?" My mind was racing. "No, wait, wait. First, whatever it was, did you tell Coach Parkins about it, too?"

"No. And I don't think she did either, 'cause she told me not even to tell the Coach. So I didn't."

"So he couldn't have told anyone about it," I thought out loud. "Now, tell me about the envelope. Where did it come from? What's in it? Where is it?"

"It was Scott's. Or I guess it was really Amy's—his lady, you know? But Scott had it. What happened was, a couple days before he was drowned, Scott showed me where he had hid this envelope—just a regular white envelope like you send letters in. He told me it was some very important papers or something that his girlfriend gave him to keep for her and he promised her he wouldn't open it because it was some secret of hers or something. I said why you showing it to me if it's so secret and he said he was just worried about it and in case something happened to him or something I'd know where it was and I could give it back to his lady. I didn't think too much about it. Thought it was some love letters or something. Plus, I didn't think anything was going to happen to him or anything so I kind of put it out of my mind, you know?"

Jason paused to take a breath. I kept my mouth shut. I didn't want to break the spell.

When he spoke again, though, what he said was, "Man, I'm hungry. Can't we get something to eat?"

By this time, we were approaching the western edge of the city. I turned south on Austin Boulevard, the street that divides Chicago from neighboring Oak Park, and headed for the Eisenhower Expressway.

"We'll stop pretty soon," I said, pulling on to the westbound ramp of the Eisenhower. "But I want to get a little farther out before we do. In the meantime, keep talking. So Scott showed you where this envelope was hidden so you could give it to Amy if something happened to him."

"That's right, man. And then, damn, something *does* happen to him. And something happens to Amy, too. But I didn't even know anything about them being killed until after these gangsters or whatever came and turned our room upside down."

"But they didn't find the envelope?"

"Sure didn't."

"Why not? You said they looked everywhere."

"They did. But it wasn't in the room." He paused and I swear it was for dramatic effect. "I had it with me."

"You mean in the bathroom? But if you didn't know anyone was going to search your room, why would you want to take the envelope with you to the bathroom?"

"Who said I *wanted* to take it to the bathroom? You see, what happened is I got this real sensitive skin and sometimes when I shave I get a rash. And Scott had got this new electric shaver that really worked and he used to let me use it. He kept it in a little leather shaving kit, you know, with shaving lotion, and toothpaste, and all that. It has a plastic lining so if something spills or something it won't ruin the leather, I guess. And Scott hid the envelope in the bottom of it. He slit the plastic lining and put the envelope between the leather and the lining. So I had taken the shaving kit with me to the bathroom. So the dudes didn't find the envelope, man, because it wasn't there. Just luck, I guess."

"Yeah, but not very *good* luck, not for you."

"I know," he answered. "So anyway, after they're gone I'm thinking about what they were saying. And then it hits me. I figure it's got to be the envelope they're looking for. So when they left and said they were coming back, I figured I better get out and take the envelope with me. So I took the shaving kit with me when I took off. I still had it when I went up to Pepper Mill."

"And?"

"And what? Oh, you mean where is it. It's still in the bottom of the shaving kit."

"But you don't have the shaving kit with you, Jason. So where is it? Not in Wisconsin, I hope."

"Course not. I brought it back with me. But before I dumped my car I went to one of those storage places where you rent a space, you know, and take the key with you. The only lockers they had left were these big ones that look like garages, but not really big enough for cars. I told the dude I only had a few things with me but I was gonna be bringing more stuff pretty soon. All I had was a suitcase with some clothes and the shaving kit, and I put it in the locker. It's the only thing I could think of to do with it."

"I can't think of anything any better, either," I said. "I wonder if anyone else could."

"Yeah, well, I don't know. Thing is, I wish I didn't know anything about the damn envelope." His voice was taking on a more conversational, less challenging tone.

"Which gets us to what *do* you know about it? I mean, did you open it?"

"Yeah, I opened it. Felt kinda funny doing that, too. But Scott was dead, Amy was dead, and . . . I don't know . . . it seemed like I should find out what it was. I mean maybe it would turn out to be nothing, or maybe it was something important and I could find out who the dudes were that wanted it and just *give* it to them, you know? So when I was up at the Coach's house I opened it."

"And . . . ?" I prodded.

He was silent for a moment. "When we gonna get off and get something to eat, man?"

I hadn't been paying attention to where we were, but I turned onto an exit ramp that was coming up fast. We ended up in a suburban shopping area that had every food franchise outlet known to humanity clustered in a three- or four-block stretch.

"Take your pick," I said.

"How about Taco Bell?" Jason asked, pointing up ahead and to the right.

"If you want Mexican, how about Chi-Chi's?" As far as the food went, it didn't matter much to me. But I preferred some place we could have a booth and a little privacy.

I didn't press Jason any further while we were seated and the waitress brought me a root beer and Jason a Coke. When she left with our food orders, I couldn't wait any longer. "You were going to tell me what was in the envelope," I said, dipping a taco chip into the salsa. I do love Chi-Chi's salsa.

"Well, I told Coach's wife I wouldn't tell anyone."

"Jason," I said, "that was before they killed the Coach. Besides, I thought we crossed that bridge already, a long time ago. The die is cast."

"What?"

"Just tell me what was in the envelope."

He scooped more salsa onto a taco chip than it was designed to hold and brought it to his mouth with the balance of a juggler, never spilling a drop. Having negotiated that, he was ready to answer. "Just some sheets of paper. Letters, I guess, or notes, really. One was to Amy. I don't know who it was from. It just had the letter D for a signature."

"What did it say?"

"I don't remember the exact words. But it was like an apology, like they'd had a fight or something and he was telling her he was sorry and it would never happen again and stuff."

"He? Why do you say he? Couldn't D have been a woman?"

"I don't know. Just seemed to me it was a man. It was pretty good handwriting. I guess it could have been a woman. But it sounded like a man to me. And Coach's wife, I'm pretty sure she thought it was a man, too."

"Can you remember more exactly what it said?"

Jason overloaded another taco chip. "Not really," he said, between crunches. "Just things like this time he really meant it, and it wouldn't happen again, and not to do anything real drastic. That was about all. It wasn't very long."

"You said there were more sheets, more letters. What were they?"

"Just one other page. It didn't say 'Dear anybody' or anything. It had a list of dates, with things written beside them like 'my birthday' and things."

I left the chips to Jason, and concentrated on my root beer. "That's it?" I asked, waving my empty cup at the waitress. "Just a list of dates? Was it in the same handwriting?"

"No. It was different handwriting. Like a woman's writing. And at the top of the page she had put something like she was afraid, and whether people believed her or not she was going to tell the truth. Like I say, I don't remember exactly. Oh, and off on the side, there was a woman's name written—Nicole."

Jason had reached the bottom of the chip basket and was gathering up the crumbs with the tips of his fingers. He looked up at me and said, "You know, I got the envelope. We can look and see what the letters say for sure. Thing is, I don't even know if the envelope is what this Josey Whoever is after. But I can't think of anything else, that's for sure."

"Lauren Parkins," I said. "Did she read the pages?"

"Sure. I showed them to her at Pepper Mill, on the morning of the day that . . . that the phone calls came and we left and went to her sister's farm. It seemed like she thought she understood. But she didn't tell me. She just said the letters might be worth a lot of money and we shouldn't tell anyone, not even Coach Parkins. She said we could talk about it later. And then that night we went to the farm and, well . . . I took off from there and I haven't seen her since then."

The waitress arrived with our food. When I apply myself, I can eat as fast as anyone, even Jason. And since he ordered twice as much as I did, I finished first.

As I laid my napkin on the table and pushed my chair back, Jason looked up. "What? You gonna leave now? I haven't finished my lunch yet."

He'd fallen back into his old pain-in-the-ass tone of voice. Must have been the food. I thought maybe if I withheld nourishment we'd get along better.

"Relax, will you? Finish your lunch. I just want to make a few phone calls."

I was surprised to find a message on my "Entertainment Division" line. I took that one first, and it was Becky, wanting to know why I hadn't shown up at her place on Friday night. I was just happy she'd noticed I wasn't there. Becky can talk to a recorder as though it were a live person. "You comin' in this week or not? Actually had a guy complainin' about no piano player. Course, he was drunk as hell and smelled like a raccoon in heat and we tossed him out. Anyway, lemme know. Some young guy wantsa come in, with a bass player. Says they have a more contemporary sound than you. But you know me. I don't care what it is, long as they don't interfere with the drinking. I might just give 'em a try. Gimme a call."

A more contemporary sound? Hopefully, that meant loud

and fast, or improvising so far from the melody no one recognizes it. Becky's crowd would never go for that.

The only other caller was Mr. Troublesome. His message was predictable. Translated, it meant if I didn't cooperate, and soon, I'd have far more to worry about than the gig at Miz Becky's. He left the same Union Station number.

I called the number. Halfway through the second ring, a man answered. "Yeah?" It was the Lumberjack.

"It's Foley. Here's the message. Listen hard, because I'm not going to repeat it. I'll call back at six o'clock tonight. You tell him I'm not dealing with munchkins. Mr. Troublesome either answers the phone himself, or I hang up."

"Wait a minute, asshole, you—"

"That's the message. Tell him to answer personally. Six o'clock." I hung up and checked my watch, wondering if he noticed I'd repeated myself, after all.

I called the Lady and told her I had Jason and we'd checked into Happiness Haven.

"I know," she said. "I hear you ran into Renee and LaToya on the front steps. I forgot to tell you, there's never any street parking, but you can park in the alley by the garbage containers if you leave room to get by. They never give us a ticket if we have to do that."

"Okay. But yesterday we found a place right away, behind an abandoned wreck of a Cadillac. Gotta go now, but I'll call you when I know more."

"That's fine, Malachy. Be careful. Good-bye." Before she hung up, she added, almost to herself, "Abandoned cars . . . such eyesores."

Finally, I tapped out Breaker Hanafan's private number. A recording told me the number was out of service and no further information was available.

Back at our table Jason was ready to go.

On the drive north to the storage locker Jason asked what we were going to do when we got the envelope.

"First, it's not *we,"* I said. "It's *me* . . . I mean *I.* You're not going to do anything except go back to Happiness Haven and stay hidden. Second, I don't know what I'm going to do. You got any ideas?"

"Nope. Like Coach Cartwright said, you're the genius. But I tell you one thing. I can't sit around that little room very long. I need exercise. I gotta play some ball."

That was it for a while for conversation. I was wrestling with myself about what to do with Jason. Keeping him with me was dangerous for him and dangerous for me. We still made a pretty conspicuous couple, and I had to keep an eye on his back as well as my own. The problem was, he'd become my responsibility. If I left him somewhere, even at the Haven, I'd lose control over what he might do, or what might happen to him. I kicked this around for a while, but got nowhere.

I tried to find something to fill in the silence. The two of us didn't have a whole lot in common. "You always eat so much?" I finally asked.

"Usually a lot more. But I don't feel like eating, you know? I feel . . . I don't know . . . like tired or sluggish or something. It's been a long time since I worked out or anything. My body just doesn't feel right somehow. I need to get back to practice."

"Well, this'll all be over pretty quickly," I said, adding silently, *I hope.*

"Yeah, sure," Jason said. He was silent for a while, staring straight ahead through the windshield; then he said, "You made some calls from the restaurant. You hear anything about Sharon? Or, uh, your wife?"

"Nothing."

"Where are they?"

"I don't know."

He turned his head and looked out the window to his right, then asked, very softly, "Is Sharon . . . dead?"

"No. Sharon's not dead."

"How do you know?"

"Because I know, that's all. Plus . . . she's with Cass. And Cass certainly isn't dead. She can't be. I won't have it that she's dead. So Sharon's not dead, either. But something's happened. I don't know what."

"This Josey has them, doesn't he? Like as hostages."

"I think so."

"Yeah, well, if he wants to make a deal, I'm giving the envelope to him."

"We'll just have to wait and see," I said.

There would be no deal. It was too late now for Josey to be satisfied with only the envelope. If it was important enough to kill for, then once he had his hands on it Josey would take out everyone involved, including Jason, Sharon, Cass, me . . . everyone.

CHAPTER 25

WHAT THE WEATHERPEOPLE CALLED "a surprisingly early arctic cold snap" had settled in to stay, with the air clear and bright, the temperature hanging just below freezing. Traffic was light, and by two o'clock we were near O'Hare Field, in an area that was mostly truck docks and light-industrial buildings. The sign at Luckett's Lockitt shouted: Always Locked! Always Available! 24-Hour Security on Premises!

There was an office with diagonal parking in front, and a large fenced-in lot with row after row of long, low cinderblock buildings divided into storage lockers, each with an overhead garage door for entry. I pulled in near the front door of the office and parked next to a Chrysler LeBaron, the only other car in sight.

"I gotta show 'em my ID before they'll open the gate," Jason said.

I sat in the car while Jason went into the office. The bright sun made the car warm and I rolled down the window. I listened to the cooing of a couple of pigeons perched on the roof of the office and studied the heat waves wiggling above the hood of the LeBaron. Through the office window I watched a man in a guard's uniform checking Jason's identification. A second man, who'd been behind the counter with the guard when we drove up, stretched, yawned, and disappeared through a door behind the counter. Finally, Jason and the guard—an overweight, middle-aged black man—left the office through a side door that opened into the lot behind the fence and walked together to the gate. The guard fumbled interminably with about a dozen keys, but finally managed to unlock the gate and push it open. I drove inside and Jason got into the car.

The guard blew noisily into his cupped hands. "Damn keys all look alike. Y'all go past the office there and turn left and then right at row two. Say, how long y'all gonna be?"

Jason started to answer. "We just—"

"We'll be awhile," I interrupted. "We've got a full trunk to unload."

"What—," Jason started to say, but I drove off with him before he finished.

We moved slowly down row two, Jason comparing the numbers stenciled on the doors to the number on his key. "Number two-thirty-seven," he said. "There it is." He started to open the car door.

"Hold on a minute," I said. "You said you couldn't store a car in that locker, but it looks wide enough to me."

"Yeah, well, maybe just barely. But once you got the car inside, wouldn't be enough room to open the doors and get out of it. Why?"

"Just wondered," I said. "Close your door and I'll back up to the door."

"For only one little suitcase, man?"

The locker was on our right. I pulled just past it, then swung to the left to position the Cavalier to back into the locker. As I did, the guard appeared at the far end of the row of lockers and strolled toward us.

"Want some help with your stuff?" he yelled.

"That's all right," I called back. "We got it." The guard stood and watched, as I backed the car up—and bumped the closed overhead door of the locker.

The guard started walking again and called, "Hey, be careful there."

"Sorry," I called back. I pulled forward, then backed up and bumped the door again.

"What the hell you doin'?" the guard puffed, as he urged his fat body into a trot to cover the remaining yards between us.

Jason was staring at me. "Yeah, man, that's what I'd like to know," he said.

I yelled to the guard through the open window. "Sorry. Just trying to get this thing lined up so we can unload." Then, slipping into park, I turned to Jason and hissed, "Get down."

Jason didn't move a muscle.

But the guard did. He moved his right hand uncertainly toward the gun at his belt. He was very slow. I was out of the car with the Beretta in his face before he could unsnap his holster.

"Way up," I said, keeping my voice very soft.

"Huh?" He looked confused.

"Your hands. Over your head. Way up." Whispering now. "Not a word or you're dead. And turn around."

His hands shot up and he turned his bulky back to me. I switched my gun to my left hand and drove the barrel, hard, into where I thought a kidney might be hidden beneath the fat. I took his gun from its holster and slipped mine into my jacket pocket.

Grabbing his shoulder, I made him face the storage locker and put my mouth close to his ear. "Is he in there?" I asked softly.

"The fuck you talkin' 'bout, man? Is who in where?" Despite the cold, there were beads of sweat appearing on the back of his neck.

With the barrel of his gun pressed under the right side of his jaw, angling upward, I leaned forward and spoke again quietly into his ear. "The man with the LeBaron. Is he?"

"Fuckin' LeBaron's the manager's car, man. Been in his office all day. You musta seen him when you drove up."

"No good. That car's engine was still warm when we got here. So"—pressing the gun into his skin—"is he in there or not?"

His body tensed, then slumped. "Well, shit. Yeah, I think so."

"And the suitcase?"

"I don't know 'bout no suitcase. But look, man, this ain't none of me. I don't know nothing about this shit at all."

"You should have warned us."

"I couldn't man. The dude . . ." His voice started rising above a whisper.

I scraped the gun barrel across the skin of his neck. "Keep it down, friend. Don't mess up—maybe you'll come out alive."

Jason was out of the car now, standing nearby, silent.

"All right, Jason," I said, now in a louder voice, "let's get these boxes out of the backseat first and stack them by the door."

As I spoke, I motioned to Jason to come closer. I kept the gun at the side of the guard's neck and he didn't resist as Jason, starting to get the picture, shackled the man's hands together in front of him with his own handcuffs. Following my gestured directions, the guard lay on the ground on his stomach.

I moved the car about a foot and a half out from the overhead door. Jason and I opened and closed the car doors a few times for effect. I needed somehow to get the suitcase out of the locker without getting us killed—either now or later. Once Josey had the suitcase, he'd find the envelope. Jason and I would be expendable. And Cass and Sharon as well.

The man inside the locker had to be suspicious by now. "Okay, Jason," I said, in a voice I hoped wasn't too artificial. "That's about it. The guard'll open the door."

I got the guard to his feet and gave him Jason's key to the locker. Pointing to the rear of the car, I whispered in his ear. "Squeeze in there and put the key in the lock. When I start to back up, you throw that door up in a hurry and get inside, because I'm coming in after you. You got that?"

He nodded vigorously. The beads of sweat on his neck had turned into streams that were soaking his shirt collar.

The overhead door was less than a foot wider than the car, so with the Cavalier blocking the doorway there'd be no way out except over the top of it. I motioned Jason to the side, out of sight, and got into the car. I started the engine and, with my left foot on the brake, moved the shift lever into reverse.

I watched the guard through the rear window. As he felt the car slip into gear, he turned the handle and clumsily raised the overhead door. He started screaming, "It's me, man! It's me! It's me! Don't shoot!"

Holding the steering wheel at the bottom, I lay over sideways on the seat. Working the accelerator and brake pedals together, I moved the car, slowly and smoothly, back into the storage locker. The guard and another man were shouting. If it was human langauge they were using, I couldn't decipher it. I concentrated on moving the car straight backward. I wondered if I'd be able to tell when the rear bumper was pressing human bodies against the back wall of the enclosed space. Time expanded, and it took long seconds for the car to slide back into the stall. I lay on the seat and watched the open overhead door come into view at the top of the windshield.

Words finally broke through out of the confused shouting behind the car. It was the guard's voice. "Stop the car! Stop! Please!"

I didn't stop.

There was a scuffling and scraping and I knew the two men must be clambering onto the trunk of the Cavalier. There was more angry shouting and scuffling, but I didn't dare raise my head to look.

Suddenly, the closed-in space was rocked by the explosion of a gunshot, followed by a howl and then what I knew was the sound of someone being pushed off the back of the trunk. There was no more shouting after that. The Cavalier met a soft resistance. I couldn't back up any farther, and I didn't dare raise my head.

For a moment there was silence. Finally I heard someone climbing onto the roof of the car, then sliding forward above me. I pressed my left foot on the brake pedal, shifted into drive, and waited. A face appeared, upside down in the windshield above me. It was a pale face, and it frowned as a shoulder and arm swung around to join it. In the hand at the end of the arm was a pistol. The frowning face broke into an ugly grin.

Sitting up, I slammed my right foot on the accelerator and then, a split second later, my left foot on the brake. The man on the top of the car slid forward and bounced onto the hood. Instead of continuing his slide and getting off onto solid ground, he instinctively fought his momentum and managed to scramble to his hands and knees on the hood of the car, facing me. I hit the accelerator again. This time he came sliding, face forward, straight at me. He twisted his body to his left and threw his arms out to regain his balance. With a thud, he pounded into the windshield, then fell off the hood onto the ground. At the same time I heard something solid scrape backward along the top of the Cavalier and clatter against the trunk.

"The gun!" Jason yelled, pounding on the passenger window of the car. "He lost the gun!"

It was true. As the man scrambled to his feet on my side of the car, he was without his gun. He wasted only an instant looking frantically around him, then turned and ran. I climbed out of the Cavalier, the Beretta in my hand, and started after him. He pulled away from me and was going to get to the end of the row of lockers and around the corner. I stopped and planted my feet, raised the pistol, and drew a bead on the back of the running man—just above waist high. He had just shot a handcuffed man. He'd have killed Jason, too . . . and me.

I lowered the gun to my side and stood watching as he disappeared around the corner.

I sprinted after the man and, when I rounded the corner of the row of lockers, saw him turning away from the locked office door. He caught sight of me and ran through the open gate to the LeBaron. Kicking up two sprays of white gravel, he sped away.

I trotted back to the Cavalier. Jason had moved it out of the doorway and was inside the locker. He had a small suitcase in his hand, and held it up toward me as I approached. In his other hand he held the guard's key ring. The handcuffs were lying on the floor. A few feet away, also on the floor, lay the gunman's pistol. The guard himself was on his feet, leaning against the cement block wall, his left hand pressed to the side of his belly. He was breathing hard, but was conscious and talking.

"Ain't nothing," he was saying to Jason. When I got there, he turned his head to me. "Dude said he was a cop, man. But he wasn't no cop, was he?"

"Don't worry about it," I said. "You should sit down."

With his hand still pressed to his side, he walked unsteadily out of the locker and into the sunlight. "Shit," he said, between harsh gasps of breath, "I took worse'n this in Nam. Ain't even no blood." He took his hand from his side and stared into it. "At least, hardly none." He sagged back against the closed door of the locker next to Jason's, then slid slowly down until he was sitting on the concrete apron.

I pointed at the pistol on the floor. "You didn't touch that, did you, Jason?"

"Not me, man," he said, shaking his head.

I kicked the gun out of Jason's locker. Jason's suitcase wasn't locked, and I took the tan leather shaving kit out of it, then left the suitcase in the locker as I closed and locked the door.

"What about my clothes?" Jason asked.

"You can always get more clothes." I turned back to the guard. "Don't try to move. We'll get an ambulance here right away."

I put the guard's gun back in his holster, and we left him sitting there, his back propped against the wall. I slithered the Cavalier around the end of the row of lockers and pulled up to the door of the office.

"Jason, you'll have to make the call. Try to sound like the guard." As we searched through the guard's ring for the key to the door, I told him what to say on the phone.

Inside, Jason called 911. "I been shot!" he cried into the phone. "I'm bleedin'. Skinny white fucker in a black LeBaron shot me." He recited the Chrysler's license number.

While he talked, I scanned the office. There was a box full of keys on a shelf, and I added Jason's locker key to the group. On the counter there was a book to log customers in and out of their lockers. I tucked it under my arm. If the guard lived, the cops would eventually piece the story together. If he died,

Jason didn't need his name tied in to it. There was a computer sitting on the counter. Jason was probably in there somewhere, too. There wasn't time to figure out how to delete him, so I sent the computer crashing to the floor and put the metal leg of an office chair through the monitor screen. Probably useless, except maybe to slow things down. We wiped the phone clean, and then the door handles as we left.

Outside, I yanked open the back door of the Cavalier. "On the floor again, Jason."

He didn't argue. I threw my jacket in the backseat and got behind the wheel, cramming the White Sox cap onto my head. Not wanting to leave another set of skid marks, I backed slowly into the street, and drove away.

CHAPTER 26

SIRENS SCREAMED AND SNARLED, gradually drawing closer. Two or three cars were in front of us, stopped at a traffic light, although it was green. Suddenly, a huge mobile trauma unit lumbered around the corner, and—seconds behind it—a police cruiser. In my mirror I saw another police car approaching Luckett's Lockitt from the opposite direction. The light turned red, then green again, and I drove through the intersection.

Jason's face appeared in the rearview mirror. "I didn't like leaving him there like that."

"I know," I answered. "But what could we have done—except sit there with him and wait."

"You think he's okay? I mean . . . is he alive, you think?"

"Of course he is. He's got a lot of fat for a bullet to get lost in."

"I guess. I hope so. But . . . I don't understand. How could someone know I stored anything at that place?"

"Well, think about it. When you were trying to figure out a safe place to hide something you didn't want to carry around, how many places could you think of? Once you eliminate your home, and the homes of friends, what's left?"

"I guess you're right. At first I thought of a locker at the airport. But I heard somewhere they open those things every twenty-four hours. I couldn't think of anywhere but a storage-locker place."

"Right. Another idea would be a safe-deposit box at a bank.

But an awful lot of people would have come up with the same choice you did. You needed a credit card, so the locker would be in your own name. All Josey had to do was check the storage facilities. You'd be surprised what you can learn over the phone. So, your name turns up and, well, his man beat us there."

"Too bad you, well . . . Couldn't you have shot him before he got away?" Jason asked.

"What was the point? His being dead wouldn't help us. And he was running away from us. How would I explain shooting him in the back to the police?" *And sending the unarmed, handcuffed guard to face death—to save myself? How do I explain that to myself?*

"So, why not just shoot him in the leg or something?" Jason persisted.

"Well, let's say I was a sharpshooter and I could have wounded him. We'd have to have left him there, right? And who knows what story he'd have come up with for the cops?"

"But he shot the guard. He'd go to jail."

"Maybe he would. Maybe not. Anyway, that doesn't help the guard. Besides, the guard'll be all right."

"Yeah." A moment later he said, "You know, man, I don't like this kind of shit. I don't like it at all."

"Nobody likes being afraid," I said. "Not in real life, I mean."

He was offended. "I said I didn't *like* this shit, man. I didn't say I was scared."

"I know. But you were scared back there. And you still are."

"What makes you think I'm scared?"

"Because *I'm* scared, for God's sake. I'm scared as hell. And I've been here a lot more times than you have."

"Here?" he asked.

"I mean around trouble like this—greed, lies, people hurting people . . . trouble."

"And it makes you scared?"

"Of course it does, scared in lots of different ways."

"Different ways?"

"Sure. Scared somebody might get hurt . . . scared *I* might get hurt. And, I guess, scared I might hurt somebody else once too often and something might happen to me inside myself and—" I stopped talking. I didn't like the way the conversation was going. "You're young. You don't understand."

"Well, I don't know about the 'inside yourself' business. But if it bothers you, then why do it? I mean, you oughta just stay away from trouble."

Stay away from trouble. There it was again. Great advice. This time it was coming from the center of the storm himself. But he was wrong. They were all wrong, damn it. Jason, Harvey Cartwright—even Cass and Barney Green when they said it. You can't do it, that's all.

You really can't stay away from trouble.

About all you can do is pick your brand. There's that quiet, sneaky kind of trouble that hangs around and picks at you, dogs you along the daily routine of job and home and job again. You can never quite get a handle on it, so you try to push it away with lots of TV, sports, booze . . . whatever. Or you can break out of that rut, and then you run into another kind of trouble, the kind that jumps up and smacks you—hard and sudden. Maybe a piece of pipe, or even a rolled-up *Good Housekeeping*. Not exactly a welcome visitor, either, but at least it's more tolerable when trouble shows up because you stepped forward and took some action, and not because you tried to—

"Hey! Wake up, man! The light changed." Jason was yelling in my ear, and the guy in the pickup behind me was leaning on the horn.

"Sorry about that," I said, punching the accelerator.

On the way back to Uptown and Happiness Haven, we stopped at Sundborg's Bakery in Andersonville, the neighborhood around Clark Street and Foster Avenue. Sundborg's was a survivor from the days when Andersonville was the hub of Chicago's Swedish community, and was still run by a large, no-nonsense matron who probably wiped her hands on the same flour-dusted aprons her grandparents wore when they first warmed those predawn ovens over fifty years ago. At a Mexican grocery nearby, we picked up a few basics, but the fresh loaf of limpa bread from Sundborg's was the prize that made the short detour worthwhile.

Then it was south to Lawrence Avenue, and a Sears store that seems to hang in there forever. At the men's department, Jason took another forever to replace the clothes we'd left behind in his suitcase. I wandered around, finally stopping at the toiletries counter. When we left, Jason complained bitterly about the lack of selection, although I'd easily found what I was looking for.

We got to Happiness Heaven about five o'clock and there would have been no parking places, except that as we pulled up a tow truck was maneuvering the abandoned Cadillac away from the curb. Once it had driven off, I pulled forward to park in the newly vacated slot.

When I started to back into the spot, Jason stopped me. "Hold on." He climbed out of the Chevy and with the sides of his shoes he swept away the shards of broken glass that had gathered along the curb. When he finished he had a serious look on his face. "It's okay now," he said. "But you gotta be careful, man, in neighborhoods like this."

I thought maybe we were making progress.

Back in the room, Jason relaxed with the newspaper while I emptied the grocery bags and stowed various things in the refrigerator and freezer compartment. Then, fortified with a

Pepsi for Jason and a cup of instant coffee for me, we sat down with Scott Strelecki's leather shaving kit on the kitchen table between us. Jason emptied the contents onto the table—electric shaver, aftershave, comb, toothbrush, and toothpaste. Then, showing me where Scott had slit the plastic inner lining along one side of the bottom, Jason removed a white envelope and handed it to me.

There was no writing on the envelope and it was unsealed. Inside, as Jason had said, there were two folded sheets of paper. One was a piece of expensive, ivory-colored notepaper, with the name *Amy* engraved at the top in a flowing, flamingo pink script. Below that, in careful feminine handwriting, was a note, not addressed to anyone:

> Probably no one will believe me. I'm scared, but I'm telling anyway. I'm not waiting until I'm forty or something. These exact dates are stuck in my memory for sure, because of the special days. Those are the worst. There were others in between these, and I think some earlier times that are like lost in the fog.

Then there was a list of seven dates, spread irregularly over an eight-year period beginning some ten years earlier. The first two were about a month apart. Next to the first date was written, "Around then"; next to the second, "Two weeks after Mother's funeral." Each of the remaining five dates also had notations: "My birthday," "Valentine's Ball," "The lake," "His birthday," and "Last time." That was it, except that on the right margin, angling upward, as though jotted down at a later time, were the words "Nicole G. Thurs 10:30. Scott???"

The second sheet was plain white bond. I agreed with Jason that this one was probably in a man's handwriting:

Amy,

I promised you before, but I broke my promise. I'm so sorry. This time for sure, so help me God, never again, not even close, nothing. Please, honey, don't even talk about doing something like you said. If anything happened I couldn't stand it. You have to believe me. You're all I have. Please forgive me. Give me another chance.

D.

I laid the two pages side by side on the table.

"Well," Jason asked, "make any sense to you?"

I swirled my coffee around in the mug, then tasted it. It was lukewarm, but I drank some, anyway. I didn't want to answer. I thought the pages did make sense. I thought I saw in them what Lauren Parkins must have seen. I wondered about Lauren's reaction to them. I had liked Lauren. I wanted to keep liking her. But I wondered.

"What did Mrs. Parkins say when she saw these?" I asked.

"She seemed like she knew what they meant, and she said not to tell anyone. I told you that before, man."

"I know you did, Jason. But what I'm asking now is what did she *say?* Can you remember exactly what she said?"

"She said . . . she said something like they might be worth a lot of money. And that we shouldn't tell anyone about them and we'd talk about it later. But, man, I can't remember her exact words."

"Did she say who they might be worth a lot of money to?"

"She didn't say who. But I thought she meant they were worth a lot of money to whoever was after me."

"Well, how do you know she didn't mean the letters could be worth a lot of money to you and to her?"

Jason's eyes widened as it gradually became clear to him

what I was talking about. He drained the Pepsi from his can and flipped it across the table and into the sink.

He shook his head and said, "Man, you sure don't know Coach's wife. She's like Coach, you know? I mean, I never even *thought* what you're thinking about. And you know why? Because it isn't possible. You're talking about her saying maybe her and I could squeeze some money out of someone by using the letters, aren't you? Like blackmail or something?"

Lifting my hands from the table, I spread them in front of me, palms up. "Well, it's a thought I had."

He stood up and glared down at me with mixed anger and surprise. "She didn't mean that, man. She doesn't think like that. Coach doesn't either. . . . I mean, he didn't. Why do you think I went there? I mean, they just help people, man. They don't think about money all the time." He stopped, then added, "Maybe you wouldn't understand that."

"I can understand that there are people like that, Jason. It's just, well, I don't run into them very often. And I don't know Lauren Parkins at all."

"Yeah? Well, I know her pretty good," Jason said.

I got up and dumped the rest of my coffee in the sink. "Well then, what you say about her is good enough for me." But I still wondered.

Jason dropped onto the couch and sat there, elbows propped on knees that stuck up far higher than the edge of the cushion, hands clasped together. He lifted his head and looked at me and said, "I don't know what's going on, man, but we got to get this over with. We got to find out where Sharon is . . . and your wife, too. Plus, you know . . . plus, I gotta play some ball or I'm gonna go crazy or something."

"Right," I said, looking at my watch. "But just now let's have something to eat. I have to make a call at six o'clock."

CHAPTER

27

It's not easy—cooking in someone else's kitchen. You have to make do. I dumped a couple of cans of pork and beans into a too-large saucepan and set it on the stove. The only other pan was too small. Opening a package of eight hot dogs, I dropped four of them into the beans. Not exactly health food. I paused for a moment, listening in surprise at Jason noisily bouncing knives, forks, and plates onto the table.

More progress.

As I slid the remaining four franks into the pan, thoughts of Cass flooded my mind. Maybe slipping hot dogs into a pan of warm, moist beans holds some Freudian symbolism. But on a conscious level I was recalling her recipe for "fixing up beans and franks."

I couldn't remember everything she puts in, and the cupboards were pretty bare, anyway. But I pulled open all the drawers until I found the inevitable catchall drawer. There were rubber bands, expired discount coupons, pieces of string, dozens of twist-ties for plastic bags, various unsuccessful inventions for keeping the fizz in an open soda container—the usual. Rummaging through, I collected quite a pile of packets of ketchup and mustard, discards from who knows how many carryout meals. Taking a handful of each, I tore off their corners and squeezed their contents into the pan of beans. I'd bought an onion, but not a green pepper. I'd forgotten brown sugar, too, but the jumble in the drawer gave up three little packages of pancake syrup from some long-past breakfasts from Wendy's. I peeled back the tops. One of them hadn't been airtight, and the contents were mostly mold. The others I emptied into the beans and franks.

While the concoction heated, Jason hacked the loaf of unsliced limpa bread into pieces with a butter knife and I set out a quart of low-fat milk for him and a can of beer for me.

Not a bad meal.

What it lacked was human conversation. Jason pulled the television set close to the table and flipped from channel to channel through the various news programs, expertly avoiding commercials. On three different networks, we watched three different ex-athletes painfully extract interviews from three young football players about three different upcoming games. The comments they made were nearly identical.

As the beans and franks disappeared with gratifying swiftness, we meandered through the channels. On one, an attractive woman with lots of hair and a husky, earnest voice recited a few vague statistics about sexual abuse, then urged us to watch the late evening news for "explicit details about this pervasive problem that's destroying our children." Moving on, we learned about the perpetually worsening state of the juvenile court system, watched as firefighters struggled with another spectacular fire in an empty warehouse, and heard two experts estimate how many homeless people in Chicago had Ph.D.'s. Not many, as it turned out.

By that time, I had drained the last of a second beer and was clearing the table. Jason was lying on the couch, his homemaking energies clearly exhausted. I rinsed the dishes and put them away, made myself a cup of instant coffee, and went to the phone.

It was just past six o'clock. Seeing that Jason had fallen asleep, I went over and turned off the television. He woke up immediately.

"What's up?" he asked.

"I'm calling Union Station. I think you should listen."

I tapped out the number. There was one ring and the phone was picked up.

"Foley?" It was Mr. Troublesome.

"Listen to me, I've got—"

"Hold on a min—"

"No, I'm not going to stop talking"—when he tried to break in again, I kept talking over his voice, pushing forward without any pauses—"and you can listen or not and it's up to you. Tell your man Josey I've got the kid and I've got the letters and I'm ready to deal and it's got to include the kid and the two women because . . ." I had to take a breath, but he kept quiet. "Because if the women are dead, Josey's worse than dead. And you tell Josey I'll be in touch."

"Look here you—"

"Don't ask me where I am or how to reach me or when I'll be in touch or how or what kind of deal I want." I didn't have most of those answers, anyway.

"Foley." The ice-cold tone of his voice finally stopped me. "Listen to me. It's too late for you to say what kind of deal you want."

My stomach started to turn and shrivel at the same time. "What do you mean?" I asked.

"I mean we set the terms, not you. We have something very dear to you, and you'll do what we say. Now first, we want—"

"Put my wife on the phone. Or the Cooper girl. One of them, now!"

He chuckled. "Not now. First—"

I hung up the phone. My whole body was shaking by then, and bitter, warm vomit had crept up the back of my throat. I swallowed it back down.

Jason was sitting up and staring at me. "You don't look so

hot," he said. "You want another cup of coffee or something, man?"

"I want another beer." But I didn't move.

Jason went to the refrigerator and got out a beer.

"Thank you," I said, taking it from his outstretched hand without looking at him.

"Yeah, sure, man. But, uh, I don't know . . ." He didn't finish, but dropped back onto the sofa.

I drank half the can without stopping. "Don't worry about it," I said, standing and walking to the kitchen sink. "I'll be all right." Sure.

With one more long pull I finished the beer and set the empty can on the kitchen counter. *Slow down.* Opening the freezer compartment above the refrigerator, I poked around inside. I had left it on its coldest setting. Everything I'd put in there was solid as a rock, including the quart of butter pecan ice cream I'd bought in Andersonville. When I tapped it with a spoon it sounded like a chunk of wood. Leaving it on the counter to thaw, I got out another beer.

"That stuff won't help you figure out what to do next," Jason said. He sounded a little worried. That made two of us.

Sitting down at the table, I stared at the can, then popped it open before I spoke. "Figuring out what to do next is not the problem. What the hell, more than half the time I don't know what to do next. I can deal with that, and something usually turns up." I drank some beer, but in swallows, not in gulps. Talking out loud helped slow me down. "Like I say, that's not the problem. The problem is they won't put Cass or Sharon on the phone."

Jason stood up and started walking around the room.

I took another drink, only a mouthful, and swirled it around in my mouth slowly before I swallowed it and said, "What does that mean?"

"I don't know what any of this means, man."

"Josey's so weird."

"Was that him on the phone?"

"No. Josey thinks he's important. Important people don't answer phones."

I lifted the can of beer and stared at it. The small print told me that if I was pregnant it was risky to drink the contents, and warned of other health problems. The government makes them tell us. Otherwise they wouldn't say a word. They don't care if the stuff hurts us, or our children. But we read the warnings and still drink it, don't we? So I guess we don't care, either.

I put the can down and made another call.

When the Lady came on the line, we'd scarcely gotten past the hellos when she said, "You sound as though you're not well, Malachy."

"I'm fine," I lied.

"Oh," she said. "Well then, what progress are you making?"

I quickly reviewed the events of the day, ending with the call to Mr. Troublesome. I knew she could hear my voice tighten up when I told her he wouldn't put Cass or Sharon on the phone.

"I understand exactly, Malachy," she said. "But you only know now what you've always known—that Cass and Sharon have disappeared, that their disappearance is connected to Jason, and that Jason's difficulty is connected to Amy's envelope. Am I right?"

"Of course."

"Well then, there's nothing to do but press forward. You'll find out about Cass and Sharon. You just have to move ahead and not sit around drinking beer or something and letting anger and fear paralyze you."

"Have I said anything about fear or paralysis, Helene? Or beer?"

"Haven't you? Well, anyway, would you read the two notes to me?"

I read everything to her, first from Amy's notepaper and then the letter from D. When I finished, she asked me to reread them.

After the second reading, there was silence for a moment. Then the Lady said, "Nicole Grant."

"What?" I asked.

"I'm sure most of the dates can be verified easily enough. But my goodness, Malachy, don't you know Nicole Grant?"

"No."

"Well, I don't actually *know* her, either, of course. She's that awful woman on television—Nicole Grant. Her latest atrocity is a series on child abuse."

"I don't know the name, but . . . was she on the news just a while ago? The dark-haired one, with the bedroom eyes and the husky voice?"

"I suppose that's an accurate description. I didn't see this evening's news. But she's on all the time with some salacious material or other. She even called me once. She was doing a series on sex crimes and wanted to *interview* me about the connection between child abuse and prostitution. Promised I'd get *great coverage.* Awful woman." Helene paused, then added, "Although, maybe that's unfair. *Unfortunate* is probably more accurate. I suppose she's had quite a difficult life herself." By this time, the Lady seemed to have forgotten I was on the phone.

"Did she leave a number when she called you?"

"She said just call the station and she'd call back."

"It's getting late," I said. "Oh, by the way . . ."

"Yes?"

"That abandoned Cadillac's been towed."

"Yes," she said. "Well, it helps to know whom to call." The Lady's list of helpful people is interminable. "It's such a shame, though, that you have to *know* people to get anything done."

We said good-bye and I went for the ice cream. It was just right—firm, but scoopable. Taking a minute to ease my bursting bladder, I left Jason to divide the quart. When I returned, he was already eating—and his bowl still held more than mine.

"You don't watch it, you'll get too heavy," I said.

"Yeah. I gotta play some ball, you know? At least get to a gym and work out. I just don't feel right."

I considered pouring the rest of my beer down the sink. But then, I wasn't getting my share of the ice cream. So I brought the beer back to the table.

Jason finished quickly and went back to the television. Dawdling over the butter pecan and the beer, I worried over what to do. I couldn't come up with anything concrete, other than that it was Tuesday night and I wanted to be back at Miz Becky's piano by the weekend. Not much of a plan—but a clear enough goal.

CHAPTER 28

WONDERING WHETHER example is really the most effective way to teach—or just the easiest on the nervous system—I washed up the bowls and spoons and stowed them away, while Jason watched television. He ignored me as I opened and closed drawers and cabinets, refrigerator and freezer doors. He took no interest as I poked around and arranged things in my gym bag.

I made a big deal, though, of refilling Scott's shaving kit, with the envelope back under the lining, and—with a flourish—dropping the kit into the gym bag. That got his attention.

"What's up?" he asked.

"We're going out."

"Now? Where to?"

"Back to Cragman. That's one place I don't think they'll be looking for you anymore. I'll call Coach Cartwright. You can use the gym for a while. Then you can spend the night right there, in his office or something. You need exercise. Besides, I have things to do and I can't stand leaving you here alone at the mercy of the television."

"But what are *you* going to do?"

"Try to push things along."

"You taking that shaving kit? With the letters?"

"Sure. We can't leave it here. And you'll be better off if you don't have it."

He didn't argue.

Harvey was at the gym. He wasn't very enthusiastic at first, but agreed it would help Jason to loosen up and take a few shots. The team would be gone before we got there. By the time we hung up, Harvey'd warmed to the idea. He even decided that afterward Jason should go home with him for the night and wait for me there.

With the gym bag in the trunk, we set out in the Chevy. At Cragman, I circled the gym a few times and saw nobody. The team van was parked near the door. I pulled up next to it and Harvey let us inside the otherwise empty building.

"You know, Harve," I said, as Jason hustled off to change, "I can't guarantee there won't be trouble. So—"

"Cut the bullshit, Mal. Can't just abandon a kid with problems, right? Besides"—and he flashed the famous grin—"he's my chance for a conference championship."

It was about nine o'clock when I left the gym and drove to my favorite neighborhood In'n'Out. It was still bitterly cold as I stood at the outdoor phone.

A man answered.

"Nicole Grant, please," I said.

"I can only take messages, sir. If you leave a name and number, I'll see that Miss Grant gets the message."

"Tell her it's very important, an emergency. Tell Miss Grant my name is Foley and that I have Amy's letters." I made him repeat the phrase "Amy's letters" and gave him my phone number. "Tell her after tonight it'll be too late. I'm not home, but I'll keep calling in for messages and she should tell me how I can reach her."

"Very good, sir, but I have to tell you, I don't know whether I'll be able to reach Miss Grant tonight."

"Listen," I said. "This is a big one. This is *very* important to Miss Grant. And Miss Grant is *very* important to your ratings. And Miss Grant will be *very* unhappy if you don't reach her tonight. Do you understand what I mean?"

"I understand, sir."

I hung up. I didn't know if Nicole Grant was important to the station's ratings or not, or—if she was—whether the man on the phone would care. For all I knew, they got a dozen crank calls just like mine every day, and all of them *very* important.

I wanted to call Breaker, but he'd changed his number after I'd showed off and let him know that I knew it. I got on the Kennedy and headed southeast. Fifteen minutes later, I left the expressway and drove farther east, all the way to the No Parking sign in front of the Monumental Theatre.

That night's "lust-filled double bill" included *Maiden Japan* and *Boobs in Toyland*. Only country music can match the porn industry for titles. Ignoring the ticket window, I pulled open one of the glass doors and walked inside. A perfectly respectable-looking senior citizen in an usher's uniform sat on a stool, looking like he might doze off any minute. I brushed past his outstretched hand. The small lobby was dimly lit and, except for the two of us, empty. The door from the ticket booth into the lobby suddenly opened and a woman's head jutted out at an angle. Her bright orange hair clashed with the dull look on her face. There were a few seconds of silence as she pulled back her head and my eyes adjusted to the semi-darkness.

"Feature don't start for forty-five minutes," the old man finally said, scratching his thigh halfheartedly, "if that matters any. Myself, I can't see much difference between the beginning, the middle, and the end."

When I didn't respond, he scratched his other thigh and said, "I don't s'pose you want a ticket, huh."

"I want the manager."

"Uh-huh." Lifting his hand, he waved it limply toward the end of the lobby to my left.

The walls, like the floor, were covered with maroon-and-gray carpeting, as though a van-conversion company had done the decorating. A brass doorknob poked out of the wall the usher had waved at, without any door that I could see. But as I headed that way, the doorknob—and with it a rectangle of carpet—swung outward from the rest of the wall about a foot, leaking fluorescent light into the lobby.

A tall, cadaverous man slid sideways through the crack in the wall, closing it behind him. His thin white hair was parted in the middle of his skull and hung limply over half of each ear. His gray sport jacket looked healthier than his skin. It was freshly pressed and had *Manager* embroidered in maroon thread on the breast pocket. The ends of his mouth angled downward, matching the slump of his shoulders exactly. His glance darted nervously around the lobby, looking for any other trouble that might have come in with me.

His eyes flitted across my face, then moved on before he said, in a tired voice, "Haven't seen you before. Any identification?"

"Into the office," I said, and took a step straight toward him.

If he stiffened for an instant, he sagged again just as fast, and nodded his head in the direction of the usher. As the doorknob clicked behind him, he turned and pulled the door slightly open. I went through first and he quickly closed the door behind him, as though not to let too much light leak out into the lobby.

The carpeting ended at the door and we stood on a freshly painted concrete floor in a bright hallway. The walls and ceiling were bare white plaster and looked as though they'd been recently scrubbed. To our left, a stairway led upward, probably to the projection booth. About ten feet ahead, a lighted sign above the door at the end of the hall said EXIT. To our right, its door standing open, was the manager's office.

There were only two chairs in the office. At the desk against the wall, I spun the swivel chair around to face the room and sat down. That left a comfortable-looking armchair for the manager. He stood. In addition to the desk and chairs, there was a wall of shelves loaded with neatly spaced stacks of papers, a couple of steel gray file cabinets, and a large floor safe that must have weighed half a ton. The top of the desk was bare, except for a few thin manila folders and a telephone.

"You're a very tidy person," I said.

"Fuck you," he answered, in a weary monotone. "Who are you from?"

"Whom," I said. "It's clumsy, I know, but technically more correct. 'From whom are you?' Of course, the modern trend—"

"You're not a cop," he said. "What do you want?"

"Breaker. I want to talk to Breaker."

"I don't know what you're talking about. I don't know any Breaker. You must be crazy."

"I've often thought that myself," I said. "I want to talk to Breaker and I don't know his new number. So I want you to get him on the phone for me. Very simple."

He didn't answer.

"You could call the cops," I said, "and they might take me away. But the local neighborhood association will be very interested in how often I've seen you let young kids in this place when you thought no one was watching."

"That's absurd," he said. "I'm not that stupid."

"Maybe not. But when did I promise I'd always tell the truth? You know, I think Breaker would be very unhappy with an interruption in his cash flow."

"Yeah, he'd be unhappy all right—with *you.*"

"Oh? So you do know Breaker, after all."

"I heard of him."

"Well, as you say, unhappy with me," I answered. "But with you, too, since you could very easily have avoided the problem. So, unhappy with both of us. But, you see, I really don't care. You do. And that, as they say, makes all the difference."

"Breaker'll kill you, you mess with him."

"I don't know that he'd actually kill me. But for sure he'd try to, oh, put the hurt on me a little. He might even succeed. More important, though, he'd certainly succeed with you. And, at our age, friend, these bones don't heal the way they used to. Think about it. All you have to do is call him. Tell him Foley wants to talk to him."

"Suppose he doesn't want to talk to Foley?"

"Well, then he just hangs up, right? What's the problem?"

"The problem is he hangs up and he's pissed I even called him."

"Well then, later you tell him you couldn't help it. You tell him I had a gun to your head."

Getting to my feet, I showed him the Beretta and said, "Don't worry, Mr. Manager, he'll believe you all right." I stepped away from the desk and gestured with the gun, first at him, then at the phone.

That did it.

He went to the desk and, turning his back to me, tapped out a number on the phone. After a pause, he said, "Yeah, it's Biggins, at the Monumental. There's a little problem here. Guy named Foley. Yeah. Talkin' about shuttin' us down. I gotta talk to Mr. Hanafan. I think—"

Pushing him gently away from the desk and toward the door, I lifted the receiver from his hand without resistance and spoke into the phone. "This is Foley. Get Breaker on the phone. He wants to talk to me."

I closed the office door, shutting the manager out in the hall.

Breaker's voice came over the line sooner than I expected.

"Whadda you mean I wanna talk to you, Foley? I didn't wanna talk to you in the first place. Plus, I don't like crazy talk about shutting down places, and I especially wouldn't like it if I had any places, which I don't."

"If you'd list your phone number I wouldn't have to talk crazy to get to you."

"Yeah? Well—"

"Hold it, Breaker. Just humor me for one more minute, and one more piece of information. Is there some connection between Josey and a TV newswoman named Nicole Grant?"

"What the hell you talking about?"

"I just want to know, that's all, if there's some connection."

Breaker chuckled. "You're really something, you know, Foley? How the hell do I know if there's any *connection* between those two?"

"I don't know *how* you know, but if there's something to know in this town, you know it." What I was saying was true, and Breaker knew it. But he still liked to hear it said. Human nature is pretty consistent, and flattery's still right up there with fear and greed—even if it's at a distance—as a motivator. I poured it on. "If *you* don't know of a connection, then there *is* no connection."

"I don't know why I waste my time with you. But I'll tell you this. I hear this Grant broad's been *connected* to a whole lot of people. On the tube, she talks moral fiber and all that shit. But the way I hear it, when she's not out exposing corruption in high places, she's exposing something else—and not always in high places. And it ain't always guys, either. Makes no difference to her. If it was horny and knew the right people, she'd jump on a muskrat's lap."

"The right people? Who are they?"

"Anyone who can help her keep her face on the tube," he said. "She's bright, and as crafty as they come, they say. But she makes a lot of enemies. So she needs friends, too."

"But Josey Creole? Does he know the right people?"

"Josey's gotten pretty big. Some say too big, too fast. I wouldn't know about that. But he's getting to know a lot of people, one way or the other. As far as him and the Grant broad, who knows? Money means business, business means advertising, advertising means TV." He paused for a moment, then asked, "This have something to do with that kid you're looking for?"

"Yeah, something to do with him, or at least something he had that I've got now. Thing is, I don't know what it all means yet."

"Well, I don't either. And I'm not interested in finding out. I already gave you my best advice. Anyone messes with Josey Creole these days is fucking crazy."

"You're right. You already gave me that advice."

"But you don't listen. That's your problem."

"Breaker—"

"That's all I know, pal." He hung up.

I put the receiver in its cradle and rested my hand on the phone while I took a deep breath. Then I lifted the receiver again, and tapped out my own number.

There was a message on my machine.

"This is Nicole Grant," she said. "I'd very much like to talk to you." She breathed her phone number as though she were reading for a part in *Boobs in Toyland.* "Call me tonight. I'll be here. We'll make an appointment."

I called and she was there. We made an appointment.

CHAPTER 29

THIRTY MINUTES LATER, I was almost to Astor Street. Just a few blocks long and a stone's throw in from Lake Shore Drive, Astor's a street that murmurs tastefully of money—old money, new money, other people's money. Coming at it from its north end, at Lincoln Park, I passed North State Parkway. There were lights on all over the mansion with the thirteen redbrick chimneys where the cardinal-archbishop of Chicago lives. A little farther on, it was dark at the old Playboy Mansion.

On Astor itself, an occasional ugly high-rise juts up to remind its neighbors that even money can't always save you from "development" in the City of Backroom Deals. But mostly there are trees and tiny yards fronting vintage brick two- and three-flat buildings and elegant stone city-homes nestled complacently against each other on both sides of the street—with a couple hundred thousand dollars' worth of wrought-iron fencing running up and down the sidewalks.

The address Nicole gave me was a two-story graystone with a sloping tile roof and plenty of beveled glass. Its wrought-iron gate stood slightly open onto a brick walk leading to the front steps. In a covered cement stoop, a bulb burned softly, dropping an inviting mixture of light and shadow across the front door, a massive oak masterpiece with its window divided into small panes by a gridwork of lead. Lights glowed gently behind drawn curtains at windows on both floors.

I parked in a lot about a half mile to the west and walked

back. I had told Nicole I couldn't make it before midnight. When I reached the corner of her block, it was barely ten o'clock. With the collar of the leather jacket turned up against the cold, and the gym bag hoisted over my shoulder, I imagined I looked like any other up-and-coming mogul heading back from an evening of tennis or squash or racquetball or whatever was in at the time.

Except there weren't any other moguls, or anyone else, in sight, which made me a pretty obvious figure on the sidewalk.

I walked past Astor and turned into the alley that divided the rear ends of the lots on Nicole's street from those of the lots on the next street. A bright orange glow spread from sodium vapor lights set high on utility poles, but the varying setbacks and heights of the walls and fences along the alley created shadowed areas on both sides. In dark jeans, brown leather jacket, and black running shoes, I tried to stay in those shadows, yet walk as though I had no reason to hide.

It was cold—probably just below freezing. The calm, clear night was alive with the constant muffled din of city sounds—a hum of flowing traffic from Lake Shore Drive to the east; a more distant, homogenized mixture of shouts and sirens, slamming doors and honking horns, music and laughter from the blocks of restaurants, theaters, and bars to the south and west. In the alley itself, though, there was only the soft sound of my running shoes against the pavement.

From the front sidewalk, I'd counted the buildings from the corner to Nicole's. From the rear, though, it was surprisingly difficult to identify her building behind the garages, the coach houses, and the high walls and fences of brick and wood that lined the alley. I found it by her street number stenciled on the side of a large, wheeled garbage bin set back in an alcove in a high brick wall. There was no gate into her backyard. The only entrance was through the two-car garage.

I stared at the garbage bin for a moment. Then, feeling a little foolish, I took a flashlight from my bag and cautiously raised one of the two hinged lids a few feet, shining the flashlight beam into the bin. Real investigative work. Seth Green would have loved it.

I don't know what I thought I might find in the bin. But the contents consisted of one bulging black plastic bag and—on top of the bag, picking at the yellow twist-tie—one very startled gray rat. It wasn't very big, as Chicago rats go, but it scared the hell out of me as it leaped past my shoulder and skittered off into the shadows.

I dropped the metal lid, and, though it didn't have far to fall, I'd have sworn the clang spread five miles in all directions. As the echoes subsided, I stood and waited for my brain to tell my lungs it was okay to exhale.

Then the silence was suddenly broken again, this time by the whirring of an electric motor and the scraping of metal wheels in their tracks. Just one house down and across the alley, a garage door rose slowly, spreading an expanding rectangle of white light on the reflected orange of the pavement. Pressing back into the dark alcove beside Nicole's garbage bin, I watched a strange, bulky shadow move out across the patch of light from the garage. The shadow's puzzling shape was explained when a man stepped into sight, carrying a stuffed garbage bag in each hand. He glanced up and down the alley, then went to his own bin. Setting one bag on the pavement, he raised the lid and tossed the other bag inside. As he reached down for the second bag, there was a scurrying at his feet. He jumped, dropping the metal lid. Another clang echoed through the night.

"Goddamn fucking rats," he muttered, and deposited his second bag into the bin.

He returned to his garage, the door slowly lowered, and

the alley fell silent again. No one came to investigate the noises. No one hollered out an upstairs window. No one cared.

So, what's a little noise? I waited a few minutes and then, with my gym bag sitting on the closed lid, I dragged Nicole's garbage bin out into the alley and pushed it—squealing and scraping—over to her garage, placing it directly in the center of the double overhead door. A moment passed and, when no one responded to the noise, I climbed on top of the bin. Again I paused and listened. Nothing.

Standing and stretching at full length, I could barely reach the garage roof with the tips of my fingers. There was no rain gutter, but a thin, sharp metal ridge ran along the edge of the overhanging eave. Bending, I opened my bag, removed a pair of thin leather gloves, then closed the bag and flipped it up onto the roof. With the gloves on, I leaped up slightly to get a firm grip on the edge of the roof, hung there momentarily, and then, feet waving wildly, heaved and scrambled myself to the roof of the garage.

Leaving the garbage bin in front of the garage door was a pretty obvious sign to anyone who happened by. But there was nothing to be done about that. The alternative was to go around and ring the doorbell and seek admission to the spider's front parlor. My contact with beautiful investigative reporters was minimal, but I doubted it was standard operating procedure for them to interview unfamiliar sources in their homes at midnight—at least if they were otherwise alone, as she had claimed she'd be.

I found myself exposed under the alley light on the flat garage roof. A brick parapet wall, about two and a half feet high, ran around all but the east side of the roof, the alley side. The rear of Nicole's graystone building loomed above me, possibly thirty feet in from the garage. All the second-floor windows were dark. I couldn't tell if someone was watching from one of them.

The nearest alley light was to the north, making the only available shadow on the garage roof a narrow band of darkness along the north parapet wall. Dropping to my belly, I squirmed to the corner where the north and west parapet walls met. Lying flat, with the side of my face pressed to the tarred roof, I lay partially shielded from view from the house by the parapet, and partially hidden in shadow.

Long, silent moments passed before I raised my head, then got to my hands and knees and peered down from the corner. To my right and below, the north garage wall stretched down to the ground, unbroken by any window or door. In the west wall, facing the house, there were two small windows, and a service door almost directly below me.

Except for the garage, the backyard would have been a square, formed by the rear of the house and the ivy-covered brick walls on both sides and along the alley. The garage, taking up the southeast corner, made the yard L-shaped. There was no grass, only flagstones and ground cover and carefully tended ornamental trees and shrubbery. There were a couple of wrought-iron benches, probably neither moved nor sat on since they were put in place by the landscape architect.

Much of the yard lay in shadows, shielded from the alley lights by the high walls. The sole illumination from within the yard itself came from a bare low-watt lightbulb glowing dimly above a solid-looking, windowless back door.

To the right of that, a pair of French doors opened onto a stone patio that was raised a couple of feet above the rest of the yard. On the patio was a round glass-topped table, with a hole in the center for an umbrella pole. The umbrella itself was off the patio to the right, lying on ground level near the corner formed by the house and the yard's north wall. Back up on the patio level, a gas barbecue grill sat on its post, shrouded in gray plastic—like a miniature catafalque draped and waiting for burial. Although it was far too cold for coffee on the patio, a cup and saucer sat on the table, and a pair of wire-rimmed glasses. There were four wrought-iron chairs with cushioned seats.

Three of the chairs were empty.

The woman sitting stiffly in the fourth iron chair should have been shivering, wearing only a shirt and dark-colored pants, no coat. But she made no movement at all that I could see. Even her pale, bare feet rested still and motionless, as though frozen to the cold patio stones.

I was the one who shuddered, and not from the cold.

The emptiness of her stare and the tilt of her head took my breath away. Suddenly it wasn't her I saw, but Frank Parkins, tied to his chair. I squeezed my eyes closed to shut him out. When he wouldn't go away, I opened my eyes and saw the woman again. She was sitting up, tall and straight, and she wasn't tied to her chair. She was alive, breathing rapid, shallow, nearly imperceptible breaths. If she saw anything, though, it was inside her head, and not through those wide-open, somnambulant eyes.

CHAPTER 30

I DROPPED THE GYM BAG from the roof. While it fell and landed with a soft thud at the base of the blank north wall of the garage, I kept my eyes on the back of the house. All the windows remained still and dark. Nothing moved that I could see, not even the woman on the patio.

Edging over the parapet wall, I lowered first my legs, then my body, until I was hanging over the side, hugging the top of the wall between my elbows and my chest, shoes dangling eight to ten feet above the ground. The wall was about a foot wide and topped with glazed roofing tiles that offered even gloved hands little to grip. I lifted myself up with my arms, unhooked my elbows, and—managing to keep a hold on the smooth tiles only momentarily—slid down the face of the bricks to the ground. I was too close to the wall to hit the flagstones in a crouch and cushion the shock, and the little bit of cartilage left in my knees didn't take the landing well at all.

Returning my gloves to the gym bag, I left it at the base of the wall and, gun in hand, moved toward the woman on the patio. She began turning her head very slowly from side to side, but with no indication that she saw me. Her skin seemed thin and taut across her face and neck, with a waxen glow, almost blue in the dim light. She hugged her shirt tightly against her body, as though it offered some real cover or shelter against the cold.

As I approached, she finally managed to focus on me. Her eyes filled first with a glint of terror, then dimmed again in dull recognition. As though with a great effort of will, she unwrapped her arms from her sides. With dramatic, exaggerated gestures that belonged in a silent film, she pressed her left forefinger to her lips and pointed with her right hand to the house. Only then did her body begin to shiver.

Shoving the Beretta into the holster at my belt, I moved quickly up the three stone steps to the patio and went to her side. I stripped off my jacket and wrapped it around her. She pulled it close to her, leaving its empty sleeves hanging limply from her shoulders.

"It's okay," I whispered as I took her arms and placed them into the jacket's sleeves. "Don't worry, Lauren. It's okay."

"No," she whimpered, shaking her head slowly. "Not okay, never be okay. No more Frank. I thought I could . . . She's inside. She . . . she gave me something, and . . . and I was asleep and not asleep. And a man came . . . and they were . . . *doing* things to me. Not okay."

I pulled her to her feet and walked her to where we couldn't be seen from inside, against the back wall of the house to the side of the patio doors.

"Why are you out here?" I whispered.

"I don't know. I was asleep and she . . . she—"

"You mean Nicole?"

"Yes. She woke me up. Said the man was gone. . . . She wanted to take a bath. She locked me outside. Gave me coffee. Said I had to stay outside until . . . until his friends came back. I thought . . . something in the coffee, but . . . but it was warm and I was cold and I drank it."

"How long have you been out here?"

"I . . . I don't know. Five minutes . . . an hour . . . I don't know."

"Stay here against the wall," I said, "out of sight from inside."

With the automatic in my hand, trying to watch the French doors and all the windows at once, I backed across the yard and tried the service door to the garage. It was locked with a dead-bolt lock and seemed heavy and solid. Decorative iron bars covered the windows. The only way out of the yard was over the wall or through the house itself. I tried the patio doors, and the other, windowless, back door. Everything was locked.

The iron patio chairs were surprisingly heavy, but I lugged one from the table, stood on it, and was able to reach the bulb above the solid door and loosen it until it went out.

Replacing the chair at the table, I picked up Lauren's glasses and took them to her. She was sitting on the stone patio, her back against the wall of the house and her knees pulled up to her chest, trying to wrap her entire body in my jacket. She was shaking uncontrollably, but she seemed more alert.

She took her glasses with two hands and put them on. "Frank was . . . he was . . . cremated yesterday. He didn't want any funeral. Later, I snuck away from my sister. Drove down here in the afternoon, and . . ."

"Lauren," I said, "you can explain later. Right now we need to figure out how to get from now to later. Is Nicole alone in there?"

"Yes. At least . . . Well, I don't know. No one came in through the back, unless I blacked out or something. But I don't think—" She stopped suddenly and a wild look of panic swept over her face.

I heard it, too. A car had stopped in the alley.

"It's them. He . . . he might be with them," Lauren whispered. She stood up, eyes darting in every direction and cringing as though remembering some malevolent, deranged creature from a nightmare.

The sound of a car door opening came from the alley, followed by low, unintelligible conversation. My eyes swept around the yard. Although the light was dim and broken by shadows, there was no niche, no corner that couldn't be seen from the patio.

From the alley came the grating, metallic sound of the garbage bin being dragged away from the garage door.

"Lauren," I said, "come on." I grabbed her by the wrist and pulled her to the edge of the patio. Jumping down to ground level, I turned and lifted her down next to me.

She lowered her head and concentrated as her cold fingers fumbled with the jacket zipper. She seemed to have lost interest in me—unwilling or unable to move. When I heard the raising of the electrically operated garage door, I took her by the shoulders and shook her, hard. She opened her mouth as though to cry out. I clamped my hand over her mouth and dragged her a few feet to where the patio umbrella lay in the shadows along the wall.

Shaking her again, more gently, I whispered, "Listen to me. You've got to lie still and not move a muscle. No matter what happens. Can you do that?"

A car door closed in the alley.

Lauren stared at me, openmouthed but silent, and finally nodded her head. She neither cooperated nor fought me as I sat her down on the cold flagstones and maneuvered her, feet first, into the folds of the patio umbrella, managing to cover her legs and most of her body. It was like stuffing a life-sized Raggedy Ann doll into a huge stiff Christmas stocking. When I finished the job, her head and shoulders stuck out. Frantically, I tugged at the jacket, trying to pull it up over her head. She had it zipped up and it wouldn't budge.

I could hear the driver maneuvering the car in the narrow alley—forward and back, forward and back—getting it into position to pull into the garage.

I stood up and stared down at Lauren. She lay on her back on the ground, looking up at me, as pale and still as a corpse. I spun around and suddenly saw again the gas grill, covered like a shrouded coffin. I jumped up to the patio, snatched the gray plastic cover from the grill, and brought it back to Nicole.

I crouched and whispered, "Whatever happens, just don't move. It'll be okay. Trust me." I couldn't even look her in the eyes as I said it, but I pulled the cold, stiff plastic across her face.

Grabbing one of the patio chairs, I stumbled clumsily with it to the north side of the garage, just around the corner from the service door. The car was in the garage now, and the overhead door was closing. They would move carefully, not knowing whether someone was in the yard.

Holding the back of the heavy wrought-iron chair in front of me with two hands, I tilted it backward with two of its legs resting on the flagstones, ready to lift it into the air.

The tumblers of the dead-bolt lock *ka-chunked* softly into place. The hinges were not quite soundless in the still, cold air as the service door was opened. My fingers tightened on the iron chair.

There was a long, silent moment when nothing at all happened.

Then the whisper of leather against stone announced softly that someone had stepped out of the garage and into the yard. I rolled my shoulders, loosening the tensed muscles of my arms and hands, waiting for him to move cautiously around the corner.

When it happened he was too fast for me. In one leap he was suddenly around the corner and facing me, crouched and sweeping the yard next to the garage with the elongated barrel of a pistol with a silencer attached.

I had the heavy chair barely an inch off the ground when he swung the gun toward my chest. It flashed across my consciousness that if I dropped the chair he might not pull the trigger. But the cold fire in his eyes told me to keep on. He wasn't paid to think twice.

Suddenly a woman's voice called from an upstairs window, "Lauren? Is that you?"

The gunman barely flinched.

But it was enough. As I stepped forward, swinging the iron chair upward and driving it into him, he squeezed off two rounds. There was the silenced *chud* of the discharge, and an almost simultaneous *ping* of lead against iron as the first bullet caromed off the chair and into the city skies. The second round came as one of the chair's leg braces caught his wrist and twisted it up and back. Again the *chud,* and almost simultaneously . . . a sickening grunt and the sound of cracking bone. The second bullet, too, carried on toward the sky, but it wouldn't go so fast or so far as the first, slowed as it was by its passage through the soft underchin of the gunman and out the top of his skull, and by the bits and pieces of his life clinging to it.

By the time he hit the ground, I had the Beretta in my hand. A second man had been behind the gunman but had stepped back around the corner of the garage. I moved out to my right away from the garage, and forward to get a view around the corner. The man's back was disappearing through the service door. He was large, and wore a fur cap, as though it were winter in Siberia and not just a very cold autumn night in Chicago. I raised the gun.

Maybe it was because an unsilenced gunshot might have raised an alarm that the clanging, screeching garbage bins had not raised, or maybe because I didn't know who he was and whether he might somehow lead me to Cass and Sharon. Maybe I didn't have the stomach for it. Whatever the reason, I watched the door slam behind him.

Maybe it was just a dumb mistake.

CHAPTER 31

I TRIED THE GARAGE DOOR. It was locked with the spring lock. The dead bolt wasn't thrown and, given an undisturbed five minutes and a little luck, I might have been able to open it. In the meantime, I heard the car back out of the garage and disappear down the alley.

I turned to the dead man. He lay on his back, his face strangely untouched by the bullet that had torn through his skull. Tucking the Beretta in my holster, I took his pistol, barrel-heavy with its silencer, in my right hand, and with my left hand swept his body for more weapons. There were none.

It must have been Nicole who had called out, but I couldn't see her at any window. As though looking for a way out of the yard, I walked along the north wall and paused near the patio umbrella, too close to the house to be seen from inside.

"It's me," I said softly. "Are you okay, Lauren?"

"I was watching," came the muffled reply. "I saw. I'm very cold, but I'll be okay, I think."

I thought she'd be okay, too, someday—if I could just get her out of there alive.

And why not? Any self-respecting amateur piano player ought to be able to think his way out of a locked yard and whisk a barefoot, nearly frozen lady through city streets half a mile to his car, past what might soon be Josey's gathering militia. That wasn't the problem. The problem was, to get Lauren out of there, I'd have to get myself out. And I didn't *want* out. Not yet.

I wanted to talk to Nicole, and I wouldn't get a second chance. The answers were here—the answer to the search for Jason and the letters in the shaving kit, the answer to where Cass and Sharon were.

There really wasn't any choice.

"I'm going in the house," I said. "You can stay here or come with me."

She pushed the plastic cover off her face and wriggled her way out from the folds of the umbrella. I pulled her to her feet. The effects of the drug were wearing off. While her right hand tugged down on the jacket like a miniskirt, her left hand pushed her glasses higher up on the bridge of her nose. She danced and hopped on the cold stones with her bare feet, like a hyperactive child.

"I'm coming. I'd rather be near someone," she said. "Besides, I have to go to the bathroom."

First hiding the gym bag within the folds of the umbrella, I helped Lauren up to the patio and led her to the French doors. If they couldn't be kicked in, there was always the silenced pistol to blow the lock away. I stepped back and raised my foot.

"Wait," Lauren said. She pulled down on the brass handle and pushed the door open. "While you were trying the garage door, I thought I heard the latch."

"Probably not a good sign," I whispered as we stepped into the spider's back parlor.

With the dead man's gun in my right hand, I reached back with my left and pulled the patio door closed behind us. The effect was dramatic. The steady, throbbing backdrop of city noise was suddenly and completely absent, replaced by a soft, almost palpable stillness. Like eyes adjusting to a withdrawal of light, my ears adjusted to the new silence—only gradually picking up the whispering notes of a flute, playing a seductive melody. It sounded vaguely Japanese.

The only light in the room was a soft reflected light coming in from the backyard, spreading through the wide, multi-paned French doors and rolling in rows of trapezoids, first across a wide-boarded pine floor, then over a tightly woven, mostly red-and-black rug. I'm not up on my Navajos and Hopis, but the rug looked like serious American Indian to me—and serious American dollars.

Taking Lauren's hand, I pulled her to the side, into the shadows. The sweetly acrid scent of a recent birch-log fire mingled with the perfume of freshly cut flowers and floated around the room with the sounds of the Japanese flute. If there was a hint of hashish as well, it could have come in through my imagination—but I didn't think so.

Much of the north wall of the large room was taken up by a massive fireplace, the stone chimney continuing up through the high wood-beamed ceiling. The wall opposite the patio doors was mostly bookshelves. The higher shelves were lined with rows and rows of books; the lower shelves—the ones a person could reach—held photographs, vases of various sizes, and figurines and knickknacks not identifiable in the darkness.

A grand piano filled the end of the room to the left of the patio doors. Its top was propped open, but the leather-cushioned piano bench was off to the side, with several weeks' worth of newspapers stacked on it. Chairs and tables—pseudo–hunting lodge style—sat here and there around the room, with some comfortable-looking sofas and armchairs gathered in front of the fireplace.

It was a library, a music studio, a den. It looked like a great place to come home to—as long as you didn't actually read, or play the piano, or mind an occasional body leaking blood and other fluids onto the backyard flagstones.

Suddenly, a soft purring sound came from our left, in the area of the doors we had just come through. Lauren's hand tightened around mine, and I dropped to the floor, pulling her down with me. We knelt there and watched as heavy drapes moved across the French doors, drawn by electrically driven cords, slowly squeezing the flow of light into the room down to a narrowing ribbon, then snuffing it out entirely.

For a long moment, we crouched near the floor in near total darkness. Then a table lamp clicked on near the corner of the room diagonally opposite from us. Instinctively, I moved the barrel of the pistol in the direction of the light.

"Don't shoot," the woman said. "It's just me, the newsperson." She'd come in through a doorway near the far corner of the wall that was otherwise shelves.

I had seen only her face on the television screen, and she was taller than I would have guessed. But it was Nicole, all right. She wore a long robe type of thing, flowing from her neck down to her feet. I noticed it looked like sweatshirt material, and that it was light purple. And I noticed how nicely the shape of her body showed up under the robe.

She was toweling her hair, gently massaging the sides of her head with both hands. She arched her back slightly, just enough so her breasts were outlined clearly, the two of them sliding gently up and down—not quite in unison—under the robe. Watching me watch her, she put a hint of a smile on her lips. She continued to rub her hair with her right hand, dropping her left hand and resting it on her hip. As she did, she tightened the robe across her breasts, outlining all their high, hard features clearly.

She could have been slightly more subtle, and the hair she was toweling was as dry as my own. But she was a pro, all right, and she knew what she was doing.

Lauren interrupted my analysis. Whatever she'd taken had

lost its effect and the dreamy tone was gone from her voice. "Excuse me, but I have to go to the bathroom."

"That way," Nicole said, stepping farther into the room and nodding toward the door behind her. "Incidentally, honey, you'll find your coat and your boots in there." Without taking her eyes off me, she laid the towel on the lamp table, next to a red telephone.

Lauren started to cross the room. I touched her arm. "Just a minute," I said, and waved the gun at Nicole. "Sit down, Miss Grant."

"Oh, don't be silly. Put that nasty thing away before you hurt somebody." She wagged her hand, smiling patiently, understanding teacher to mischievous little boy.

Part of me almost wanted to obey.

"Sit down," I repeated.

"My, my," she said.

But she sat down, choosing one of two sofas facing each other across the front of the fireplace, her back to the wall of shelves. Legs crossed under the robe, she spread her arms out in both directions along the back of the sofa, and leaned her head back lazily to look up at me. The breasts appeared again—though with some of the hardness gone.

"You *are* Mr. Foley, aren't you? Or, may I call you Malachy? You can call me Nicole." She lifted her chin and gave her head a little shake—coquettishly, I guess you'd say. "Do you like flute music?"

"It's great," I said. "Japanese music always relaxes me."

"Good. After all, I want you to feel comfortable."

Most of what I was feeling I was trying to ignore. I went with Lauren to the doorway. Other than the patio doors, it was the only entrance to the room, and led into a hall. Leaving me the jacket, Lauren went into a bathroom a few feet down the hall.

I turned back to Nicole. "Anyone else in the house?"

"Of course not, silly. Why should there be?" Another lift of the chin. Another coquettish shake of the head.

"I'd take it easy on the neck muscles, Nicole. Your tendons are getting prominent. They show your age on the tube."

Her smile froze, as cool and distant as the Japanese flute music that still drifted through the air.

I slipped my jacket on. "Tell me about Jason Cooper," I said.

Leaning forward, she clasped her hands around one of her knees and looked up at me. She sighed. "You're in over your head, you know."

I raised the gun, aimed it high on the wall to the right of the chimney, and squeezed the trigger. *Chud.* A hole appeared in the plasterboard wall, a few inches wide of the grid of a built-in wall speaker. Every gun is a little different.

Making a slight adjustment, I fired again. The grid exploded, leaving a gaping hole in the wall. Flute music came now only from the speaker to the left of the chimney, as I went and sat on the sofa opposite Nicole.

"Tell me about Jason Cooper," I said.

She yawned. "You're wasting your time. There's so much you don't know. Like that flute, for instance. It's not Japanese at all. It's Indian. Or *Native American,* I guess we're supposed to say now. Anyway, you're in over your head."

Waving the gun at the piano, I asked, "Do you play?"

"I don't believe you said that," she answered. "Do I *play?"* There was mockery in her voice, and no humor.

A white plaster figure, the head and shoulders of a man, sat on a pedestal near the piano. "Do you know who that is?" I asked, gesturing with the gun barrel.

"Couldn't care less," she said. "I'm sure he's dead."

"Right," I said. "His name was Haydn."

I was staring straight into her eyes when I squeezed the trigger. The bust of Haydn off to my left disappeared in a shower of chips and plaster dust.

Maybe she flinched a little. "You don't have much time," was all she said. "I'm surprised he's not here already."

"Josey Creole?"

"You should have killed the other man. He'll have called. Josey will be here."

"Good. I can ask *him* about Jason."

"He won't be alone. And he'll be . . . angry." Something sparkled in her eyes. Fear, maybe the thrill of anticipation, and maybe a little chemical something, too. "He's . . . well, Josey can be a little crazy, you know."

"Maybe," I said. "But then, who's to say who's *normal?* I mean, take me, for—"

"If you had any sense, you'd go away," Nicole interrupted, playing the schoolmarm again. "There's still time to take that woman with you and get out."

"There, you see what I mean? You're absolutely right. If I had any sense, that's what I'd do."

Lauren appeared in the doorway. She had a raincoat over her arm, and I suddenly noticed she was wearing the same rust-colored shirt and dark corduroy pants I'd first seen her in, at Pepper Mill. It was a nice outfit. She probably didn't have many nice outfits.

"Well," I said, "now we can—" I stopped.

We had all heard the front door open.

"Lauren," I whispered, "into the bathroom. And turn out the light. Fast!"

"But—" she started, then switched off the table lamp and retreated silently back into the bathroom and turned off that light as well.

In the darkness I went and stood behind where Nicole sat on the sofa. "Don't move," I said softly.

A man's voice called from the front of the house, "Nicole? Are you there? *Nicole!*" The impatient, fatherly voice was all-too-familiar.

I heard her breathe in.

"Say 'I'm back here.' Say anything else," I whispered, "and you'll say hello to Haydn."

"I'm back here," she called.

"Remember," I said, "say anything and I'll kill you."

I moved backward away from her until I stood against the wall of shelves, with the doorway to the hall some fifteen feet to my right. The hall light came on, spilling through the opening into the room, then went out almost immediately. Footsteps came softly down the hall.

Taking a smooth porcelain statuette from a shelf behind me, I laid the pistol, with its silencer, in its place. With the statuette in my left hand, I drew the Beretta and pointed it at the doorway. A little noise might not be a bad idea.

It was very dark, but I saw the outline of a man ease carefully into the room, his knees bent, his hands out in front of him, as though waving a gun. I heaved the statuette across the room, smashing it against the wall behind the piano.

As the man turned toward the crash, Nicole screamed. He dove to the floor and, aiming high, I squeezed the trigger. I didn't want him dead. The shot echoed in the high-ceilinged room as the man scrambled for shelter behind the piano. I crawled around the end of the sofa and found Nicole huddled in a ball on the floor in front of the fireplace.

When I got near her she whispered, "He'll kill you . . . me . . . all of us."

"One word about Lauren and I'll kill you myself," I replied, my lips close to her ear.

Wrapping my left arm around her neck, I stood her on her feet and held her in front of me, my back to the fireplace.

When she opened her mouth as though to speak, I yanked my forearm tight across her throat. No more struggle. In fact she settled back against me, in an unsettling sort of way. There was something about violence she enjoyed.

The man crouching behind the piano finally spoke. "You're finished, Foley. It's over."

It was the voice that had called from the front door. It was the voice I had spoken to on the telephone so many times.

"Well," I said, "Mr. Troublesome. I told you I'd be in touch, and here I am. So where's that ugly insect of a boss of yours, in a specimen jar in your pocket?"

A moment passed when no one spoke. Nicole's body shuddered against mine. She was afraid. I was afraid, too. Afraid for Cass, for Sharon, for Jason, for me—even for Nicole, but not so much.

The click of a wall switch suddenly cracked through the silence, and light filled the room. "The ugly insect, Mr. Foley, is over here. And if anyone's in a jar when this is over, it will be you. Probably several jars."

CHAPTER 32

MAYBE FIVE AND A HALF FEET TALL, he stood just inside the door to the hall and peered out at the world through the circular lenses of enormous black-framed glasses. His magnified eyes were set wide in an almost round, olive-skinned face that might have been just slightly higher than it was wide. His head had shiny black hair pasted across the top of it, and was attached, without any visible neck, to a body the shape of an acorn squash. Thin arms and legs stuck out in approximately the right places, as though he'd been designed by a child drawing a four-legged beetle dressed up to look like a man.

He should have looked ludicrous. Instead, he looked like someone to be reckoned with.

The custom-tailored suit helped, and the silk shirt. And it helped that his eyes, myopic as they were, shone with intelligence and a cold touch that might have been madness. What helped most, though, was the snub-nosed revolver that he carried in his hand as though it were a natural appendage.

"Stand up, Harold," he said, nodding toward the piano, "and relieve Mr. Foley of his gun."

The man stood up and started around the piano.

"Harold," I said, "keep coming and I'll kill you, as sure as I'll kill that beetle if he comes toward me."

The man looked at Josey.

"Try him, Harold," Josey said, keeping his eyes on me and breaking into a grin, "because if you don't, *I'll* kill you."

I felt a shiver run through Nicole. Probably anticipation.

"And remember, Harold," Josey added, "I prefer that Mr. Foley not die until I find out where the letters are."

That was comforting.

"As for Nicole," Josey continued, "well, I don't suppose I care that much one way or the other." No one in the room doubted him.

"No letters, Josey," I said, "not until we've got a deal."

"I don't need a *deal,* Foley. I've got you, I've got the Parkins woman, and I've got—"

"Wrong," I broke in. "Lauren Parkins is long gone."

Josey's eyes moved to Nicole. "I left her here, with you."

Nicole stiffened, frightened of us both, not sure how to play her hand. "I . . . Well . . . I mean, you shouldn't have left me here without any help."

"Shut up, bitch." Josey's tenor voice rose a notch. "Don't ever tell Josey Creole what he shouldn't do. Nobody tells Josey Creole what he shouldn't do."

"I . . . I'm sorry, Josey. I didn't mean . . ."

Josey ignored her and spoke to me. "Where is she?"

"Hell, I don't know. I put her out in the alley with directions to my car. But she was stoned out of her mind. I don't even know if she heard me."

"Well, fuck her," Josey said. "I'll find her." His mind seemed suddenly to switch to a new track. "It was fun trying to see if she had anything to tell us, though, wasn't it?" He leered at Nicole. "You can be such a *mean* girl, when you put your mind to it."

My mind raced. Harold and Josey were on opposite sides of the room, and I couldn't handle both of them without Nicole being hurt. I didn't want that. She'd earned something by keeping quiet about Lauren. Besides, I needed Josey alive, at least until I found out where Cass was.

Harold had been happy to stay where he was by the piano

while Josey mentally played with himself. But suddenly Josey switched tracks again. "Harold," he said, "what are you waiting for?"

Harold started toward me and I fired. The bullet went into the wall behind him and to his right. He stopped and looked at Josey.

"See what I mean?" Josey said. "He won't kill you. He can't. I can. I will. Believe me."

The look in Harold's eyes spelled belief.

"Don't believe him, Harold," I said. "Killing you would leave him here alone with me. He doesn't want that."

A new look in Harold's eyes gave me a bit of news I wasn't happy to learn. But there wasn't time to fret about it, because something happened then that I'd been afraid of. Lauren appeared, creeping silently down the hallway behind Josey.

Wanting to keep everyone's attention, I spoke rapidly. "It's a problem, isn't it Harold? I say I'll kill you if you come for my gun. Josey says he will if you don't. The way I see it, you got just one choice. Take Josey out."

"Shut up, Foley," Josey said.

"It *is* a little complicated," I continued. "But since Josey's the only one in the room who will *certainly* kill you, I'd say your best bet is—"

Lauren was close to Josey now.

Nicole made her choice. "Look out, Josey!" she screamed.

Josey started to turn just as Lauren lunged at him, pushing him hard with two hands. The two of them crashed to the floor, Lauren landing on top of him.

I threw Nicole away to my left. Harold took a step toward me, his gun raised. I shot him. For an instant, he stood still. Then he sank to his knees, staring up at me in surprise.

I stared back at him—too long.

"Drop the gun, Foley, or the bitch is dead meat."

I turned my head. Josey was kneeling on the floor, with Lauren lying beside him. He held the barrel of his gun pressed into her neck.

I dropped my arm to my side. The Beretta slid out of my hand and landed with a thud on the woven rug.

"Now kick it over to me," he said.

As I sent the gun skidding across the rug, I said, "Harold needs a doctor."

"Fuck Harold. *You* shot Harold, not me. It's not my fault. It's your fault." He sounded like a child blaming someone else for a broken window.

Harold moaned. "Please . . . Josey." From a kneeling position, he had sunk back on his haunches. Blood seeped between the fingers of his left hand, pressed to his right shoulder. "A doctor . . . I'm dying. Please."

"Shut up, Harold," Josey said, his voice becoming more agitated. "If you'd done what I told you, this wouldn't have happened. It's your own fault."

Harold looked at me. "Foley," he said, "do something. I'm gonna die."

"It's all right," I said. "It's just your shoulder. You'll be all right."

"No . . . bleeding. Please . . . Josey's . . . not right . . . crazy. . . . You don't know how crazy."

"Shut up I said! You fucking prick!" Josey was nearly screaming.

"I can help you," Harold pleaded with me. "Don't deal with Josey. Your wife . . . she's—"

Harold's head snapped backward as bullets tore through his chest and throat. Terrible liquid sounds rolled out of him, and he fell forward onto his face on the rug.

In the momentary silence that followed I heard again, as though for the first time, the lonely music of the flute.

Josey had the gun turned back to Lauren's neck. He scrambled to his feet and pulled her to a standing position. "There," he said, as though the routine preliminaries had been concluded. "Now let's get down to business."

He sat down on one of the couches, pulling Lauren down beside him.

"Thank you for the warning, Nicole," he said. "Now, for your reward, you may remove Mr. Foley's jacket and search him, please. I'm sure that's something you'd enjoy." To me he added, "And if you try anything, Mrs. Parkins is dead."

Nicole stepped behind me and peeled the jacket from me. When she found nothing in the pockets, she tossed it to the floor, and moved close behind me again. She breathed gently on the back of my neck and, as her hands moved in slow circles over my back.

"Doesn't she do good work, Mr. Foley?" Josey asked, smiling. I thought he trembled a little.

I said nothing. But in my head I screamed at Harold to finish his sentence. *Your wife . . . she's*—she's what? Why not deal with Josey? Was she dead?

Nicole moved closer, her breasts gently rubbing against my back. She reached around and from behind did a similar slow massage of my chest and belly. Whatever she thought she was doing, anger and revulsion wiped out anything else she might have stirred up.

Both arms around my waist, she loosened my belt buckle.

When she started fumbling with the button of my jeans, Josey broke in. "Now, now, Nicole, it's a search, not playtime."

She abandoned the button and simply slipped her hands inside the waistband, groping with her fingers.

"Oh my," she said, "I think I found something."

She paused, then slid her hands, still under the waistband,

around my sides and to the back. "But nothing unusual," she added, moving back away from me.

"Do his legs," Josey said, "all the way down to his shoes."

She found the ankle holster and handed the minirevolver to Josey.

I'd been counting on the NAM, and when it was gone something strange happened. Maybe I bottomed out. But the raging, competing feelings—dread and anxiety about Cass and Sharon, anger and disgust for Josey and Nicole—drained away. There was nothing left but a cold, hard calm.

Smiling, Josey dropped the mini over the back of the sofa onto the floor behind him. "No papers?" he asked.

"Nothing," Nicole replied.

"Now," Josey said, "sit down. Let's talk."

I sat on the sofa opposite him and Lauren. Nicole stood behind Josey's sofa. My mind was clear and cool, all my senses wide open and alert. Cass might be dead, and Sharon, too. But I was here, and Josey was here. And only one of us would walk away.

"Cozy," I said. "Cozy with Josey. What shall we talk about, Mr. Bug?"

If my comments bothered him, he didn't show it. "Just one question. Where is that—what is it, a shaving kit?—with the girl's letters?"

"And just one answer. I'm not talking. Period. If you had some bigger bugs with you, you could try to beat it out of me, but that's been tried before. No one's ever made me talk and no one ever will. Not talking has become sort of a specialty of mine."

I kept talking stupidly about not talking because I'd heard a noise from out on the patio. Blowing leaves? A nocturnal squirrel? Josey didn't seem to notice.

"Yes sir," I continued. "Mr. Not Talking. That's me. That's what got my law license suspended, which has led, by a rather tortuous path, to my being here with you tonight to tell you that I'm not talking. You see—"

"Shut up. You're not funny," Josey finally said.

"Not funny," I agreed. "But not talking, either. At least not until I know the two women are safe." I wasn't hearing any more sounds from the patio.

"Ah, yes," he sighed, "the women. We will talk about the two women. But not yet. Not until I have the letters."

"Then there's nothing to say."

"No, you will tell me where the letters are." He turned to Lauren beside him, and gently touched her cheek. "And I won't have to beat it out of you."

Lauren swallowed hard, but said nothing.

"Get my drift, Foley?" Josey asked.

"I get it. But guess what? That woman means about as much to me as good old Harold here meant to you. So drift away, pal."

"I think you're lying, Foley. But we're going to find out, aren't we?"

He put the gun to the side of Lauren's neck again. "My dear," he said, "you're slouching. Sit up straight and put your hands down beside you."

Stifling a gasp, Lauren did what he said.

"Now, Nicole, why don't you give the lady a reminder? But be gentle, at first."

Nicole reached around from behind Lauren and slowly swept the hair back from the side of Lauren's face, gathering and twisting it behind her head. Lauren had stopped trembling. She sat as still as the statues on the shelves behind her.

"Now, Mrs. Parkins, I realize you may have been a little—oh, shall we say—'under the weather,' this afternoon. But do you remember our little question and answer session?"

When Lauren answered, she talked straight at me. Her voice was strangely flat. "I remember enough. The truth is, I don't care anymore. He can do whatever he wants to me. It doesn't matter. Frank's dead. This man can hurt me, kill me. I want you to understand. It doesn't matter. Believe me."

I did believe her. Right then she didn't care. But that wasn't much help. Because I cared. Seeing her victimized rattled me and started the feelings churning again. What happened to her mattered to me. I wished it didn't. I tried to make it not matter. The letters were my only road to Cass—if there was a road—and I tried to blot out Lauren with Cass. But what happened to Lauren mattered, too.

I met Josey's eyes. He knew it mattered, and that made him smile.

His smile turned the tide. The anger surged again.

Something exploded inside me. I spoke slowly, scarcely recognizing the sound of my voice. It was a bad sound, the sound of hatred. "Listen to me, beetle-man. It's just you and me. Something's going to happen now, something very bad. Nicole will get hurt, Lauren too. They may both die. And my wife and Sharon Cooper as well. Chances are, you'll kill me. But—gun or no gun—you're going down with me."

The hint of fear flickered in his eyes for a second.

But then it was gone and he smiled again, and said, "Fortunately, we won't have to put your anger to the test, Foley. Because, you see, it's *not* just you and me. It's you and me . . . and the Russki."

I remembered again that look on Harold's face.

When I didn't answer, Josey laughed, pleased with himself. "What the hell? You think I'm gonna walk in the front door with just Harold and not have someone in the back?"

He rose and, dragging Lauren with him, moved toward the

patio doors. He kept his eyes on me. "Nicole, open the drapes."

Nicole went to a switch near the door to the hall, and the drapes drew back slowly. The glass panes of the French doors were mirrors, reflecting back only the lighted interior of the room.

"The light, goddamn it. Turn it off," Josey said.

When she switched off the light, the patio came into view through the doors.

"See?" Josey said. "There he is. Straight from Moscow, or some goddamn Russian place. There's thousands over there want to come here. No fear, no conscience, and they work cheap. Imported muscle." If he hadn't had a gun in one hand and Lauren's arm in the other, I think he would have clapped with glee.

I stood and looked out through the glass doors.

There was a man out there, all right. Arms folded across a massive chest, he sat leaning back in one of the patio chairs, huge booted feet stretched out toward the round glass-topped table. With his black fur cap tipped forward over his eyes and his black-bearded chin resting on his chest, he seemed to have found a way to get comfortable despite the iron chair. He sat just a few feet outside the French doors, at a forty-five-degree angle, where he could watch the doors, the garage, and the entire backyard.

But only, of course, if he stayed awake.

His imported muscle's indifferent attitude infuriated Josey. He grabbed the door handle and shouted, "Sit up, you damn Russki! Sit up!"

But he didn't sit up, and as Josey yanked the patio door inward, the Russian toppled toward him, pulling his chair over with him and crashing heavily to the patio stones just outside the door. The black fur cap tumbled off. There was a small, clean bullet hole just above and between his black-browed eyes.

Josey instinctively slammed the door closed. And when he did, another door swung open, in my mind. I saw in an instant what had been wrong, why Josey hadn't simply offered Cass and Sharon for the letters. All along I'd been used, all along working with only half the truth.

"Look out!" I yelled, diving headfirst toward Lauren and Josey. The three of us crashed to the floor in a tangled heap.

Nicole screamed, while the glass in one of the two French doors exploded and scattered through the room.

I couldn't hold both Josey and Lauren down on the floor. Josey wrestled free and scrambled to his feet. He still had the gun in his hand.

"You bastards!" he screamed, to no one. He looked confused.

"Josey," I yelled instinctively, holding Lauren with me on the floor. "Get down, Josey. They're outside!"

He blinked, then turned and peered out through the door that still had glass. Understanding froze him motionless for an instant. That was too long. A silent flame of light flashed in the shadows near the garage, and one glass pane in the French door exploded. Josey returned the fire, but couldn't have seen anyone. Another pane of glass exploded, then another, and another, until I lost count. Josey's beetlelike arms jerked outward from his body, flailing and flopping. The gun flew out of his hand, landing with discordant bounces on the strings of the open grand piano.

Then, arms hanging limply at his sides like an Irish stepdancer, Josey skipped backward into the room in short stuttersteps, stopped, and fell onto his back. Maybe he felt his head slam with a sickening thud against the pine planks. Or maybe the scraps of lead that had shredded his chest had already obliterated feeling. He'd never let us know.

Never more than a psychopath with inflated ambitions, now he was just another dead creep. There was no final word, no dying statement. Nothing came from Josey's lips but a large, bubbling clot of blood-tinged vomit that erupted, slid down the side of his jaw, and dripped onto the floor.

There was one more crash of broken glass, and a gun sailed into the room and landed on the floor next to Josey. Whoever tossed it in had removed the silencer.

CHAPTER

33

By the time I scooped the Beretta from the floor and pulled open what was left of the patio door, the garage door had slammed shut. A car's engine roared to life in the alley, and the car drove away.

I looked down at the dead Russian. They must have followed him through the garage and right into the backyard. Both ends of a thin dark cord were tied to the outer handle of the patio door. The cord had been looped around his body as it sat slumped in the iron chair, linking him to the door. Stepping around him, I went to my left across the patio, past the gas grill, and down to ground level. My gym bag was still hidden in the folds of the patio umbrella.

Back inside, I turned on the light and closed the heavy drapes to shut out some of the cold coming through the shattered French doors. I tossed the gym bag on one of the sofas. Nicole wasn't in the room.

Lauren stood near the wall of bookshelves, as far from the two bodies on the floor as possible. She looked across at me and said, "That woman, Nicole, she . . . she said she'd be right back. She wants to talk to you."

"I bet she does," I said. "But first she's calming her nerves."

"I don't understand."

"Cocaine or . . . whatever."

"I want to go away from here."

"Me too."

I went around the sofa and found the NAM and returned it

to my ankle holster. "Lauren," I said, "since you've been here, have you seen or heard anything about two other women? Two women that Josey might have been hiding here, or even hiding somewhere else?"

"No, nothing. I'm almost certain no one else was in the house." She stared at me. "It's your wife, isn't it? And Jason's sister."

"Yes. Harold said not to make a deal with Josey. It sounded like he was going to tell me that they're dead."

Lauren's eyes widened. "Oh my God," she said, speaking through her hand cupped over her mouth.

Nicole appeared in the door from the hall. "Shall we sit down, Mr. Foley? We need to talk." Her tone said she was ready for business, but her eyes said she was flying.

"I'll stand," I said. "There isn't much time."

"Well then, the shaving kit, and the girl's letters. I want them. I'll pay you."

"Where's my wife? Where's he put her?"

"You poor, sad, stupid man," she said, shaking her head. "Josey wasn't holding any women. Harold was to offer you money for information about that nigger kid, Cooper. Then all of a sudden you start talking about the two women. I mean, even Josey was impressed by the way Harold handled that, acting like he knew what you meant. Josey never had your wife."

"You're lying," I said. But she wasn't lying, not about this, anyway. She wanted the letters too badly. I was learning more about how I'd been used, was still being used.

"You kept babbling all the time about your wife, and that Cooper girl, too, the bitch who thinks she's such a big-time violinist. This whole thing's her fault. Josey was pissed out of his mind when Harold couldn't get anywhere with her. Harold called her sometimes from here. I saw how hard he tried. What a snob she must be!" Nicole's eyes shone. "Christ, I hate the niggers. It's the same at the station. Every goddamn one that gets anywhere at all in the world, I mean, you can't even *talk* to them."

"My God, you're disgusting," Lauren said. She stared at Nicole in disbelief.

"My, my," Nicole said. "Sensitive, aren't we? Anyway, whatever you call her, she was a disgusting snob. She disappeared right after Josey had the rat put in her violin case. Josey went nuts when he couldn't find her."

"You knew about the rat?" I asked.

"Knew about it? Honey, that was my idea. I only wish I could have seen that bitch's face." She flashed a conspiratorial smile, fooled by the chemicals into believing I'd admire her creative thinking.

Stepping across the space between us, I reached out with my left hand and slapped her across the side of her face, harder than I thought I'd intended. I wanted to bring her down to earth. But there was anger and frustration, and fear for Cass and Sharon, in there, too.

"I want the letters," she whined, holding her hand to her cheek, her eyes still flashing strangely.

"What's Josey to you?" I asked.

"Josey?" She looked across the room at his body. "He's a rotting corpse, a piece of garbage, to me."

I slapped her again, just as hard.

Some of the sparkle went out of her eyes. "I need to sit down," she said.

We sat, Lauren and I on one sofa, our backs to the bodies, Nicole on the other. Now we were getting somewhere.

"Tell me about Josey and you and Jason Cooper," I said.

"Fuck you." So much for getting somewhere.

I remembered what the Lady had said. *I suppose she's had*

quite a difficult life herself. Standing up, I leaned across and slapped her again. I knew no other way to bring her back to reality. Tough as nails, that's me. If this kept up, I'd hate myself more than I hated her.

Her shoulders sagged then, and she started to cry. I couldn't believe it was for real. I didn't know what was real and what wasn't.

"Tell me," I said. "It'll be easier on both of us."

"Okay," she said, still sobbing. "If I talk to you, will you make a deal for the letters?"

"If you don't talk, no deal. If you talk, maybe."

"I met Josey five or six months ago, at . . . well, at a private event. He . . . I guess he fascinated me. A weird little man, but exciting, and dangerous. Big ideas and, of course, lots of money. I knew he was, well, *connected.* I guess I thought he could help me, you know, get ahead." She paused. "I really don't know what I thought. Anyway, I started seeing him. Not actually out in public, of course. Then he set me up in this place. It was great fun for a while. He had some interesting habits, sexually, that is. I mean, you can't imagine." She got a dreamy look in her eyes, then caught herself. "Pretty soon, though, I started to see how crazy he really was. And then . . . and then I couldn't get rid of him."

"And the cocaine?" I asked.

"That? That was nothing at first. I'd done coke now and then through the years. With Josey, though, it was different. It was getting to be all the time. It was so . . . easy with him, and it seemed like I needed it more." She looked across at Josey's body. "You don't know how glad I am that the little shit is dead. I'm free, you know? I don't need the stuff anymore."

"That's why you were in the bathroom," I said, "almost before he hit the floor."

"That's different," she said. "Anyway, now I've told you everything. I need those letters. This story's going to turn the corner for me. I know what the letters mean. I've got the girl on tape. She called me. I mean, the quality's not that good, and she's kind of vague. But the tape and the letters together, if the letters say what I think they say, will prove that that creep Radcliffe had been fucking—and God knows what else—his own daughter for years. Had her so messed up she couldn't think straight. When she called, she could hardly even talk about it. My God, what a break! It was the answer to a prayer, the story of a lifetime."

"But what about the girl?" Lauren asked. "What about Amy?"

"I'm a reporter, honey, not a therapist. She had plenty of money for shrinks. That wasn't my job. My job was the story. But I blew it. I made a big mistake."

"You told Josey," I said.

"And good-bye story," Nicole said. "Josey had other ideas for the information. Radcliffe was going to be U.S. attorney."

"And Josey was going to control Radcliffe with those letters," I added.

"Yeah, but then, when she was supposed to bring in the letters, she didn't show. Got cold feet. Called and said she didn't want to go through with it. I told her that was okay, she could trust me, I was her friend. I said, 'You didn't destroy the letters, did you?' She said no, that her boyfriend had them."

"And you told Josey," I said.

"I had to. Anyway, Josey got impatient, started having her and the boyfriend followed. I told him to wait, she'd call again. I knew I could change her mind. Give her some time. But he couldn't wait. Stupid little shit. Anyway, his people chased her, and she ended up on the bottom of the lagoon.

Josey went berserk. He wanted the letters and he couldn't find them. When the Cooper kid disappeared Josey figured he took the letters with him."

"But how did Josey know about Pepper Mill?"

"Pepper Mill?" Nicole asked. "Oh, you mean that military acad—"

"That was me." Lauren's voice was very soft. "I . . . I told her."

I stared at her. "You wouldn't—"

"I work with abused women and girls all the time. When Jason showed me the letters, I knew what they must mean. The school has a satellite dish and I'd seen Nicole's reports. I knew who Amy's father was. I wanted him exposed for the terrible things he'd done. And . . ." Her voice trailed off.

"Go ahead. Tell him the rest," Nicole said. "Tell him about the money."

"You brought that up. I didn't ask for anything."

"Make all the excuses you want, honey," Nicole said, her voice harsh and brittle. "But you know goddamn well you called up and said you had the letters and they're hidden in a shaving kit and I said I'd try to get you two thousand dollars and you said fine. That's what happened. And I told you I'd check with the station."

"But . . . but I wasn't even thinking about money when I called," Lauren said. "You brought that up and I just said okay." She looked at me, then lowered her head. "Anyway, that's what happened. And now Frank is dead. I killed Frank."

I couldn't think of an answer.

Nicole turned to me. "Where are the letters?"

I reached into the gym bag next to me on the sofa, pulled out the tan leather shaving kit, and spilled its contents—electric shaver, comb, aftershave, the works—on the floor in front of me. Then, from beneath the lining, I removed the two sheets of paper.

Nicole started to get up.

"Sit down," I said. "I'll show you from here." I held each piece up toward her with two hands, and she read them.

Her breath came heavily. "I want them," she said. "I'll give you five thousand dollars."

"No," Lauren said. "You can't do that, Mal."

I looked at Lauren, then slipped the letters back under the lining and put the shaver and everything else back in the kit. I zipped it closed.

"No," I said. "You're right. I can't do that." I looked down at the kit in my hand, then across at Nicole. "The price is fifty thousand."

Both Lauren and Nicole gasped.

"Fifty thousand gets you the shaving kit," I said. "And Lauren and I walk out of here and never say anything to anyone. You call the police. You call your TV station. You make up whatever story that hopped-up little mind of yours can think of to explain all the dead bodies lying around. And the station gets you explaining everything on tape, an exclusive. Maybe you open the shaving kit right there, on screen. The story of a lifetime. You'll be bigger than Barbara Walters ever was. Fifty thousand. Otherwise, it's good-bye TV. Good-bye everything. You go to jail."

"But I don't have fifty thousand dollars," Nicole said. "Make it ten."

"Well, that's it, then," I said. I dropped the shaving kit into the gym bag and zipped the bag closed. "No fifty, no shaving kit. Let's go, Lauren."

I started to my feet.

"Wait—wait," Nicole said. "I've got money, but not that

much. Twenty-five, maybe thirty thousand. It's right here, right in this room." She got up and, making a wide berth around Josey on the floor, went across to the piano stool. She swept the newspapers onto the floor, raised the hinged seat, and withdrew a fat brown envelope from among a clutter of sheet music. She handed the envelope to me. "There," she said. "You count it. Whatever it is, you can have it, all of it. But that's all there is."

I counted out the money in the envelope. Large denominations, but it still took quite a while. "Twenty-eight thousand, seven hundred," I said.

"That's it. And maybe a few dollars in my purse."

"Not enough," I said. "Try Josey."

"What?"

"Try Josey. He was always a big spender."

She shuddered, then crouched beside Josey's body and gingerly removed a wallet from his tattered suit coat. She gave it to me and I counted out the bills. The amount surprised me. "Seven thousand, four hundred. Not bad," I said. "Now, how about Harold?"

She went through Harold's pockets, too, and then the Russian's. She came up with about three thousand more.

Stuffing all the additional cash into the envelope, I said, "Almost forty thousand. But . . . too bad. The deal was fifty."

Nicole was pacing nervously back and forth in front of the piano. "That's all there is," she insisted.

"Well," I said, "maybe I'm being too greedy."

Lauren spoke up again, her voice shaking. "Please, Mal. You can't make a deal with her like this."

"You're right again," I answered. "I did say fifty, and if I don't stay with that I lose credibility." But then I opened the gym bag and dropped in the envelope filled with cash. "Lauren, call the police. Tell them there's been a shooting."

Nicole stared at me from across the room. "There's forty thousand dollars there," she cried. "You can't just take it!" When I didn't answer, she started walking back and forth again.

Lauren went to the phone.

"Wait," I said. "I've got a better idea." I gave her the number I had called earlier that night. "Call Nicole's station. Tell them there's been a shooting and to hurry up because the police are on their way. We'll wait a few minutes, *then* call the police."

Lauren made the call. Then the two of us sat and waited, while Nicole continued her frantic pacing, now making circles around the piano. I knew what I wanted to do, and couldn't think just how to pull it off.

Then Nicole stopped walking and faced me. "You . . . you bastard," she said. Then, shoulders heaving, she began to cry. Huge gasping sobs. Phony sobs. Suddenly I knew she had a plan, and I knew what it was. And I had a plan, then, too.

"It's not as though it's your money, Nicole," I said. "Look on the bright side. You're rid of Josey. You've got a great exclusive story. What more do you want?"

She turned away, her body racked with sobbing, leaning over the insides of the open grand piano and heaving as though she were going to vomit onto the strings. "Take the money," she managed to say between sobs, "but I want the goddamn shaving kit."

Standing and hoisting the strap of the gym bag over my shoulder, I said, "I guess it's time to call the police."

As Lauren started toward the phone, I half turned and reached through the drapes to pull open the patio door. As I did, Nicole swung around from the piano and faced me.

"Step away from the doors," she said.

And I did. I was staring into the barrel of Josey's gun.

Nicole must have circled it half a dozen times before she fished it out of the piano. Her plan was unfolding. Maybe mine would, too.

"Open that bag," she said, "and give me the shaving kit."

I fumbled with the zipper on the gym bag.

"Don't do it," Lauren said. "The TV people are on their way."

"I have to," I said, "or we'll be dead before they get here." I put my hand into the bag.

"Throw it on the floor between us," Nicole said, "and step back to the fireplace. No tricks."

"No tricks," I repeated.

The leather shaving kit hit the wooden floor as we backed up toward the fireplace.

Nicole watched it slide across the pine boards, up against Josey's stiffening body. She stopped and, reaching carefully over him, picked up the little leather bag. Straightening, she said, "And now—"

"No!" Lauren screamed, and she dove at Nicole.

That wasn't part of my plan.

Caught by surprise, Nicole swung the gun around clumsily. She never got off a shot. Lauren took her to the floor in a tangled heap. There wasn't much of a fight. Nicole released her hold on Josey's revolver and I grabbed it, while Lauren pinned her down. Wiping the gun hastily, I placed it on the floor near Josey.

Meanwhile, Lauren and Nicole got to their feet, Nicole holding fast to the shaving kit with two hands.

I went through Josey's pockets and found his keys.

Nicole turned suddenly and ran out through the patio doors, dodging the Russian. We followed her to the locked garage door, where she pulled and pushed fruitlessly on the knob.

She turned from the door and glared at me. "You can't have

these letters," she said. "It's my story. I'll put that fucking Radcliffe in the toilet."

I stepped toward her. Her eyes darted frantically around the yard, looking for somewhere to run. But there was nowhere.

As I reached out, she was afraid I'd snatch the shaving kit from her hand, so she stepped sideways and, with a desperate, clumsy hook shot, flipped it up into the air.

The little leather package cleared the parapet wall and plopped onto the garage roof.

For a moment we all stood, motionless, staring upward. We hadn't called the police, but the television station must have. We heard sirens approaching.

"It'll still be there," Nicole said, "when the police and the cameras arrive." She smiled. "What a story!"

The sirens were getting closer.

I found the key from Josey's ring and unlocked the door. Pulling Lauren with me into the garage, I tossed the keys at Nicole's feet and closed the door behind us.

CHAPTER

34

IT WAS TWENTY MINUTES LATER when Lauren finally said, "You shouldn't have done that."

We were in my car, headed south on La Salle Street, in the direction of the Loop. Those were her first words since we'd left Nicole in the backyard. They seemed a little negative to me.

"I don't know," I said. "I thought it was a rather dramatic rescue. I suppose you wish I'd left you there, with the spider and the beetle."

"No. I'm thankful for that part. You know what I mean. I mean we shouldn't have left Amy's letters there with Nicole. We should have waited for the police."

"I can't afford the time it would take them to sort things out, if they ever do. And you've seen how well I get along with law officers."

"Well, besides leaving the letters, I guess . . . Oh, I don't know. It seems wrong to have taken the money."

I looked over at her. "If you say that again, slowly, you'll see how dumb it sounds. Anyway, that money was *earned.* And I'm sure you can use it."

"Me? I don't want it."

"Well, then, I'm sure I can use it. Or I suppose I could give it to the Lady. She can use it."

"The Lady? Is that . . . is that your wife? The one—"

"No. It's too long to explain. But you'll meet her . . . if everything goes well."

We drove in silence for a while, crossed the bridge over the Chicago River, and waited for a red light at Wacker Drive.

I pointed up and out through the windshield. "Cal Radcliffe's office is in that building. I don't suppose he's there at this time of the morning."

She didn't answer. We drove on, leaving the building behind.

"So," I said, "suppose we hadn't left the shaving kit with Nicole. And suppose now *you* had Amy's letters. What would *you* do with them? You're the one who tried to give them to Nicole in the first place."

"Yes. I know. I killed Frank. That's not something I'm going to forget."

"I'm sorry," I said. "I didn't mean it that way. Besides, you couldn't have known what was going to happen."

"No. But it was my desire to hurt that killed Frank. I was anxious to help destroy a man's life."

"Radcliffe, you mean. But he'd destroyed his daughter's life."

"Yes. And then I destroyed Frank's. And my own."

"Frank's dead. You didn't do that. But you're not dead. And your life's not destroyed. It just seems that way right now."

She didn't answer.

I was right, of course. She could have a wonderful life someday without Frank. But why should she believe me? I didn't believe myself when I told myself that without Cass I could still have a life. With me, somehow, it was different. Lauren had a legitimate career. The women at her crisis center probably depended on her. She . . . Well, it was different, anyhow.

I turned west onto Randolph Street.

A little later, I said, "Anyway, you didn't answer my question."

"What question?"

"You objected to my leaving the letters with Nicole, and I

asked you what you'd do with them if *you* had them."

"I don't know anymore. I hated that man for what he did to his daughter. I wanted to expose him, to destroy him. But now, I seem to have run out of anger and hate." She paused. "You know, I really thought Nicole was doing good with her investigations. I'd only seen her on TV. But I admired her so much."

"The Lady never knew Nicole except from television, either. But she called her 'that *awful* woman.' "

"Maybe the Lady's smarter than I am."

"I don't think 'smart' is the right word, somehow."

"Whoever she is, she was right about Nicole. Now I know she's . . . she's an evil person."

"But then the Lady said maybe 'awful' wasn't the right word. Maybe 'unfortunate' was better. That Nicole probably had a difficult life herself. Or something like that."

"You know, I'm not sure I'm going to like—"

I threw a sudden hard right and rocked to a stop only inches short of the metal overhead door, then leaned on the horn, loud and long, three times.

While we waited, I said, "Not everyone likes the Lady. She irritates some people. But *you'll* like her." If we live that long, I thought.

Lauren looked up and down the wide deserted street, then gaped at the metal door as it started to rise in front of us. "What are we doing here?"

"We're looking for Cass and Sharon," I said.

CHAPTER

35

I PULLED FORWARD INTO THE WAREHOUSE and the metal door rolled down behind us. As it had been the last time, the huge indoor dock was as dark as a mushroom cave. My headlights cut a swath of brightness that ran smack up against the opposite wall, but didn't penetrate the black on either side. Before the car had stopped, I had my door open, with the interior light on, showing that it was just Lauren and me.

I cupped my hands around my mouth and called out, "No bullshit searches, Breaker! We're coming up."

I had no doubt that he'd be there, all right—expecting me.

Suddenly, the high ceiling light came on.

"Get out of the car, Lauren," I said.

I got out. I drew the Beretta and laid it on the roof of the car.

"I'm clean," I called. "The woman's clean. I'm bringing up a gym bag. No weapons in it, but it'll be at arm's length, anyway."

Reaching into the backseat, I withdrew the bag, held it out from my body, and headed for the metal staircase that led up to Breaker's office, motioning Lauren to follow. We were a few steps up from the floor when the door swung open above us and Fat Wilbur stepped out onto the platform. He held the door open as we continued up and past him into the office.

Breaker was at his desk. A sleek new telephone sat looking out of place amid the rest of the rubble on the desktop. Breaker wasn't on the phone. He rose to greet us. He was wearing black shoes, black pants, and a black windbreaker over a black shirt. They matched his black eye-patch.

"Lauren Parkins," I said, dropping the gym bag on the floor just inside the door, "meet Breaker Hanafan. Don't let the outfit fool you. He's no priest."

"What?" Breaker asked. Then he looked down at his clothes. "Oh. Well, I been out doing the Lord's work."

I never heard Breaker tell a joke before, and decided he must be in a good mood.

"Anyway, pleased to meet you," Breaker said to Lauren. "My sympathies about your husband."

Lauren jumped a little, startled. "Thank you," she said. I could hardly hear her.

"Breaker's not a priest," I repeated. "But he does know a lot of secrets. Actually, he sells things—maybe a few fruits and vegetables, but mostly lots of other things people think they want. He's . . . well, he's a purveyor."

Lauren looked a little confused.

"So, Breaker," I said, "you mean *personally?"*

"What?"

"Personally doing the Lord's work?"

"Oh," he answered. "Yeah. Well, 'You want a thing done right' and all that, you know." He leaned over and peered through the picture window onto the dock area below. "What the hell? You ever hear about conservation of energy?" Turning to Fat Wilbur, he said, "Go and turn off the lights in Foley's car. And wait there."

Fat Wilbur went out the door and we heard him clump heavily down the iron steps.

"Sit down. Sit down," Breaker said. "You want a beer or somethin'? Or maybe some coffee, huh?"

While I went to the refrigerator for a bottle of Moretti, Breaker poured coffee into plastic foam cups for Lauren and himself. Lauren and I took the two metal armchairs and Breaker sat in the swivel chair, his back to the desk. He reached into a lower drawer at his side and came out with a bottle of bourbon.

Holding the bottle up, he asked Lauren, "You want something in your coffee?"

"No thanks," she said.

He dumped a slug into his own cup and dropped the bottle back into the drawer. "Cheers," he said, lifting his cup and drinking.

"You shouldn't use that stuff, Breaker." I took a long pull on the Moretti.

"Jesus, you sound like my doctor or something. And what the hell are you drinking, anyway?"

"I don't mean the bourbon. I mean that plastic foam crap. Damn stuff doesn't biodegrade for seventy million years or something." I poured more beer down my throat. "Glass, now, that's recyclable."

"Yeah, well, we'll get together sometime and talk about the future. But right now, what are you doin' here?" He knew.

"Josey Creole's dead," I said.

"Is he now? Well that's a shame. Can't say as I'll miss him, though. Can't say as anyone will. Quite a few people in town will be much obliged to you, I suppose."

"I didn't kill Josey," I said. I finished the beer and went for another.

"You didn't?" Breaker looked at me over the rim of the plastic foam cup. "You mean it was that TV girl—Grant or something?"

"No." I popped the cap off the beer. "It was you, Breaker."

Breaker turned his head to Lauren. "Your friend here's got a great imagination, ma'am. Incidentally, did you know this guy, Josey Creole?"

"I . . . I met him," Lauren said.

"Well, then, maybe you know the type of guy he was. I mean, he was gettin' to be more than just a pain in the, uh, neck. But Foley knows I don't go around killing people. Especially nobody who's a kind of a, well, a kind of a business associate, I guess you'd say. Oh, I don't say there weren't times when I kinda wished Josey was out of the way. But for *me* to do something like that? Well, it's just not smart. You know? Killing a business associate? That kind of stuff just gives other people ideas. Then, well then there's just no end to it, you know?"

Breaker kept directing his words to Lauren, as though she were his student or something. "But along comes some outsider like Foley, or this girl Grant or whatever—or maybe even *you,* God forbid—and they get into it with Josey about something that's just between Josey and them, and Josey happens to get killed. Well, those things happen. People in the business understand, you know? But it's nothing that reflects on anybody that's a kind of an *associate.* Doesn't make the other associates nervous, or jumpy—like maybe it would if *I* killed Josey or something. So I might be much obliged if someone got rid of a pain in the neck for me. But I'd never do something like that myself. No way. Uh, would you like more coffee?"

Lauren looked down into her cup. She hadn't drunk any coffee. "No thanks," she said, holding the cup out toward Breaker, "but, maybe, some bourbon?"

Breaker obliged. Then he turned back to me. "So," he said, "I'm glad we got that straightened out. Now, have you got something for me, Foley?"

I'd been wondering how long it would take him to get around to it.

"Something for you?" I asked. "Like what?"

"Oh, I don't know. Some papers or something? Josey was after something the kid had. You found the kid. So you had what Josey was after. You didn't make a deal with Josey, 'cause he died. Now you're on my doorstep. I don't think you stopped by at this time of the morning just to tell me someone died. I think you came to make a delivery."

"No," I said, leaning over to set the empty beer bottle on the floor, "not a delivery, a pickup." I straightened up, with the NAM from the ankle holster pointed at Breaker. "I'm here to pick up Cass and the Cooper woman. And if anything's happened to them, I'll kill you."

"You might want to. But you couldn't do it. That's where you and I are different." Breaker chuckled. "Besides, I thought you said you were clean."

"I lied," I said.

"I didn't believe you, anyway. Put that goddamn little thing away, before you shoot your dick—I mean before someone gets hurt."

I held the gun steady.

Breaker added more bourbon to his cup. "Well then, maybe you're here for a delivery *and* a pickup. A trade, maybe."

"Maybe," I said. I stared at him. "Not bad, Breaker. Pretending to try to scare me off. But using me all along, feeding me bits of information. It was you that grabbed them, wasn't it? Making sure I stayed in the game to the end."

Breaker shrugged. "I really didn't think you'd give up in the first place. But in business, you know, a little insurance never hurts. Plus"—his voice hardened—"now I got something to trade."

"Are they . . . all right?"

"Hey, of course they're all right." He smiled. "I mean they're a little worried, 'cause they don't know what's going on." He drank from his cup, and when he spoke again he wasn't smiling. "You want something. I want something. Simple."

"You got what you wanted. Josey's dead and you're not involved."

"Well, you know, just when we get what we want, it always seems like there's something more, doesn't it? Human nature, I guess. Josey's dead, and now I want what Josey was after. Anyway, I had no deal with you so far. But now, we got a deal, a nonnegotiable deal. You give me the letters, and I give you your wife and the kid's sister. You don't give, you don't get." He tilted his cup toward the gun in my hand. "That little thing don't mean shit—pardon the expression. I want the letters."

"But—" Lauren said.

"Quiet, Lauren," I interrupted.

Breaker turned his head to her. "But what?" he asked.

Lauren looked from him to me, and was silent.

"Answer me," Breaker insisted. There was a new, harsh tone to his voice. It wasn't a tone that was easily ignored.

"There were two letters," Lauren said. "But he . . . he doesn't have them anymore. He left them with Nicole."

Breaker's smile returned. "Pardon the expression again, ma'am, but that's bullshit. Foley knows it's the letters that count. He wouldn't part with the letters without getting his wife. And if Josey didn't have her, well, Foley knows I'm a man of business. I don't let my emotions get involved with business decisions. And so"—he swung his head to me and returned to his business voice—"he wouldn't have left the letters with this Nicole person. Because if he did, no wife. Simple."

"I could drop you right now, Breaker," I said, "even with this little thing."

"Maybe. So I'd be dead. And then . . ." He didn't finish, and didn't have to.

No one said anything for about a hundred years. Then I said, "How do I know you've got Cass and Sharon? And that they're all right?"

"You'll have to take my word for it. Have I ever lied to you, Foley?"

"Yes."

"Well, now I'm telling you I got 'em and they're all right. But"—and his voice came cold and mean—"I'm also telling you they won't be all right if something happens to me, or if I don't get the letters. You think I'm lying now?"

I stared down at the floor. Even when everyone lies to you every day, and it's part of your job not to believe, there are times when you *do* believe. Not because you have a hunch, or some sixth sense or something. But because there's just no other way. You either believe, or it's all over. And you know that one time maybe you'll be wrong. One time it *will* be all over.

"No," I said, putting the mini away, "you're not lying."

"Good. Then we got a deal. The women for the letters."

"A deal," I said, getting up and going over to the door.

Returning to my chair, I sat down with the gym bag on the floor beside me. Lauren was saying, "But I don't understand. It's not—"

"But let's be clear about something, Breaker," I said, my right hand already in the bag. "All I ever had were two letters. I never told you they'd do you any good. They don't identify the writers, although a handwriting analyst probably could. And they don't identify who's accusing who, or what they're accusing someone of. There's another piece of the puzzle, a tape, a conversation with one of the writers. I don't have that, and I've never had it. Someone else has that."

"The Grant woman?" Breaker asked.

I didn't answer.

"It's her," he said. "But I said the letters for the women. And a deal is a deal. You give me the letters. If I need more, that's my problem."

"And Cass and Sharon?" I asked.

"They'll be at your place before you can get there."

Withdrawing my hand from the bag, I tossed the leather shaving kit across to Breaker. He looked down at it in his hands, then opened it. He spilled the electric shaver and the rest of the contents on the floor and felt around inside. He looked up.

"Under the lining," I said.

He found the letters, took them out, and glanced at them.

He looked up at us, smiling, and said, "Nice to have met you ma'am. See you again some time, Foley."

"Breaker," I said.

"Christ. Now what?"

"Radcliffe. What about Radcliffe?"

"Clean Cal? He's mine." Breaker winked his one good eye. "Been mine for some time now. But this shit sure won't hurt any. Now, I thought I said good-bye."

Lauren and I headed for the door. Swinging out my left hand to push it open, I nearly broke my wrist when the panic bar didn't budge.

I yelped and swung around. Breaker looked up, startled, from rereading the letters. "Oh," he said, "sorry about that." Reaching behind him, he touched something hidden in the mess on his desk and said, "Try it now."

We went out and down the iron stairs.

Fat Wilbur was standing near my car. He had turned it around to face the door. As Lauren and I got into the car, he leaned over, scraping his palm across the grease on his head, and said, "Jesus, Foley, scratches all over the hood, dents in the fuckin' roof. I don't see how you can drive a piece of shit like this."

Lauren slept most of the way to Evanston.

Once, she woke up and said, "I suppose you can buy those tan leather shaving kits anywhere."

"From Bloomingdale's to Sears," I said, "and they all look pretty much alike, if you don't look that close. And Josey's gun, it was a five-shot revolver, you know? I mean, when Nicole took it from the piano it was empty."

She went back to sleep. I drove too fast in the night. My head kept nodding and I held my left arm stretched out the window to try to keep myself awake. I kept thinking that I'd forgotten something, but I was too tired to figure out what it was.

A little later Lauren stirred again. "What if they're not there?"

"You mean Cass and Sharon?"

"Of course," she said. "What if they're not there?"

"They'll be there. They're fine."

CHAPTER 36

THEY WERE THERE when we got there. They were fine.

We called Jason and made coffee, and there was plenty of talk for a while, until the sun rose red over the lake and I finally convinced Sharon and Lauren to get out of there and leave Cass and me alone. I was hoping, then, for more talk, and who knows what after that?

Instead, I collapsed on the couch and when I woke up Cass was gone. It was nearly five in the afternoon and the phone was ringing.

It was Jason.

"I just called," he said, " 'cause we got a game Friday night, preseason. Coach says with me bein' gone and all, I might not start, but I'll play some. I just thought, uh, you know, maybe you might—"

"I'd like to. But Fridays I play the piano at a bar, and I've been missing—"

"Yeah. Well, okay, man, maybe some other time." He hung up.

Maybe I wouldn't have made such a wonderful father, after all.

The doorbell rang.

By the time I got downstairs, a Jaguar was disappearing down the crushed-stone drive. Sitting on the cement stoop was the gym bag I had forgotten at Breaker's office. I took it upstairs, dumped the contents on the kitchen table, and then called the Lady for a consultation on how to split the forty thousand dollars. She was out looking at her new building in Hyde Park.

I called Miz Becky's. But before I could tell her I was thinking of skipping Friday that week, Becky said they'd given the new piano player a tryout, and the crowd liked him, and his bass player, too. They'd play this weekend, but she'd saved Friday night for me. "Feel like I owe you, y'know?" she said.

"Becky, I—"

"That's okay. I know Friday's your favorite night," she said, "and I appreciate how faithful you been."

"Uh . . . thanks. Friday, then."

Jason would have other games. Meanwhile, I needed to practice, run a few riffs. I turned toward the back room and the piano—and finally saw the note from Cass, on the counter by the toaster.

It was a sheet of paper folded in quarters and—I don't know just why—something about the look of it hit me hard even before I opened it.

The way I always thought the story went, the brave but simple warrior rescues the lady in distress and the two live happily ever after. And even though my rescue of Cass was a little convoluted, I'd been brave—and certainly simple enough—and I thought I qualified.

Not this time.

A short note it was, and not very explicit. Phrases like "time to think" and "only fair." Decoded, it seemed to say another warrior had wandered into the story a while back. Possibly brave, for all I know, and maybe not so simple. Deserving of a tryout, anyway.

I sat down and pressed the paper flat in front of me on the kitchen table and stared at the note for a long time. It didn't get any better. Finally, I reached across to the stove and turned on the front burner. I held the note over the flame and watched most of it dissolve into smoke, and the rest fall black onto the white of the stove. I should have let go of it before I did, but I suppose for an instant I somehow enjoyed the searing pain in the tips of my forefinger and thumb.

While I ran cold water over my right hand, I tapped out a number on the phone with my left.

"It's me, Becky," I said. "About Friday. I . . . there's something important that's come up. A basketball game, and one of the—"

"Jesus H. Christ, Mal. Why . . . ? Fine, then. I'll call you sometime."

What she meant was she probably wouldn't.

I turned on the television, mostly to remind myself that the world was very large and most of it was going to keep right on going—however I felt about what happened in my own little corner. The fact was, the world didn't know, and didn't care. Sounds depressing maybe, but the reality of it seemed to help somehow. We're on our own here, and we have to make our choices.

I'd missed much of the evening news, but caught a sportscaster explaining how he'd be doing a series of profiles next week on local college basketball players—kids that just might have a chance at the pros. Jason's name was mentioned, along with something about an attitude problem.

"Not to worry," I said to the face on the screen. "He's handling that."

After a commercial, I learned that it wouldn't be long before the new U.S. attorney was confirmed. As expected, investigations were turning up nothing but good about Calvin Radcliffe.

That time I didn't say anything to the face on the screen.

More commercials. Then the weather. The arctic cold snap was over and there were warm Indian summer days ahead.

Finally, just before sign-off, there was a lengthy recap of the day's top story, that "dramatic shaving-kit shoot-out" between a reputed mob figure and his own bodyguards on the city's near north side. Police had identified the four dead bodies, but seemed perplexed by inconsistencies in the story told by an unnamed woman who said she'd seen Josey Creole shoot his bodyguard, Harold Greenleaf, after Greenleaf shot Josey.

They replayed an on-the-scene report, taped earlier that day. It showed the house on Astor Street, and some chalked outlines where the bodies were found. Then there was a man backing down a ladder that was leaning against the side of the garage behind the house. All very interesting.

But the segment I liked best showed a woman's hands opening a tan leather shaving kit, something the man had retrieved from the roof. They were Nicole's hands, even though they never showed her face as she dumped the contents out.

The camera zoomed in.

In a voice-over, the commentator said that what fell out of the shaving kit had been frozen. But it plopped onto the ground. And when they picked it up and peeled back the plastic, you could see that the little dead rat was already starting to thaw.